D1612777

Strike!

Books by
DOUGLAS SUTHERLAND

BURGESS AND MACLEAN
THE YELLOW EARL
AGAINST THE WIND
THE LANDOWNERS
BEHOLD! THE HEBRIDES
TRIED AND VALIANT

STRIKE!

A novel by

Douglas Sutherland

HEINEMANN : LONDON

William Heinemann Ltd
15 Queen Street, Mayfair, London W1X 8BE

LONDON MELBOURNE TORONTO
JOHANNESBURG AUCKLAND

First published 1976
© Douglas Sutherland 1976

SBN 434 75202 9

Printed in Great Britain by
Northumberland Press Limited
Gateshead

This novel covers a period of ten months towards
the end of the present decade

'The unacceptable face of capitalism ...'
The Rt Hon. Edward Heath, Prime Minister, 1970-1974

'We must be mugs. We allow ourselves to be manipulated, tricked, misled, misrepresented, agitated, frustrated and when senior stewards cannot get their way at mass meetings, we are left leaderless.
'We put at risk our livelihood, our dependants' welfare and our way of life because we are too bloody petty, helpless and short-sighted.'
Organization to represent Moderate
Opinion of Trade Unionists

'The destruction of a capitalist Society is an end in itself.'
Karl Marx

I

Robert Clancy-Smith sat in the cocktail bar at Prestwick Airport sipping his third tomato juice and waiting for the metallic voice which would come over the tannoy to announce the arrival of flight 703 from New York. It was already half an hour behind schedule but he felt no irritation.

From time to time he got up and strolled over to the window which overlooked the general arrival and departure area. A party of nuns sat like a flock of solemn birds, clutching their rosaries as they waited for the charter plane which was to wing them away to Lourdes. A harassed schoolmaster counted and recounted his charges who kept darting away to the lavatory or to peer at the nudes which adorned the magazine covers displayed on the central bookstand. Businessmen sat in ones and twos, gripping their briefcases and glancing constantly at the big clock which ticked away the minutes until they would be called to start their journeys to glamorous-sounding destinations.

Clancy, as he liked to be called, although he had been born plain Robert Smith, could have hugged himself with self-satisfaction. He would have loved to have ordered himself a large gin and tonic but he did not want the liquor to smell on his breath. Instead he kept glancing at himself, checking his appearance in the mirror behind the bar. Just right, he thought. The not-too-flamboyant tie, tied in a large Windsor knot, the pinstripe suit which fitted round the back of the neck without the suspicion of a wrinkle and the slightly flared bottoms to his trousers breaking exactly right over the tops of his highly polished wedge-heeled shoes which did something to offset his lack of inches. At thirty-two years of age and the recently appointed Sales Director of the Greenbank Engineering Co. Ltd, with the Chairman's Rover parked on the tarmac outside, he was savouring one of the high spots of his career as he waited for Dick Katz III, Executive Vice-

1

President of the Camel Automobile Company of Detroit, to come dropping out of the skies.

*   *   *

The office building of the Greenbank Engineering Company stood on its own, halfway down Turk Street, Glasgow. It was by far the most important building in the street which was made up of mean dwellings with a builder's yard at the bottom end and a scattering of small shops. Because the street was a cul-de-sac with no through traffic it was a favourite playground for children who ran up and down it in ragged packs, kicked dilapidated footballs or played games of hop-scotch on the chalk-scrawled pavement. Ex-Sergeant-Major Kelly, important in his Corps of Commissionaires' uniform, his war medals making a splash of colour on his chest, did what he could to add dignity to the squalid scene. When visitors arrived at the Greenbank offices he saluted them smartly and saw to it that their cars went unmolested by the kids whose delight it was to scrawl rude words on any car with a sufficient coating of dust. The urchins called him 'Farty-Tarty' behind his back but they went in considerable awe of him.

To step inside the swing-doors however was to enter a world as decorous as a funeral parlour. The panelled walls of the spacious hall were innocent of decoration except for the Roll of Honour for the dead of two world wars. On the right a door led to the general office, through which could be glimpsed the bowed heads of the ledger clerks crouched behind their tall, old-fashioned desks. On the left a panel of that opaque glass which is associated with Victorian lavatories declared it to conceal the person of the Office Manager. Guarding the foot of the highly polished oak staircase an elderly lady, her grey hair pinned severely back, sat in a box. She divided her time between answering the enquiries of callers and operating an old-fashioned switchboard. It was only when the visitor reached the first floor that there was any concession to luxury. There a narrow strip of carpet was laid along the polished corridor off which opened the mahogany doors of the private offices of the Directors and more important executives. There was nothing to show that they controlled one of the largest private engineering businesses in Scotland.

Little had changed in the Greenbank offices since the building had first been erected over a hundred years earlier. In those days it had been quite a showpiece with a fine view from the Directors' offices over the River Clyde and green trees lining the newly laid-out street. Now the upper windows looked over the roofs of grimy tenements to a skyline of warehouses and towering cranes and the trees had long since been uprooted when the cobble-stones had given way to tarmacadam.

Sir Charles Puddefant, Chairman and Managing Director of Greenbank, stood with his back to the room looking, with apparently absorbed interest, at the view he had looked at a thousand times before. Occasionally he clasped and unclasped his hands behind his back or turned his head to glance with controlled casualness to where Turk Street gave way into busy Dock Road. Behind him three men sat at the polished board-room table each concealing his nervousness in his own way. Keith Puddefant, Sir Charles's son, lounged with one arm over the back of his chair while he employed the other in making a passable sketch of a class J sailing dinghy on his blotting paper; Roland Motion, the Director in charge of Personnel and Industrial Relations sat with his shoulders hunched, stabbing aimlessly with a ball-point pen at a sheet of paper while Jock MacKay, the Production Director, placed at the bottom end of the table, stared as if fascinated at Sir Charles's back. Every now and again he stretched his left arm out in an elaborate gesture and examined his wristwatch with minute care.

As the Rover drew up at the front door Sir Charles turned abruptly from the window. He was a tall elegant man of sixty-five. The meticulously cared-for white hair, the neatly clipped moustache and the narrow aristocratic face suggested more a successful diplomat than the head of a Glasgow engineering firm. His normally high colouring showed a little pinker as he took his seat facing MacKay.

'Gentlemen,' he announced. 'Our visitor has arrived.'

*　　*　　*

The emergency Board meeting of Greenbank Engineering had been called at the request of Robert Clancy-Smith. He had joined the Company just a year before as Sales Manager when old Aeneas Mackenzie had retired and his quick promotion to the Board rather rankled with some of the older staff but there was

3

none who could deny that he was a live wire.

It was Keith Puddefant who had found Clancy-Smith. For his last few years Aeneas Mackenzie had not been up to the game. Many of his old contacts had died or retired and he had little in common with the new generation. Few of them were members of the City Club where he liked to do business over a glass of port and a cigar and he had become something of a picturesque anachronism with his flowered buttonhole and his old-fashioned mannerisms. Only Sir Charles regretted his retirement for he liked to have his old friends about him.

Clancy-Smith was quite a different proposition. Keith had first met him when they had both been playing in a Pro-am golf tournament and he had taken to him at once. Clancy had real style. Apart from their rivalry on the golf course they shared a liking for fast cars and late nights. Sir Charles had hired him without much enthusiasm but with the warming feeling that he was moving with the times and keeping in step with the younger generation.

Clancy-Smith had gone to work at Greenbank with a will and he had produced results. In a way Sir Charles had regarded his success as Keith's success. It spoke well for the boy's judgment and he was only too willing to give credit where it was not necessarily due. There were only small contracts at first but, with business hard to find, it enabled men to be kept on who would otherwise have become redundant and there was always the promise of bigger things round the corner. 'Softly, softly, catchee monkey' was one of Clancy-Smith's favourite expressions and, if names were anything to go by, he was certainly in with the big time.

When the break came even Keith, his most ardent supporter, found it hard to believe. For months the name of Bill Hamilton, the Production Manager of the giant Camel Motors had appeared with great regularity on the expense vouchers. There had been one particular evening with ringside seats for the big fight at White City and a dinner afterwards at the Savoy when even the phlegmatic Mr Thomas in charge of accounts had been jogged out of his rut. Mr Thomas had once taken his wife for a holiday in Ayr and had ventured to the bar of the Turnberry Hotel for a drink. The expense had so shaken his thrifty soul that he had never repeated the experiment although he had talked about it

4

for a long time afterwards. To dine at the Savoy Hotel in London, the haunt, so he had heard, of film stars and millionaires was to his mind such an outrageous action that he had taken the bill to Sir Charles himself for approval before he could bring himself to pass it through the books. 'Bloody peasant,' Clancy-Smith had remarked when inevitably he had got to hear of it and went his own confident way.

The pay-off came a few weeks later when Clancy was putting for the match at the eighteenth at Sunningdale. As he was about to make his stroke Bill Hamilton remarked:

'We are going to have to contract out our automatic transmission unit for the new model to an independent firm. It might be that your boys would be interested.'

Clancy was so interested that he duly missed the putt and handed over five pounds with the mental reservation to charge it up.

'That was an unfair way to win a game,' he protested. 'Don't do it again.'

But Bill Hamilton was serious and the next day discussions opened in earnest. Clancy was summoned to a meeting with Hamilton and John Doxy, the Chairman of the whole of the Camel operations in the U.K.

The problem was by no means an easy one. For years Camel had relied on models for the British market which had the virtue of solid, middle-class reliability. Now with the new motorways spreading their tentacles throughout the country it had been decided to change the image. While the first streamlined models were being put through their paces on the testing ground outside Ayr, the lights were burning late in the Mayfair offices of Adams, Appleyard and Ainsley—'the three A's for the best in advertising' —to justify a six-figure appropriation to launch the new look with the added engine power.

It was Marvin Shick, the whizz-kid copywriter who had been brought across fresh from his triumphs on Madison Avenue, who finally came up with the idea which was at once recognized as a masterpiece on both sides of the Atlantic. The art work showed a Bedouin in a bowler hat racing at speed across the desert sands while the slogan read 'You'll get there faster with a Camel'. Now all that was required was that the performance of the car should live up to the reputation which was being created for it.

5

John Doxy explained the situation to Clancy before turning to the matter of the automatic transmission.

'We are not only concerned with producing a faster motor car. We are also concerned with giving the Camel owners a more comfortable ride. Do you realize that a man driving his car up to town in the rush hour each morning and driving it back say forty miles in the evening will probably have to change gear close on a thousand times with the conventional transmission. Hell, that takes about as much energy as his whole day's work.'

Clancy looked impressed.

'Of course most of our cars in the States have automatic transmission and whatever people say it is coming over here on a much bigger scale than you already have. Camel are going to be the first to fit it to the family car and that is what we are here to discuss.'

'We have a lot of experience supplying the motor industry,' said Clancy briskly. 'I imagine we can handle this. My only worry is price. As you know most of the automatic transmissions and overdrives fitted to our British cars are made by one specialist firm, Borg-Warner. They not only have the know-how but they could cut any price we could quote to ribbons because of the quantity they are turning out.'

Doxy held up his hand. 'Just hold on a minute. We are not offering you this on a plate but we will come to that later. As to why we are not thinking of going to Borg-Warner it is simply a matter of geography. They have their works three hundred and fifty miles from our assembly plant. Three hundred and fifty miles may not seem a long way but it is a hell of a long way if there are no trains running. Our Executive Vice-President, Mr Katz, is a little alarmed at the way you run your railways. To have a strike in the works is bad enough but if you add to that the hazard that if there is trouble with a body over whose politics we have no control then we are halting production as surely as if we have a strike on our own ground. Now what appeals to us is that your works is a matter of ten miles from our assembly plant. The train drivers can stay at home as much as they like; we are still going to get the goods.'

Clancy nodded. It cleared up the main point that had been worrying him since Bill Hamilton had approached him.

'I'd have you understand that this decision is not final. Nor is

6

it by any means certain that we will offer the contract to your people even if we go along with our present way of thinking. A lot is going to depend on how we can work out the financing of the installation of the production lines and, of course, on the unit cost being satisfactory. All that is certain is that we have to make up our minds fast. Bill here will be in touch with you by the end of the week so that we can get down to a more detailed examination of the problem.'

In fact Bill was in touch much sooner than that. The same evening he was having a pint of beer with Clancy at the Queen's Elm just along the Fulham Road.

'Bloody Yanks,' he exploded, banging his tankard on the table. 'I tell you I would just as soon resign as be dictated to by that load of bastards.'

'What's the trouble?' asked Clancy. 'It's not like you to quarrel with your bread and butter.'

'Listen. I have a car to get out and if it is not rolling off the production lines on time there will be all bloody hell to pay and it will be my head which falls. It was my idea to bring in you fellows and you can be certain they have done a good deal of checking up on your outfit before getting to this stage. Now they are pissing around looking at all sorts of alternatives. We just can't afford the time.'

'We are not going to be able to produce any figures for you tomorrow. We'll have a works study to do on the practicability of the proposition. We will have to get an agreement on the who pays for what when it comes to installing capital equipment. It's a hell of a big undertaking even for somebody of our size.'

'That's precisely the point. Unless you get the green light straight away, you are not going to get off the ground in time and we'll have to go back to Borg-Warner whether we like it or not. Personally I don't give a fig. I just want them to make up their minds. No offence to you, old lad.'

'Listen,' said Clancy, alarmed. 'I don't want to put a bomb under our boys to get them moving and then find that it's all a lot of pie in the sky. There is a hell of a lot of work and quite a bit of money to be spent before we get to the stage of giving you a costing. If it blows up at that stage I won't be the most popular boy in the class.'

'I was coming to that. As you can imagine we have done a lot

7

of work on this ourselves. We've had specifications from Borg-Warner and we have internal estimates of how much we can afford if we contract out. I shouldn't do this but I'm going to give you the file. It will save you a hell of a lot of groundwork.' Bill unzipped his briefcase and handed over a bulky envelope. 'You've got my life in your hands Clancy, old son, so for God's sake don't lose it.'

Clancy took the documents with the reverence of a first communicant receiving the Holy Sacrament and caught the earliest aeroplane in the morning to Glasgow.

Sir Charles examined Clancy-Smith's prize with something akin to distaste, holding it as if with sugar tongs.

Eventually he said, 'I am not sure if this is playing quite fair. I mean after all those are confidential papers. What do you think, Keith?' He turned to his son who with Clancy-Smith and Jock MacKay were sitting round his desk.

'Good Heavens, Dad, it's the chance of a lifetime. These sort of things happen all the time in business nowadays. Bill Hamilton is playing his own game and he would not have given it to Clancy if he did not want him to have it. Let's play it for all it is worth.'

Clancy-Smith cleared his throat as if to say something and decided against it. Sir Charles ignored him.

'What do you think, Jock?' He turned to his Production Director.

Jock MacKay stared down at his feet before replying. Then he said, picking his words carefully, 'If we get this contract, it is going to mean a lot to us. I'm not saying I approve or disapprove. If it was not us it would be someone else. I'm for having a go.'

'Very well.' Sir Charles got to his feet. 'Get the costings out as soon as you can. I'm going out to lunch.' He was helped on with his coat. At the door he turned. 'I suppose I ought to congratulate you, Mr Smith,' he said with a thin smile.

Clancy did not look up. Inside he was boiling with suppressed rage. For one thing he could not stand being called Mr Smith.

It was over three months before matters were finally settled. Oddly enough the quotation was the least of the hurdles to be overcome. Within a few weeks of the Greenbank figures being submitted they were provisionally accepted subject to overall financial approval by Camel of the extent of their investment in

8

the new plant required. Camel were to provide the new machinery and Greenbank were to modernize and re-fit numbers 3-4 sheds to provide additional space on the shop floor. In the end Bill Hamilton was beginning to show signs of exasperation.

'You blokes want to have your cake and eat it,' he complained to Keith and Clancy. 'Here you are with the whole bloody thing in your lap and you're arguing about who's going to pay for a new restroom.'

'I don't come in at that level,' said Clancy. 'I'm only the dogsbody around here. If I was in Keith's shoes I wouldn't stand for it. After all it's his family business.'

Keith peered into the bottom of his glass and sighed.

'I think Dad is softening up on the whole thing. He's set in his ways. Give him time.'

'Time! I've got to get agreement in the next ten days or my head is on the block. When it comes to the crunch you can't fart around with the Yanks about money. We may have our own show over here but they hold the purse strings. What do you mean "softening up". Backing out?'

'No. I think he is going to agree the terms. I've got Mummy on my side and that means a lot.'

'Jesus, what a way to run a business,' breathed Clancy and ordered another round of drinks.

Keith proved right. Twenty-four hours later Sir Charles finally approved the draft contract. Clancy rang from London. 'The Big White Chief, Richard Katz, is flying over tomorrow. I have to meet him at the airport in the morning.'

*   *   *

'Gentlemen,' announced Sir Charles turning back to the room, 'our visitor has arrived.'

The three men at the table sat up in their seats and fingered their collars to see if their neckties were straight. It is an odd thing that the first thing a nervous man thinks about is his tie. It seemed a long time before the visitors could be heard at the top of the stairs. Sir Charles wondered yet again whether he should have been in the hall to greet them and again discarded the idea. He didn't want to appear too much of a lick-spittle.

'Good morning, gentlemen,' Clancy-Smith threw the door wide open and almost bowed his visitor over the threshold. In spite of

9

the overnight train from London he looked as if he had just stepped out of the barber's shop.

When he was introduced Sir Charles looked with some surprise at Richard J. Katz the Third. For all his sophistication Sir Charles had met few Americans. There had been the Servicemen he and Lady Puddefant had had in their home for short periods during the war and the charming couple they had both met on a cruise in the Greek Islands but otherwise his experience was limited. Somehow he imagined that an American tycoon would be larger than life with a sunburst tie, a big cigar and hornrimmed glasses. Richard Katz was none of these things. He was a tall man in his early forties with clear blue eyes and a craggy face which spoke more of the great outdoors than a life spent closeted in an office. His suit might have been cut in Savile Row. His dark blue tie was innocent of tie clips or pins and no battery of pens obtruded from his breast pocket. He was instantly likeable. He was also direct and to the point.

'I don't mind telling you, Sir Charles, that I have had lots of second thoughts about this project but you seem to have everything tied up pretty thoroughly at this end. Even Vice-Presidents don't always have the final say in our organization.' He permitted himself a brief smile. 'Bill Hamilton has been around your works and he reckons you can do the job. I'm here because I like to know the people I'm working with and we are going to be alongside each other a great deal. I don't need to tell you that this is an important operation for us and we can't afford for anything to go wrong. Now what I suggest is that you and I, Sir Charles, take ourselves off to where we can have a little private chin-wag and let the rest of them get on with the real business.' He waved his hand to embrace the room.

Sir Charles took his guest to his club.

'I certainly like your British clubs,' said Katz. 'Of course we have something like them in New York. The Harvard and the Knickerbocker for example but somehow they're not quite the same.' He looked round the fine panelled dining-room and the portraits of long-dead dignitaries hanging round the walls. 'Yes, great style.' Sir Charles glowed with pride. Everything was going far better than he had expected. It was not until they sat over their coffee that Richard Katz turned conversation to business.

'This contract is going to turn your company upside down,

10

Charles. This is a big deal for you and it means a hell of a lot to us as well. We are putting ourselves in your hands. Anything goes wrong and we are in the manure right up to our necks.'

'I have been into the matter thoroughly and I can see no difficulties,' said Sir Charles stiffly. He felt suddenly irritated that this American, twenty-four years his junior, should presume to question his ability to run his own business.

'I was just thinking,' pursued Katz, gazing at the ornate ceiling of the smoking-room. 'We are footing the bill for putting in the production machinery for you. That is reasonable enough. Frankly we'd like to go a little further than that. Sort of hedge our bet. If you would let us put up some more cash and have us take a share in Greenbank, I know my financial boys would be a lot happier. Give us some sort of control over our investment.'

'All the equity is held by me or my family. I don't think any of us would be likely to sell at this stage.'

'Or at any stage?' Katz did not give up easily. 'I mean that if I were in your shoes I would not want to go on for ever. In a year or two you might want to start taking it a bit easier and let that boy of yours have his head. They tell me he is something of a go-getter. Maybe then you would want to spread your risk. Engineering is a chancy business nowadays. If anything went wrong with our deal you'd be out on a limb, you know.'

'What could go wrong? The terms of the contract are quite satisfactory.'

'Oh I don't know. I don't much care for the industrial scene over here. Take these strikes all over the place. You haven't got your labour force held down like we have in the States. Do you know we haven't had one strike worth mentioning at Camel since the big walk out in Detroit in 1967? The Unions do not have the same power that they have in Britain. Do you know why? We pay the men what they want within reason. Over here you can't do that and make a profit. Look at the car industry in Britain. You're losing out all along the line. One Commie agitator and you're in the soup.'

'We haven't had a strike at Greenbank in our whole history,' said Sir Charles. 'We look after our workers. I know most of the old hands by their first names. If they have a grievance they know they can come straight to me.'

'If your workers let you down,' went on Katz as if he hadn't heard, 'the whole damn show goes up. No assemblies from Green-bank and ten thousand men are out of work at Camel.'

'I don't think that will happen,' Sir Charles smiled thinly.

'You will have to take on a lot of new men. Maybe you'll get some troublemakers like the rest of the industry.'

'We'll just have to meet that if we come to it.'

'There's another point. How about your top management? How will they stand up to it when the pressures are on? Don't think I don't respect traditions but new situations call for new skills. There are tough men on the shop floor and you need tough men at the top. Paternalism is getting to be a dirty word with the Unions. What they want is more pay and shorter hours and they don't care a dime how they get it. They are not going to come to your office with a begging bowl and be turned away with the soft word.'

'I think you will have to let us handle our own problems our own way,' said Sir Charles almost betraying the anger he felt at being put through his paces like a schoolboy applying for his first job. 'It is a rather late stage for you to start worrying about my organization, but if you are not happy about us it is still not too late to call the whole thing off.'

Katz stood up and grinned cheerfully.

'Maybe I'm always looking for snags. I just want to say that we are behind you all the way and if you want a hand you only got to call me. I'll be right over here—and if you have any second thoughts about a stock deal the offer still stands.'

Sir Charles dropped the American at his hotel and then drove straight home. The contract was safe and he should have felt jubilant. Instead he felt vaguely irritated and flat. Maybe he was getting too old to learn new tricks.

The Puddefant family had owned the Greenbank Company ever since its foundation almost a hundred and fifty years before but their Scottish roots went back earlier than that. The first Puddefant—the name was of Norman French origin—had come to Scotland in the wake of 'Butcher' Cumberland's army sent to put down the 1745 Rebellion. They had been blacksmiths, shoe-ing the horses of Cumberland's cavalry and sharpening the bayonets on which the Highland Clans were to impale themselves on Culloden Moor. When the punitive forces had finally with-drawn the Puddefants had not gone with them. Instead Jacob

12

Puddefant had set up his forge in a small village on the outskirts of the growing seaport of Glasgow. Business had been slow in coming at first for the Scots did not take readily to the English family who had settled in their midst. However nobody could deny that they were the best blacksmiths for miles around and with time they began to prosper. The Puddefant children learned to speak with the Scottish tongue and by the time old Jacob came to die there were few who held their origins against them.

The foundations of the family fortunes were laid by William Puddefant who secured a contract to forge cannon for the war against Napoleon so that when he, in his turn, came to die there was money enough to expand the works. The latest machinery was installed to meet the needs of the industries which were springing up on Clydeside. Peace brought even greater prosperity to the Puddefants who supplied components to many of the great shipyards which were making the name of Scotland famous throughout Europe as sail gradually gave way to steam. There were few ironclads built on the Clyde in those days of which some part did not come from Puddefant's. And not only on the Clyde for their reputation as fine craftsmen soon spread to Whitehaven, Newcastle and even Bristol.

The family were lucky in another way. Each generation managed to produce at least one son who had the characteristics of his forebears. There was always somebody to step into the shoes of his parent and continue the tradition of being astute, forward-looking in business matters and hard working. True they now lived in fine houses and dressed in fine clothes but they arrived at the works punctually every morning and knew what they were about. They were models of rectitude and looked up to by their contemporaries.

It was Sir Charles's great-grandfather who had built the offices in Turk Street and who had laid out the new works on four acres of waste land on the other side of what was now Dock Road. It was said at the time that he had overstepped himself but he lived long enough to prove the critics wrong. By the time he died Glasgow had spread itself over the surrounding countryside. Industrial development had taken place on all sides and the site of the Greenbank works was not only the envy of his competitors but had increased in value out of all recognition.

13

Sir Charles's grandfather was the first Puddefant to take an interest in public life. For a time he had sat in Parliament. When he succeeded his father, he devoted much of his time to local politics and became Lord Provost of Glasgow. It was he who built the family mansion overlooking Loch Lomond and called it Cumberland Towers—a pawky reminder of the family's origins. It was not perhaps his finest memorial. Created in the Scottish Gothic style so popular with the Victorians it resembled nothing so much as a minor Balmoral, set about with spires and turrets and so designed inside as to be the despair of domestic servants of his own and subsequent generations. In the end he was created a Baronet and his funeral was one of the most impressive seen in Glasgow for many years. He had been a hard man in his lifetime. In the days when the trade unions were beginning to flex their muscles, he had refused to give an inch. 'They should be treated like road metal,' he liked to tell his fellow industrialists, 'trample them under foot.' But they all used to say he was fair.

It is always hard in examining the history of a dynasty to say when the first cracks started to show. It would be easy enough to point to the hard days after the Great War when the hunger marchers converged in despair on London to demonstrate futilely before the Houses of Parliament. They were certainly terrible days when the shipyards lay silent and the order books were empty. In fact Greenbank were not as hard hit as many others. They were already involved in the rapidly growing motor car industry and had spread their risk wisely into fields far removed from supplying the ship builders. While the unemployed in the Glasgow slums got drunk on Red Biddy with the pittance they drew each week from the 'Buroo' and their wives begged in the streets to feed their children, there were few workers laid off from Greenbank. True, many of the men in the interest of economy were replaced by lower-paid female labour but it meant that there was still at least one wage earner in the family. There was a family feeling about Greenbank so that if the management sacrificed one of their men they usually tried to employ his wife instead at a cheaper wage.

By the time Sir Charles took over as a young man from his ailing father before the outbreak of the Second World War the affairs of the Company had perhaps never looked brighter. There were forecasts of a new golden age and, if there were mutterings of war over the horizon, a war had never spelt misfortune for those who supplied its sinews.

The war came and went and Greenbank played its part by producing parts for the Bren gun, bearings for tanks, springs for anti-personnel mines and a multitude of other things besides. In the first honours list after VE day Sir Charles collected an O.B.E. He still had some years to go before he reached the age of forty and was regarded as one of the coming men.

There was, however, one small cloud to come on the horizon of Sir Charles's good content. In his only son, Keith, he did not seem to have produced those qualities which his ancestors had possessed in such abundant measure. The boy had been sent to one of Scotland's leading schools where his father and his grandfather had been before him but there had been trouble. After one or two brushes with authority there had been an incident involving one of the dining-room maids and the headmaster had decided that the school would be better off without him. The Puddefant parents had been shocked and dismayed. He had been put to a private tutor but that had not been a great success either. The boy was moody and rebellious against any form of authority. His only interests seemed to be sailing his dinghy on Loch Lomond or playing golf. When one day at the age of fifteen he had come home very drunk from the golf club his father had confined him to his room and cancelled his subscription. Keith had retaliated by tearing up his school books and refusing to eat until he was released.

The difficulty they experienced with their son was almost a greater trial to Claire Puddefant than to her husband. She was, in her own opinion and that of her friends, a model wife and mother. It was outrageous that her son on whom she lavished so much of her time and affection should not reward her by behaving like a true Puddefant. His apparent total lack of affection for his parents and his boorish manners in front of some of her dearest friends distressed her immensely. In spite of her position as a leader of local society, Claire lacked any form of individuality or imagination. She supervised her domestic staff and her gardeners, conscientiously opened whatever flower shows or sales of work fell to her lot with a graciousness which was widely admired, and entertained with a correctness which bored all but the most sycophantic of guests to tears.

15

Sir Charles, who had married his wife for the very qualities which she showed in such abundance, found her an ideal mate. He was himself a man of tidy and precise habits. He regarded his heritage as a sacred trust which was why he attended his office every day when he would much preferred to have devoted himself to growing his prize roses and developing his pedigree herd of shorthorns. This was not to say that he was not a man of ability but he believed in delegating responsibility rather than putting himself in the forefront of the battle as his ancestors had so much enjoyed doing. He was a remote figure, steering the ship with a light hand and trusting that it did not run into heavy weather.

Unfortunately there was much heavy weather ahead. Firstly his factory manager was lured away by a competitor and left a gap which was difficult to fill. Worse he took with him a contract which made all the difference to the year's profitability. Then there came a recession when the orders were hard to find. The whole pattern of the industry was changing, calling for more sophisticated machinery. A new production line which was put in in 1947 became redundant two years later with the invention of a more up-to-date process. The old factory building was declared not to be up to the requirements of modern standards and much money had to be spent to satisfy the inspectors.

Sir Charles took these blows with stoical resignation and wondered where it was all leading. It was not until Keith was thirty years old that his father put him on the board. He had served a spell in the Army and that seemed to have straightened him out. He had gained a self assurance which delighted his mother and for which she took all the credit. It was she who had suggested that he resign his commission with a view one day to taking over the reins of the business. 'Give him a chance to prove himself Daddles,' she had urged, using her pet name for her husband which she always did when she wanted anything. 'He'll soon settle down if you show you trust him.' Daddles, who seldom refused her anything, had agreed.

After his meeting with Dick Katz, as Sir Charles drove his 3-litre Rover back to Cumberland Towers at a dignified forty miles an hour, he reflected that Claire had been right as usual. He had put his trust in Keith and Keith was proving himself just as she had said he would. What was it that American had said about him? A go-getter? Perhaps that was just what the Company

16

needed. As he drew near to the ornate gates of his home he stopped the car and got out to look at his herd of cattle grazing on the young spring grass. It would certainly be nice to think that he did not have to go to the office every morning.

At least it was something which was worth discussing with Claire after dinner that evening.

2

Solly's Gym was situated in a yard off the slummier part of Dunbarton Road. A cracked sign above the door announced that it was a club for members only but there was never anybody behind the dilapidated reception desk to question any stranger who might want to intrude on its privacy.

The premises consisted of one large room. This Saturday afternoon a sprinkling of spectators watched two bored-looking pugilists sparring with one another, their heavy head-guards giving them an air of professionalism which their performance scarcely merited. In a corner a young man in a track suit was showing rather more enthusiasm assaulting a fixed punch bag with rapid hammer blows. Others stood about in the middle of the hall throwing a medicine ball to and fro and a few loners were busy with skipping rope exercises while they chewed gum and stared aimlessly at the ceiling. Over all there was a pervasive smell of stale sweat and embrocation.

Harry Birdsall was practising as usual at the top end which was reserved by tradition for the weight lifters. Since he had been out of work he had started the habit of coming every afternoon but he liked Saturdays the best. There were more spectators on Saturdays, even if they were only punters drifting in from the betting shop on the corner between races, and Harry liked being watched at his exercises. Unlike most of the others he took great pride in his appearance. His vest with the initials of the Hercules Weight Lifting Club emblazoned across the chest was always spotless and he even conscientiously scrubbed the laces of his ankle boots to a pristine whiteness. He was altogether a fine looking chap with his fair crisp curly hair and classically regular features. He loved his body. Before going to bed each night he would strip down to his briefs and stand before his wardrobe mirror. Then he would spend half an hour flexing his muscles and taking up poses. He imagined himself one day winning the Mr Universe competition and he thought about it a lot of the time.

Young Chick Brown was also at Solly's. He was a slight pigeon-chested youth of eighteen with a chronically spotty chin. He always came to the gym on the Saturdays when his favourite team, Rangers, was playing away from home for he could never afford the fare to travel to away matches. He took no part in any of the activities at Solly's because he was ashamed of his thin frame and spindly arms but he liked to watch. Now he stood hunched against the wall bars trying to extract a few more puffs from a disintegrating fag end. Smoking was not supposed to be allowed but the management had long since given up trying to enforce the rule. All the time he watched Harry as he practised the snatch lift and the presses and longed for him to get through his routine.

Improbably Harry and Chick were friends. That is to say Harry tolerated having Chick around and Chick in return gave him his unstinted admiration. Today he was particularly keen to see his hero for he had some important news to impart. When Harry finally dropped the weights with a thud on the floor and started to make his way to the changing-room Chick darted after him. He stood behind him just looking while Harry stripped off his vest and started towelling himself vigorously. The news was burning inside him but he was always tongue-tied when Harry was around. When Harry caught sight of him he said, 'Fuck off. How often have I told you I don't like having you around when I'm dressing.'

'Harry, this is important. I've got to have a word with you.'

'I suppose you've got a message from your bleedin' sister. Well tell her from me to get knotted.' Chick's sister, Betty, really fancied Harry and was always trying to use her brother as a go-between.

'No, it's nothing to do with Betty. It's something really important. Honest.'

The two boxers came into the changing-room unbuckling their head gear.

'I can't tell you here,' Chick whispered urgently. 'Will you be down the caff this evening?'

'Might do.' Harry was non-committal, but he was curious in spite of himself.

'Awright.' He pulled a cigarette out of his packet and tossed it over to the boy. 'See you.' He turned back to the mirror and started an elaborate operation with his comb.

Of course Betty Brown insisted on going down to the café with Chick. If Chick had had his wits about him he would have said nothing about the meeting when he had got home to his tea at Inkerman Terrace but he was too excited for that. It was not often that his hero would come out especially to meet him and he could not keep the news to himself.

Betty, in contrast to her younger brother, was a big square girl with unfortunate thick legs and breasts which always threatened to spill over the top of her dress. She was good-natured about most things but when it came to men she pursued her fancies with a dedication which would have done credit to a missionary. Her mother, who was well aware of her weakness, viewed it with a mixture of hope and despair. Mrs Brown belonged to the old school who felt that it was a daughter's duty to her family to get married as quickly as possible but at the same time, as she frequently remarked, things were not the same as in her day. Her husband had died of congestion of the lungs before the children had reached their teens and the struggle to bring them up in the little house in Inkerman Terrace had exhausted her spirit. Chick now appealed to her without much hope.

'You tell her, Ma. She ain't wanted. Harry will murder me if I bring her along. Besides we've got business to talk. Go on. Tell her Ma.'

Mrs Brown fussed over clearing up the tea things. 'I'm sure Betty won't go where she's not wanted,' she said. 'Will you, dearie?'

'Course I'm going,' said Betty. 'It's a free country ain't it?'

Mrs Brown sighed.

In fact things did not go as badly as Chick had at first feared. Harry was late but he came straight over to where they were sitting and bought them both a cup of tea and a wad. He even pinched Betty's leg under the table and asked her in the friendliest way who she was knocking off at the moment which made her giggle and blush deeply. The fact that she was still a virgin was a matter about which she was not sure whether to be proud or distressed.

'Well what's all the mystery about, kidoo?' Harry asked, the preliminaries having been satisfactorily disposed of. 'Spit it out.'

20

'It's what I heard at the works see. They've been talking about it for weeks but we thought it was just the usual buzzes. Then the foreman called us together just before the hooter went last night and told us all about the new contract. It's for that big motor company and there'll be lots of jobs going Harry. Real good jobs—sixty pounds a week some of them and more. And then he said we was to think if we had any mates who had experience and we were to ask them to go along. It's going to be in the papers and everything. I mean advertising for blokes but, if we was to know anyone like ... well I thought of you Harry and your not having a job at the moment ...'

He stopped uncertainly. Harry was looking at him in a way that was not very friendly.

'Who said anything about me wanting a job?' he demanded.

'I just thought ...'

'You just thought!' Harry mimicked. 'Who wants to waste their health and strength over a bleedin' bench. I got my training to think of. I might be in the Olympics next time round.' To be an Olympic weight lifter was another of Harry's dreams.

Chick could think of nothing to say. He'd been sure that Harry would have been pleased. He felt so confused that he dropped a piece of cake in his tea where, when he tried to fish it out with his spoon, it broke up into a mushy mess.

Harry took a nail file out of his top pocket and started to work carefully on his right hand. After a while he said, 'What did you say was the name of this motor company?'

'It's that American Company, Camel,' Chick told him eagerly.

Harry held his nails up to the light, the better to examine his handiwork.

'I'll tell you what I'll do. Drink up your char and I'll stand my hand at the Dreadnought.'

The offer from Harry to stand a drink was so astounding that Chick at once forgot how upset he had been.

They had a couple of pints each at the Dreadnought while Betty had a sweet sherry because she thought it more ladylike and would impress Harry with her class. Chick, who did not normally drink pints, was struggling with his second one when Harry announced that he was moving on. 'Got a bloke to see,' he explained.

They all went along to the Exchange where they drank beer

with chasers and then they went down to O'Malley's Bar in Dock Road. Chick was beginning to feel dizzy and wished he could go home. Betty was getting amorous and hanging on to Harry's arm. When he tried to shake her off she giggled and held on tighter.

At O'Malley's they found the man Harry was looking for. Barney Corcoran was a short thick-set man of about fifty. His hair had retreated and now stood up frizzy and greying like a tilted halo on the back of his head. His blue eyes, moist and devoid of eyelashes, stared out angrily at the world and with his bristly ginger moustache gave his face an expression of perpetual outrage. Harry performed some vague introductions and Betty who was now experiencing considerable difficulty in retaining an upright position let go of his arm and grabbed Barney's instead.

'Bleedin' birds,' said Harry. 'Here, give her a drink and set her down somewhere.' He pushed some money across the counter. Betty allowed herself to be led to a table where she collapsed on the lap of an elderly naval stoker.

'Cor, just look at them tits!' he exclaimed, hardly able to believe his luck. Betty beamed happily. She was unused to such open admiration.

Chick did not remember much more of the evening. For a time Barney Corcoran had shown some interest in him and asked him questions about the Camel contract and the jobs going at Greenbank but he was past the stage when the drink might have made him a little more articulate. He could hardly even remember what it was the foreman had said.

It was closing time before Harry and Barney had finished their own conversation. Betty, deserted by her stoker, was sleeping soundly, her head cradled in her arms. They had a job getting her out to Barney's car. He dropped them outside the house in Inkerman Terrace. Chick couldn't find the lock and in the end it was Harry who took the key and let them in. Betty had stumbled down the passage into the darkness and a moment later they heard her retching over the kitchen sink.

Harry steered Chick into the front parlour. Chick tried to ask him if he would like a cup of tea but the power of speech had left him. They sat together on the little settee with the flowered cushions and a little later Chick became aware that Harry's hand was feeling around inside his trousers. For a moment he stared

22

at the grinning face which hovered over him and which seemed to advance and recede with the beating behind his eyes. Then he dropped his head on Harry's shoulder and started to cry quietly with the wonder and the beauty of it all.

*   *   *

The news that Greenbank had won the Camel contract caused a considerable stir when it was announced to the Press the following week. The *Evening Post* came out with a front page banner 'More Jobs for Clydeside' and the *Clarion* saw in it the beginning of the turn of the tide of depressed industry and rising unemployment. 'This is just the sort of opportunity', wrote their Industrial Correspondent, 'which our industry needs. Greenbank Engineering have demonstrated what can be done. It is to be hoped that other industrial concerns will show the same initiative and enterprise.'

Robert Clancy-Smith read the Press reports with his feet propped comfortably on his desk in Keith's office which he shared when he was in Glasgow.

'I like it. I like it very much. Particularly that piece about initiative and enterprise. For Greenbank Engineering read Robert Clancy-Smith.'

Keith who had been celebrating the signing of the new contract with great energy for the past few nights, rubbed his eyes and yawned.

'Why don't you belt up, Clancy,' he said without rancour. 'By the way in case nobody has told you, there is a conference with the old man at eleven. Everyone is getting a bit hot under the collar about the new production lines and all that sort of rot.'

'I'm glad somebody cares,' said Clancy-Smith suddenly irritable. 'I'm getting a little bit worried about this cosy family company of yours.'

Keith stopped searching through the drawers of his desk for a bottle of aspirin and looked at his friend, surprised. 'What's biting you this morning? Old Thomas getting on to you about your expense account again? I can't say I blame him.'

Clancy-Smith swung his feet off the desk and strolled over to look down into Turk Street.

'Frankly, old boy,' he said without turning round, 'I think the whole set-up stinks.'

23

The warm affection which existed between the two men was marred only by a tendency which Clancy-Smith had developed of late of climbing on to his high horse and delivering himself of Olympian judgments. Keith realized, with resignation, that it was going to be one of those mornings.

'Take Jock MacKay for example. He is a decent enough chap but he has not got what it takes to be a Production Director. The days when thirty years' loyal service to the company were enough to keep a man at the top of the pile are no longer with us. What's needed today is a young man who knows what he wants and is prepared to be bloody minded if he does not get it. As for Ronnie Motion you could write all he knows about man-management on a piece of confetti. He's just not going to be in the right league when we start taking on new men. God knows what happens further down the chain of command but I fear the worst.'

'Why don't you go and lay your pearls of wisdom before the old man? I'm only the office boy around here.'

'It isn't my job. I break my back carrying home the bacon. Somebody else must smoke it.'

Keith tipped his chair backwards and lit a cigarette, blowing a neat ring into the air. 'You know perfectly well father doesn't listen to me. Jock MacKay is his right-hand man.'

'And you are the Crown Prince. I wish I were a rich man's son.'

'What's that supposed to be? A cue for a song?'

'Take it how you like. Sooner or later the old man is going to retire and you'll be the boss. It's time you started to assert yourself.'

Keith shrugged his shoulders. It was all very well for Clancy to talk, but he did not know the problems of being Sir Charles Puddefant's son. How could you talk to someone who would never realize that you had grown up? Certainly they had been getting on better of late but that did not alter the fact that they were as far apart in their interests as two people could possibly be. If only the old man would hit the roof occasionally, or get drunk, or pinch one of the secretaries' bottoms there might be some hope of them understanding each other. The trouble with Sir Charles was that he was too damned decent.

The office intercom buzzed and Miss Thatcher, the Chairman's colourlessly efficient secretary, announced that the meeting was ready to start.

The two men went slowly along the corridor to the Board Room each occupied with a train of thought which was just beginning to work along similar lines.

*   *   *

At exactly the same time as the Board of Directors of Greenbank Engineering were deliberating on the best method of handling the Camel contract, another meeting was being held just half a mile away at which the same matter featured prominently on the agenda. At one side of the paper-strewn desk, perspiring slightly in the overpowering heat of the room, sat Mr Barney Corcoran and at the other, his head sunk in his shoulders and with a hot-water bottle resting on the ledge of his enormous stomach, was the formidable figure of Mr Ignatius Salvatori.

Iggy, as he was known to his friends and even to those who held him in less high esteem like certain members of the Glasgow Police Force, was remarkable to look upon. His head was pear-shaped, rising to a pointed dome from which all hair had been shaved down to a bristly grey stubble. At the base the heavy jowls of his cheeks flowed into his many fleshy chins which bulged over and almost obscured the stiff white collar and carefully tied polka dot bow tie which alone marked where his neck should have been. When he walked, which was as little as possible his over-long arms hung loosely by his sides and his great belly swung ponderously to and fro so that he resembled a gorilla which had gone badly to seed. More often, as when he indulged in his favourite occupation of attending the race-tracks, he was pushed in a specially constructed wheel chair with pneumatic tyres which folded up to fit in the boot of his large black Austin motor car.

Iggy's origins were as mysterious as the source of his undoubted affluence. He had appeared out of nowhere some ten years previously and had opened The Continental Book Store in Dunbarton Road from which he purveyed a variety of literature with such alluring titles as *The History of Corporal Punishment, Ladies of the Night* and *Fetishes through the Ages*. It was this activity which had brought him from time to time to the attention of the authorities but the periodical fines and the occasional confiscation of his stock did not appear in any way to deter him from serving what he considered to be the cultural needs of his public.

25

Just now, however, the thoughts of Mr Ignatius Salvatori were very far from culture.

'Go on, Mr Corcoran,' he said, his voice silky soft, 'you were telling me about your friend Harry Birdsall.'

'Well, that's all there is to it really. He comes to me with this info about Greenbank and I tell him to go ahead and get himself in. So he goes on the Monday morning and he's taken on.'

'You did not perhaps think it wise to ask me first?'

'You wasn't here.'

'Quite so, Mr Corcoran. Quite so. I had some business which took me out of town. Exactly what instructions did you give Mr Birdsall?'

'I just told him to get himself in and keep his nose clean. The machinery won't be running for another couple of months.'

'You know of course that Mr Birdsall is a homosexual.' It was a statement rather than a question.

'Of course I know he is a bleedin' poof. There's plenty more than him the same way. Here, how do you know so much about him anyway?'

'I make it my business to know these things. I think you ought to know something else about Mr Birdsall.'

'What's that then?' Barney shifted uncomfortably on his seat while Iggy's little eyes, sunk in a mountain of flesh, bored into his damp soul.

'Mr Birdsall is one of those remarkable people who have been born completely without any brain. He is an animal with no power of reasoning. An interesting phenomenon you might think, Mr Corcoran, if it were not that you suffer from much the same deficiency yourself.'

'Don't call me names.' His ginger moustache bristled pugnaciously and the sweat was beginning to run in little rivulets. 'I don't have to sit here and listen to your crap.'

Iggy ignored the small show of rebellion. He pulled the shawl which he wore round his shoulders tighter and adjusted the hotwater bottle to a more comfortable position. In spite of his great bulk he never felt warm in Glasgow's climate. 'On the other hand stupidity can sometimes be an asset. We shall have to watch Mr Birdsall but perhaps he is not such a bad choice after all.' He smiled a bleak little smile. 'You can go now, Mr Corcoran.'

Barney accepted his dismissal with alacrity. He let himself out

26

of the front of the shop. Outside the rain was being whipped into sharp flurries by an icy wind. He shivered as he turned up the collar of his grubby mackintosh. Mr Bloomin' Salvatori he decided, not for the first time, gave him the willies.

3

Harry Birdsall had no difficulty in getting taken on at Greenbank. He had been in and out of jobs since he was sixteen but he had never been sacked for inefficiency. The fact that he had never stayed in any job for very long was because of his health. He was quite convinced that he was not suited to working. He'd stick it for perhaps two or three months and then get a line from the doctor that he was suffering from strain and go on sick pay for as long as it took his employers to realize that he had no intention of returning. Then the next time there were any redundancies, Harry's name would be on the top of the list. This treatment of a potential Olympic champion made him very bitter indeed.

Jim Cantlie, the Works Manager, knew nothing of this when he took Harry on.

'Had a bit of bad luck with redundancies in the past,' he commented, glancing over the record.

'You know what it is on Clydeside,' Harry muttered.

Cantlie nodded. 'Well if you stick in here there will be no trouble of that kind. We look after our people at Greenbank.'

Harry smiled, trying to hide his contempt. Of course Cantlie did not know about Barney Corcoran either. It gave Harry a sense of power which he found very gratifying.

Barney's record was rather different from Harry's. He had been sacked from every job he had ever held and he was well known as a trouble-maker. The high peak of his career had been when he had been the centre of a strike in the shipyards which had brought Clydeside to a halt. Then he had had his picture in the papers and even appeared on television. It had made him something of a hero but it had not got him his job back. After that he was on every employer's black list and he had never worked again.

In a way it was the best thing that had ever happened to him. With his wife and the two boys out at work and his unemployment pay to draw every week there was plenty of beer money even without Iggy. Iggy was the cream on top of the milk.

Barney's job for Iggy was to keep his ear to the ground. If there was any trouble brewing he'd get to hear about it in his daily perambulations around the bars. Then he would slip up to the bookshop in Dunbarton Road and there would be a few fivers for his trouble. Iggy could be very generous even if he was a bastard. Sometimes he gave Barney other jobs to do like organizing the picket lines outside factory gates which had been blacked. That was the job he loved. He'd had his share of knocks in life and it gave him an almost erotic thrill to be able to kick back. He hated with a dull hatred which was all he had to sustain him. He even hated his pinched little wife who got up at six o'clock every morning to be in time to clean the floors and scrub out the lavatories in the Directors' suite of the Crossfield Finance Corporation but he took her money just the same. He hated his two sons, one of whom wore a smart suit every day and was a floor walker in Drummond's the gent's outfitters in Argyle Street and the other one was a gardener with the Glasgow Corporation and went to night-school—but he took their contributions as well ...

There was great excitement at Greenbank with the taking on of the new men and the replanning of the shop floor to accommodate the new production lines. The whole of the renovated number three and four sheds were needed for the plant. There was to be a new canteen, larger rest rooms and all manner of similar improvements for which there had never seemed to have been a need in the past.

Right at the beginning of the transformation Jock MacKay came down from Turk Street and called everyone together. Not always the most fluent of orators, he had been enthusiastic about the bright prospects which lay before them all, laid it on about the need for a high standard of workmanship, welcomed the new men and finished up with some platitudes about being one big happy family. It was greeted with some clapping and a few isolated attempts to raise a cheer. There was no doubt that morale was at a high pitch.

Nobody could have been happier than Chick Brown. He had woken up in the morning after his night out with Harry with a dreadful pain in his head but a lightness of spirit which stayed with him all day. What had happened in the front parlour was only a vague recollection but the memory of it excited him no end.

It proved that Harry was really his friend and nothing could be more truly marvellous than that. He longed to tell someone but there was no one he could—perhaps not even Billy Caird. He could see nothing wrong in what had happened but he was not sure that Billy would understand.

Of course in the end he had been unable to keep it to himself. Billy and Chick had grown up together. They had shared a desk at school and had joined Greenbank on the same day. Each regarded the other as his best friend although they were really complete opposites. Chick was the practical one. Billy dreamed dreams. His favourite dream was that one day he would win the football pools. He worked on them every Wednesday night, going through agonies of mental stress before deciding which teams to mark with the magical crosses. He never went to see a match because the crowds frightened him but stayed every Saturday afternoon, glued to the television to catch the latest scores as they flickered briefly on the screen. He spent the rest of his money on motoring magazines which he studied closely to pick out which model he would buy when his coupon came up.

'You mean he actually put his hand on it?' Billy gasped when Chick finally blurted out his news. 'Actually touched it?'

'That's right.' Chick, now he had said it, was gratified by the sensation he had caused. 'What's wrong wi' that? It was only a bit of fun like.'

'Jesus!' said Billy, impressed in spite of himself. He knew Harry Birdsall and was a little frightened of him. Then, to hide his embarrassment, he changed the subject. 'How about you and Betty coming down to the caff tonight? I haven't seen her for some time.'

'Do you fancy our Betty then?' Chick gave a superior grin.

'She's all right,' said Billy non-committally. He'd been thinking a lot about Betty lately. Unlike most of the lads who talked about their birds the whole time, he had never had a steady. 'We could have a fish supper if she's not doing anything.'

'See you down the caff then.'

'Ta-ra for now.'

'Ta-ra.'

* * *

Angus Simpson, the General Manager at Greenbank, viewed

30

the new contract with his usual cautious pessimism. He was a big man with a long cadaverous face and walked with a pronounced stoop, his head hung forward as if it was too heavy for his body. When he sat behind his desk in his glass office overlooking the factory floor he looked like an elderly vulture searching for some prey to pounce upon. In spite of his forbidding appearance, however, he was a quiet man. He did his best to avoid any sort of trouble. With three years to go before he reached the age of retirement his ambition was to go on doing his job until the time came when he would be able to devote himself exclusively to solving crossword puzzles and looking after the wants of his wife whose remaining pleasure in life was to discover in herself the symptoms of new and ever more interesting illnesses.

Now he had a meeting. There was Jim Cantlie, the Works Manager, young-looking for his forty-five years, whose hobby was racing pigeons and who secretly resented Angus Simpson his job. He felt he could do it himself much more efficiently. As Ellie his wife constantly told him he could have had the job if he had not taken so much time off waiting for a favourite bird to find its way back to the loft in the garden of his neat little house in the less smart part of Paisley. There was a joke about Jim waiting for his birds coming home to roost when he had an old rooster at home who was only too keen to fly away. Ellie was not so much of an old rooster that she did not still want to look around. She was defying forty and resenting the other half of her bed lying empty so often. The third man at the meeting was Willie Jameson the senior foreman.

'I've had Sandy Gaul to see me,' Willie was now saying. Sandy was the Convenor of the Shop Stewards. 'He's not at all happy about the situation.'

Angus nodded his over-large head like a jerky puppet. 'I know fine we are going to have trouble. I've said it all along. What's Gaul on about?'

'For one thing he wants his own office. He says that with the new intake he'll have to give his full time to looking after his members ...'

'Who the hell does he think he is!' snapped Jim Cantlie. 'He's paid as a machine operator first and he's the Convenor in his spare time. That is the way it has always been.'

'Not nowadays,' said Willie mildly. 'We've got over five hun-

31

dred new men remember and we're likely to finish up with almost a thousand. There's quite a few factories of our size have a full-time Convenor.'

'Full-time troublemaker more like.'

'I don't think Sandy is a troublemaker. It's just that he wants to feel more important.'

'Well he's not going to feel important in my time. He can rule the roost as much as he likes outside working hours.'

'Steady, Jim,' said Angus. 'We don't want to start off on the wrong foot. There'll be plenty of trouble as it is.'

'What sort of trouble?' Jim demanded. 'The men are well paid. With the new building they have got better working conditions than they ever had. All I want from them is a fair day's work.'

'You won't get it if you rub Sandy Gaul up the wrong way. He'll be led but he won't be driven.'

Angus leant back in his chair and raised his hands as if absolving himself from any responsibility in the matter. 'It is a matter for the Directors,' he said. 'I'll have a word with Mr Motion.'

Ronnie Motion—'Slow' Motion as he was inevitably known to the men on the shop floor—would have strongly resented Clancy-Smith's view of his competence had he known about it. Since he had assumed the role of Personnel Manager in addition to his job as Chief Administrator he had attended a Summer Course at Oxford devoted to the study of man-management and he had read several books on the subject. He had never actually experienced an industrial confrontation but he was confident that if the situation arose he would be able to deal with it wisely and firmly.

'Management are not always without blame in these matters,' he liked to say to anyone who would listen. 'The whole thing is good communications. If management would only communicate with their workers a lot of the trouble would be avoided. Now at Greenbank we have excellent communications. That's why we have never had any trouble.'

When Angus Simpson approached him on the subject of the Convenor of the Shop Stewards having his own office he welcomed it as an opportunity to show that he was fully aware of the problems arising from the working of the new contract.

'I think we must all realize, Mr Simpson, that it is not just the new contract which is important. It is the *nature* of the contract. Working for Camel makes us a key factory. If you read Trotsky

32

on the subject you'll know that this makes us all the more vulnerable to the attentions of the militants.' Angus who had not read Trotsky nodded his head. It was what he said all along.

'On the whole I would be inclined to agree to Mr Gaul's request but it must be made clear that if we are being reasonable with him he must be reasonable with us. We are one big happy family here and I will not tolerate any militants creeping in.'

'Jim Cantlie won't like it, Mr Motion.'

'When Cantlie is sitting in my chair he can make the decisions. Is there anything else?'

'Not at the moment, Mr Motion,' said Angus and went his gloomy way.

*　　*　　*

Harry Birdsall looked forward to the meeting to elect the new shop stewards with an excitement which was slightly tinged with apprehension. Barney Corcoran had been emphatic in his instructions. He was to get himself elected to the Shop Stewards' Committee without fail. The thought of being a shop steward made him feel important. For the first time in his life he would be somebody to be looked up to. But suppose he wasn't elected.

'Dinna bother aboot that,' Barney had told him. 'There's not many men will want the job. That young mate of yours is working in the new shop. Get him to pass the word around amongst some of his pals.' Harry duly had a word with Chick. He and Billy as apprentices had both been transferred to work on the Camel contract. Chick took his duties as chief election agent for Barney with considerable enthusiasm and became indignant when he found that it was not an enthusiasm which was shared by many of his workmates.

'They can make the ruddy Pope a shop steward for all I care,' said Sam McGee. 'I won't be at the meeting anyway.' It was an attitude which reflected the views of most of the men.

The meeting was called at stopping time in the big canteen. It was perhaps unfortunate that it coincided with a replay on television of the Celtic-Milan football match which most of the men were hurrying home to watch. There were less than thirty men present when Sandy Gaul called for order.

'Brothers, the main object of the meeting tonight is to elect three shop stewards who will be responsible for all of you work-

33

ing on the new assembly lines. You know what an important part your shop steward has got to play in representing your complaints and in making sure that you get a fair day's pay for a fair day's work. Anything you raise with your shop steward will be brought by him to me as the Convenor and discussed by the shop steward committee. If we decide that it is something which should be taken up with Supervision you can be sure that we shall do so with the utmost vigour. Remember that the days when management had all the power are over. The power rests with us on the shop floor. It's your vote now that counts. So far at these works I have never had to resort to withholding our labour but if the circumstances justify it I will not hesitate to do so.' It was a little speech he always made on these occasions. It was a matter of considerable regret to him that so few of the men he represented seemed to appreciate his efforts. Much of his spare time was devoted to Trade Union matters and he could not understand why it did not bring him more respect from those he sought to serve.

As Sandy sat down, Jim Anderson, a craggy giant of a man from the Western Isles, got to his feet.

'I have just three names nominated,' he said. 'Is there anyone else would like to put themselves forward?' There was a certain amount of nudging and muttering amongst the audience but nobody spoke up.

'Very well, we'll vote on the first name. All those in favour signify in the usual manner. Jim Pocock.' All hands were raised. 'Unanimously elected. Eddie Butterworth. Unanimously elected. Harry Birdsall. Unanimously elected. Thank you, brothers. That concludes the business for the evening.'

The men broke up into little groups, chatting idly amongst themselves. As they drifted out of the room Sandy Gaul came over to where Harry was standing with Chick and Billy.

'There will be a meeting of the Shop Stewards' Committee tomorrow night to elect one of you new lads to the Works Committee. Will you be there?'

'Aye,' said Harry still a little amazed how easy it had all been. 'I'll be along right enough.' Sandy nodded briefly and passed on to another group.

'Works Committee eh. That'll be something if I make it.' He already felt taller. 'Come on lads. We'll go down to the Dreadnought tonight and have one.'

Harry was elected to serve on the Works Committee at the general meeting of shop stewards the next night. It was a one-horse race. Jim Pocock and Eddie Butterworth, the two other newly elected men, decided that they had taken on quite enough extra as it was and would not let their names be put forward. Harry looked at it a different way. The more responsibility he had as a Union man the more excuses he would have for being absent from his bench. He could not wait to tell Barney Corcoran the news. Even Barney would have to admit that he had done well, but first he had to endure a short lecture from Sandy Gaul.

Sandy was in many ways the ideal man for his job. He was a dedicated Trade Unionist. When Willie Jameson had said that Sandy Gaul wanted to feel more important by having his own office he was wide of the mark. What Sandy wanted was for his job to be recognized as more important by the management. He was constantly concerned with status and recognition. What he would like to have been was a full-time Trade Union Official but somehow the opportunity had never presented itself. There was nothing he liked better than negotiating, particularly when he was backed by the warm feeling that he was doing something for his fellow workers. He was also an elder of St Columbus Church and handed round the plate with an air of considerable unction.

After the Friday meeting was over he took Harry aside and putting his hand on his shoulder addressed him earnestly on the importance of his new position.

'We don't look for trouble, Brother Birdsall,' he said, his eyes glittering behind his heavy-rimmed glasses with a missionary zeal, 'but if we find that our labour is being misused or that we are not getting our just demands we must not shrink from our duty to instruct our members to act together to secure our aims. It may mean hardship to our families but our principles come first.'

Harry wanted to say 'Bollocks'. Instead he smiled his secret smile and escaped as soon as he could to the Dreadnought where Barney Corcoran was waiting for him.

4

It was early in April, when the work on the installation of the
new production lines had just got under way, that Keith Puddefant and Clancy-Smith were invited to visit the main Camel
works in Detroit. It was mentioned almost as an afterthought in a
letter from Richard Katz to Sir Charles.

'I'd like to have them know a bit more about our organization,'
he wrote. 'I really want them to feel that they are part of the
team here in the States as well as in the U.K. It would give me the
greatest pleasure if they would be the guests of my wife and
myself at our home in Grosse Pointe. We'll try to show them a
good time as well as have them see around the plant.'

Keith's enthusiasm for the visit was unbounded. He had never
crossed the Atlantic before and he felt the omission acutely when
with his more travelled friends. Clancy pretended to play it
cooler. 'There'll probably be a lot of bullshit and not much fun
and games,' he gave as his opinion but he did not delay in accept-
ing.

They had an overnight stop in New York where they were
met by Harry Grohman, the Camel Vice-President in charge of
sales. He took them to dinner in a restaurant forty storeys above
Fifth Avenue where they could look down at the toy cars far
below.

'One in six of all those cars you see down there is a Camel,'
said Harry proudly. His thoughts were never very far away from
his sales charts. 'You boys are really going to see something when
you get over to Detroit.'

Keith grinned vacantly. Everything he had seen since he had
arrived at Kennedy Airport had made him light-headed with
wonder. There had been many drinks on the aircraft and only
time for a quick shower and a change of clothes before they had
been due to meet Harry. Harry had insisted on the driest of

martinis as his recipe for combating jet lag. By the time they were ready to eat Keith was in a state of such euphoria that he had lost his interest in food. The martinis which kept arriving were easier to manage. It was almost midnight when Harry announced that they were moving on to a little place he knew on East 46 Street.

'Just a nightcap then,' said Clancy. 'We have an early start tomorrow.' He knew Keith's drinking moods and he was beginning to feel anxious. There were already signs that his expansive phase was changing to truculence. It would not be the first time that Keith had spoilt a good party after too many drinks and he did not want it to happen in front of Harry.

They walked the two blocks to Joe's Bar in a light flurry of snowflakes, the cold air making them catch their breath. Once inside it was dark and warm. A scattering of customers sat around at small tables drinking morosely while a television, the sound turned down, flickered unheeded at the end of the long narrow room. The bar stools were empty except for an elderly man in the corner who dozed fitfully, his hat on the back of his head and holding his full glass tightly in one hand as if somebody might try to steal it away from him while he slept.

Harry Grohman was greeted by the barman like a prodigal son.

'What's been keeping you away?' he asked.

'Must be all of three days. Long time,' grinned Harry. 'Come on, let's have some Scotch for a change. Those martinis play hell with my liver.'

They drank 12-year-old malt whisky from tall glasses packed with ice.

Harry raised his glass. 'Here's one good thing which comes from Scotland anyhow.'

'Meaning you don't think we can make good transmissions as well,' said Clancy, but he was smiling.

'God knows how you boys got that contract. You must have had the Archangel Gabriel on your side.'

'Luck of the draw,' said Clancy placidly. 'We'll do a good job and it will save you a few headaches. It's a good set-up isn't it, Keith?'

Keith was trying to focus on his glass.

'To hell with the contract,' he said. 'What about some girls.'

'One track mind,' said Clancy. 'Ignore him, Harry. Time we

37

thought of hitting the hay, old son.' He leaned across Harry and put his hand on Keith's arm.

Keith shook him off impatiently and took a long pull at his drink. The ice cascaded down the glass so that the whisky spilled down his chin and spattered over his shirt front.

'What a way to drink whisky. Bloody ice with everything.' He started hooking the lumps out with his fingers so that they slithered across the shiny counter and fell on the floor. 'Here, give me a decent drink I can taste.' He banged his glass down hard.

Harry grimaced across at the barman. 'Give the gentleman what he wants,' he said. 'No ice.'

Keith knocked it back in one quick movement, the neat spirit making him gag. 'Let's go and find some birds,' he said thickly. 'I want a bird.'

'Pack it in, Keith,' Clancy said sharply. To the barman he said, 'Can you call me a cab? I'll take him back to the hotel.'

'You can go to the hotel on your own. I'm gonna look for a bird. Surely you've got birds over here.' He looked belligerently at Harry.

'Sure we've got birds but what I reckon you need now is some sleep. Why not let Joe here call you a cab. Maybe I can get a girl sent round to your hotel.' Harry winked at Clancy. He was used to visiting businessmen who could not take their liquor.

Keith gave the proposition his grave consideration. 'Got to have a pee first,' he announced.

'It's down the end there. Mind how you go,' said Joe.

They watched as Keith weaved his way between the tables, holding on to the backs of the chairs for support. One or two customers looked up with bored indifference. They had seen it all before.

'He'll be all right,' said Clancy. 'He's a great guy until he's had too much. Then he's impossible.'

'Quite smart in business the boss says.' It was more a question than a statement.

'Yes and no. He'd been held down too long. Won't do anything on his own initiative.'

'Scared?'

Clancy shook his head and rubbed his forefinger and thumb together. 'Money. Sir Charles is the moneybags. Keith has to go to him for everything and he's got expensive tastes. If it wasn't

38

for the money he wouldn't give a damn.'

'But he'll have some of the equity. It's a family business. Surely he's got quite a heap of stock.'

'Very little. Maybe he'd have had more but there was a long time that they did not get along together. That was before I came on the scene. They are not exactly buddies now. It's more a question of live and let live. It's not to say that Keith won't get a bigger share when the old man finally retires.'

'Any idea when that is likely to be?'

'I wouldn't know. Sometimes I think it might be quite soon. He did not exactly welcome the Camel contract at first you know.' The memory of Sir Charles's attitude still rankled with him. 'So far as I am concerned the sooner the old buffer goes the better.'

'That would make you a pretty important guy in the set-up. I mean that you have more influence with Keith than anybody from what I hear.'

Clancy was flattered. He was vaguely aware that he was being pumped for information for a purpose but it made him feel important. He ordered another drink but Harry insisted that he was not allowed to pay.

'It's all on the firm. Why waste your own money? On a trip like this you want to make out of your expenses. You can do the same for me sometime.' They both laughed like schoolboys sharing a secret of stolen apples.

'We ought to keep close to one another,' said Harry. 'We may just be simple salesmen but in our job, remember, we see most of the game.' He paused long enough to light a cigarette. Then he said, 'I'm going to tell you something that I shouldn't.' He leant forward confidentially, his hand on Clancy's arm. 'Dick Katz is interested in your little company. Very interested indeed. He'd like to take a stake in it but he does not know how to go about it because Sir Charles does not look like selling but maybe the time will come. Then you might be able to help us. We'd make it worth your while, if you take my meaning.'

Clancy inhaled his cigarette smoke slowly and tried to look cool.

Harry paused for a moment as if to make up his mind about something. Then he said, 'Listen Clancy, you seem to me like a guy who has all his back teeth. Were you really taken in by all that shit that Doxy gave you in London?'

Clancy looked up in surprise in spite of himself.

'Oh, I'm not saying that there was not something in it but Dick Katz is a real smart cookie. He does not put more cards on the table than he has to. That guy collects companies like kids collect postage stamps. There is nothing he likes better than a big show where all the stock is held by the family. It's meat and drink for him and he has had his eye on Greenbank for a long time. When Bill Hamilton came up with your name, it was like manna from heaven. I was only fooling when I said I didn't know how you got the contract. It was all over from the start. The rest was only a smoke screen and a bit of jockeying for position.'

'It fooled me,' said Clancy. 'Why are you telling me this?'

'The way I look at it,' said Harry, 'you're too big a man to stay in one little pond all your life. You'll want to branch out. If we had a stake in Greenbank that would be your big chance. You'd be part of the Camel Corporation and that's really big time.'

'I don't want to bother you but your friend has been gone a long time.' Joe interrupted them just as Clancy was struggling for the right words to conceal his sudden excitement. 'Want me to go look for him?'

'I'll go,' Clancy said, half glad of the excuse. 'He'll be sleeping it off.'

A minute later he was back.

'No sign of him,' he said. 'I can't understand it.'

'Hell,' said Joe. 'There's a back way out. He's blown!'

They all knew it was pointless but they went through to the washroom and called his name.

'He's found the fire door,' said Joe apologetically. 'Have to keep it open. Fire regulations.'

'Was he carrying a lot of dough?'

'I don't think so. Mostly travellers' cheques. He'll be all right. Keith can look after himself,' said Clancy with a confidence he did not feel.

Clancy and Harry took a tour downtown more because they felt they should do something rather than in the hope of picking him up. Then Harry dropped Clancy back at his hotel.

'If he's just picked up a hooker and taken her some place the chances are he'll finish up with a sore head and a hole in his billfold. Anyway call me when he surfaces—no matter what time.'

Clancy promised.

'Oh—and Clancy. Don't forget what we were talking about.'

'I won't. We'll be in touch.' They shook hands, each putting his left hand on the other's shoulder as a token of their solidarity. If he hadn't been so worried Clancy would have gone to bed feeling on top of the world.

* * *

Clancy was up and dressed and on his second cup of coffee when his bedroom-door buzzer went. It was Keith, swaying slightly, his eyes looking like poached eggs.

'For God's sake,' Clancy said. 'Where the hell have you been.'

'Not to worry, old man. Not to worry. I'm just fine.'

'Well you don't look fine. Come in and get tidied up. I was just going to call the police.'

'You worry too much. That's your trouble. You missed a hell of a party.'

'Never mind about the party. Our plane goes in an hour. Do you think you can make it?'

'No bother old boy. Just give me a cup of coffee.'

In the end the plane left without them. Clancy rang Harry who rebooked them on the midday flight. He came down to pick them up and drive them out to the airport. By the time he got there Keith was well on the road to recovery and nursing his first gin and tonic.

'Sorry if I ditched you,' he said cheerfully. 'Clancy tells me I was bloody rude. I don't remember a thing. All I remember was meeting this girl. It was in some bar just a couple of doors down the street. We bought a bottle or two and went back to her place. Boy oh boy, did she give me a good time! Better than anything you will find in London.'

'We were just worried about you. Could have run yourself into a heap of trouble. How did you make out for money?'

'Cost me a few dollars but what the hell! This is living isn't it?'

'How much?'

'Well maybe two hundred dollars, maybe a bit more.'

Harry pulled a dollar fold from his pocket and counted out three hundred dollars. 'Here,' he said. 'Compliments of the firm.

41

Be our guest. Lucky it wasn't worse.' When Keith hesitated he said, 'Go on. You're going to need it if you go on as you're going.'

Keith took the money. 'I'll do the same for you sometime. We'll get old Harry over to London eh, Clancy?'

When they got on the plane, Keith could not get over Harry's generosity. 'Some firm to be in with, Clancy. Can you imagine old Thomas shelling that sort of money out?'

Clancy nodded. If the truth were known the gesture had impressed him far more than it had impressed Keith. In his imagination he was already growing wings.

If either of them had been able to listen in to a conversation between Harry Grohman and Richard Katz neither of them might have felt so warm inside.

'Young Puddefant is a lush and stupid with it,' he reported. 'Clancy-Smith is smart but not as smart as he thinks. Give them the royal treatment and I reckon we are more than half way home. I'd rather fancy a seat on the board of that little outfit, Dick. By the way, Clancy-Smith thought he was real clever in pulling that contract. I disillusioned him; he knows where we stand.'

Dick Katz grunted and replaced the receiver but he was well pleased. Ever since his father had appointed him to the top executive position four years ago he had dreamed dreams of power far outside the restrictions which even a giant corporation can impose. First there had been the little electronics business he had picked up on the West Coast for a song and which was now a high flyer on the stock market. There had been a rustle in Wall Street when he had bid fifty million dollars for the Mobile Trucking Corporation and won the takeover battle against all odds. He had got a foot into Europe with the acquisition of the Schwartz Company in Germany and soon they were describing him as the 'man with the Midas touch'. His interest in Britain as a future field for expansion and diversification of interests sprang from his belief in the equation of low wages and good craftsmanship and a sublime confidence that he could find the executives to handle any local problem which might arise.

In many ways Dick Katz was a model tycoon. He took regular exercise as part of his daily routine and was rewarded by looking ten years younger than he should. He was a loving husband and father about whom there had never been a breath of scandal. He was a devoted son to his ageing father, who hung on as President of the Corporation, and he had a host of friends unconnected with his business enterprises. His capacity for personally attending to the smallest detail was perhaps one of the secrets of his success and his ruthless drive was concealed behind a charm which had to be admitted even by the victims of his devouring ambition.

From the moment their plane touched down Keith and Clancy were accorded the sort of treatment to which only the very rich and famous can aspire. A uniformed chauffeur ushered them to the Katz limousine drawn up alongside the arrival bay. The Katz mansion as they approached it down a straight gravelled driveway looked like an elaborate iced confection set about with towers and turrets which glinted in the cold afternoon sunlight. Elenor Katz greeted them in the hall, a tiny Dresden-like person dwarfed by the giant chandeliers and the rows of armoured figures which lined the walls.

'Dick has had to go back to the office. He was expecting you earlier.'

'I'm sorry,' said Clancy awkwardly. 'We missed our plane.'

Her eyes twinkled briefly.

'Hell,' he thought, 'she already knows about last night.'

'I'll have your bags sent up to your rooms. Come and have some tea. You must be frozen. I always tell Dick this is no time of the year to live in this climate.' She drew an embroidered shawl about her shoulders and shivered in spite of the warmth.

By the time Dick arrived back they had bathed and changed and were standing chatting round a blazing fire in the drawing-room.

'Sorry not to be there to meet you. Something cropped up at the office. Here, what's happened to the organization, honey. Nobody's got a drink.' He was all charm, making them feel comfortable and important.

*   *   *

The following morning breakfast was served to them in their bedrooms. Dick Katz had already left the house an hour earlier. Elenor, they learned, did not appear until midday but a chauffeured limousine waited to take them out to the main plant.

Dick Katz's office was disappointingly unpretentious. No priceless oil paintings adorned the walls. Instead there were framed

43

certificates announcing awards made to the Corporation's products. There was not even the battery of telephones on his large
glass-topped paper-free desk which Hollywood has accustomed
everyone to believe to be a necessity for the tycoon. The only
personal note was a silver-framed photograph of Dick and Elenor
shaking hands with L. B. Johnson.

Dick came out from behind his desk to greet them. The some-
what antiseptic secretary with the white cuffs and collar who
had shown them in wheeled in a trolley of coffee and soft
drinks.

'Have Frank Kreisel come on up, Miss Curtis.' He turned to
Keith. 'I'm having Frank take you over for the next couple of
days to show you round. He's one of our oldest employees. Now
he's attached to our public relations office but he has been through
the mill. There is pretty well nothing he doesn't know about the
set-up. Ask him anything you like. I've given you top security
clearance.'

Kreisel was a tall, grey-haired man with bushy eyebrows and
a bulldog jaw. His suit sat rather awkwardly on him as if he
would have been more comfortable in overalls and his big
powerful hands indicated that he had not spent all his time in a
desk job. He exuded friendliness like a cosy bear.

'Of course I don't hold with these modern methods,' he con-
fided to Keith and Clancy as he pushed the descend button of the
executive lift. 'In my day we really built cars. I was on chassis
frames in the old days. They don't use them any more. It's all
monocoque construction. Fine and easy but wait till something hits
you. All the safety devices in the world aren't going to help
you.'

'How long have you been in the industry, Mr Kreisel?' Clancy
asked.

'Frank. Just call me Frank. We don't stand on ceremony over
here. You Limeys are so damned polite it takes you half an hour
to decide who's going through the door first.' His craggy grin
denied that there was any animosity in his words. 'Well I have
been in the automobile industry just on the half century. Started
just about fifty years ago with Henry Ford. Now there was a man.
You know what they used to say about him? There was a jingle
used to go:

"There was a little man
And his name was Henry Ford,
He took a piece of rubber
And a little piece of board,
A little drop of petrol
And an old tin can,
And he stuck the lot together
And the damned thing ran."

'It wasn't true of course. We really built automobiles in those days. Built them to last. Why, some of the cars I helped to build are still running. There's not a car coming off the production lines today that will be worth a couple of dimes in five years' time let alone fifty.'

'Mr Katz wouldn't like to hear you say that,' Clancy smiled.

'Aw, Dick knows it's true. It would be bad for business if autos lasted for ever. The industry is supported by the guy who only runs his bus for a year and then changes it. We are turning them out at the rate of one every fifty seconds. Somebody's got to buy them.'

When they entered A shed the noise made conversation almost impossible. They were at the start of the production line where the thin sheets of steel were fed into the vast stampings presses to be moulded into bodies.

The shed with its high-vaulted glass roof seemed to stretch away to infinity.

'From here to the finished product each automobile travels a mile and a half,' Frank shouted. Every few yards there were boiler-suited men in baseball caps who chewed gum and gazed ahead of them with blank eyes as they went through the repetitive routine of feeding the presses. Few of them bothered to glance up as they moved down the line.

'That man there feeds in 200 sheets in the hour. Every time he puts in a sheet it clocks up on this meter so that we can check his productivity. Eight-hour day with two half-hour breaks.' Frank intoned the facts like a guide showing a party round an art gallery.

It took them all day before they had seen over the plant by which time they were exhausted and deafened and looking forward to the luxury of a hot bath and cold martinis.

45

The following day was spent largely in the design department where Al Bouchier, the chief designer, showed them the blueprint for the new Camel Convertible.

'It's a completely new concept in motoring,' he said with all the pride of a father with a new-born son. 'What we are aiming to do is to produce a specialist car for the mass market. We believe that there is a big public who do not want motoring made easier for them all the time. Now this baby you really have to drive to get the best out of it. This is the all-American sports car. Europe has had a monopoly of the sports car market for too long. This is going to knock everyone's eye out. It's all part of the new Camel image.' He enthused about the gear ratios, the suspension, the steering and the other features which made it fast and manoeuvrable.

Keith and Clancy were mesmerized by it all. The very vastness of the business stunned them and the obvious competence with which the whole production was conducted made them think ruefully of their homespun efforts at Greenbank.

The highlight of the visit came on the third day when they were taken out to the testing grounds and allowed to take the new convertible round the track. Dick Katz joined them.

'Great. Just great,' he enthused. 'We'll have you both entered for Indianapolis yet.' Later as he drove them back to the house he turned to Keith. 'I've got a special treat for you this evening. We have a few folk coming in for dinner. One of them is a countrywoman of yours—by adoption at least. She is married to one of your Scottish Earls. He's a lucky guy. She's a very pretty girl and her father could probably buy me twice over.' Dick liked making modest assessments of his own wealth.

In fact there were twenty for dinner. There were two Congressmen with their wives, a professor of cybernetics who, Keith discovered, played off a golf handicap of two, and the President of a Madison Avenue advertising agency as well as several of the younger set from Detroit. Lady Juliet Ochil was almost the last to arrive. Keith was facing the door engaged in a rather dull conversation with a young anthropologist when she made her entrance. As her name was announced, she paused for a moment, her head thrown back like a mannequin about to make her trip down the catwalk. Her honey brown skin contrasted dramatically with her plain white halter-neck gown gathered at the waist with

46

a thin gold belt and devoid of any jewellery. As heads turned she bestowed a dazzling smile around the room like a queen acknowledging her just tribute. When she turned to greet her host, Keith gazed with admiration at her titian hair which cascaded down her naked back. Richard Katz had said she was beautiful but he had expected nothing like this. A moment later Dick guided her across the room and introduced her.

'This is one of our home-grown products which got away,' he grinned. 'Elenor has put her next to you at dinner so that you can talk about grouse shooting or whatever it is you Scots spend your time doing.'

'I'm afraid I bore everyone over here about Scotland.' She spoke with only the slightest trace of a Mid-West accent. 'I just can't wait to get back there.'

'I'm in no hurry,' said Keith. 'Scotland is where I work. You go there to have fun.'

'Don't tell me you don't have some fun as well. I just won't believe it.'

Keith found her extraordinarily easy to get on with. By half-way through dinner he had told her most of his life story in spite of the efforts of the Congressman seated on her left who, under the disapproving stare of his wife from across the table, was trying all he knew to draw her into conversation.

It was before Elenor Katz collected her female guests to lead them through to the drawing-room for coffee that Juliet put her surprising proposition.

'Listen, Keith, what have you got to hurry back for? Why don't you take a few days off and fly down to our place in Jamaica? I've promised to spend a few days there with my folks and catch up on some sun before I have to endure the Scottish spring. You and Pop could play golf and we could swim a bit. It will do you a lot of good and it would be fun for me. Their friends are so damn boring.'

Keith, who had been searching in the back of his mind for some way of meeting her again, could hardly believe his good fortune.

'I'd have to cable home. And then there is Clancy who's over here with me. I'll have to talk to him.' Then he added hastily, 'I don't see that there should be any problem,' for fear that she

47

should change her mind or feel that she ought to ask Clancy as well.

It was Dick Katz who eventually made all the arrangements. He called Sir Charles from the office next day and put the matter with his usual diplomacy. Then he had his travel bureau re-route Keith's air ticket and that was that. Four days later Keith and Juliet landed at Montego Bay and were driven along the dusty sun-drenched road to Ocho Rios.

'You lucky bastard,' Clancy had said without rancour as he saw him off from Kennedy Airport. It would be hard to say which of them felt the luckiest—Clancy who had had an eminently satisfactory hour alone with Dick Katz before he had left Detroit or Keith who now looked forward to a week of unalloyed bliss.

*　　*　　*

Juliet's father, Henry D. Kaplan, who had made his considerable fortune in the real estate business, greeted them on the patio of his beachside villa which stood on a secluded bay just outside Ocho Rios. In a baseball cap with his large stomach bulging over the top of his Bermuda shorts, he did not present a very elegant picture but he made up for it in the warmth of his welcome.

'I'm really grateful to you, Mr Puddefant,' he told Keith. 'Our daughter never comes to visit us unless she's got some handsome reason like yourself. I'll have to ask her if I can borrow you for a round or two of golf.'

They sat shaded from the heat and drank rum cocktails shaken to icy coldness by Joseph, the houseboy, until Mrs Kaplan joined them after a morning's shopping. She was an elegant woman, half a head taller than her husband and with a skin burned deep brown by the sun. When she spoke it was in a flat nasal monotone.

'Certainly glad to see a new face around here. Do you play bridge, Mr Puddefant? No? What a pity. Henry here can play but he won't just to spite me. Nobody wants an odd woman at a bridge party. You can't imagine how boring it is with nothing to do down here. Sometimes I think I shall go mad. Same thing day after day. Still I suppose it's better than freezing in Detroit.' She rambled on. Keith accepted another rum cocktail and settled back in his cane chair. Looking at Juliet he did not find it boring at all.

48

They did not make love until the third day. He had played a round of golf in the morning and in the afternoon when Mr and Mrs Kaplan had retired to sleep off their lunch, he and Juliet had changed into their swimming clothes and strolled along the dazzling white sand to the extremity of Mr Kaplan's private beach. They cooled off with a brief swim and then sat together watching the sea break out on the reef.

'Happy?' she asked suddenly and leant over and kissed him on the cheek.

Keith looked at her with her hair hanging in wet ringlets down her back and the salt water drying on her high cheekbones and felt a delicious tingling. His experiences of women had been largely confined to birds he had picked up in late night clubs and driven back for a frenzied tumble in a bed-sitter filled with stuffed dolls and bedside lamps made out of champagne bottles—the expensive bric-à-brac of previous one night stands. His mother's attempts to get him to take an interest in suitable girls had always ended in disaster due to his belief that if he could not make it on the first meeting there was no future.

'Would it shock you if I took off my top? Those white patches are so unattractive.' Juliet did not wait for an answer. Then she lay back with her small bare breasts pointing up arrogantly to the sky.

'In St Tropez the girls wear nothing at all,' said Keith desperately trying to maintain an air of sophisticated indifference but his throat was dry with excitement. Without a word she pushed down her bikini and flipped it away from her with a deft movement of her foot.

'And what about the men at St Tropez? Do they lie around all wrapped up?' She propped herself up on one elbow and watched him with quiet amusement as he awkwardly removed his pants.

*   *   •

On Keith's last night he took Juliet out to dinner at the Jamaica Inn. Afterwards they sat out on the balcony overlooking the dance-floor, enjoying the cool evening after the heat of the day.

'I suppose this is really goodbye,' he said. He felt sentimental and slightly drunk.

49

'Whatever makes you say that? I'll be over in Scotland soon.' Juliet took his hand and squeezed it.

'Well, I mean about your husband and all that.'

Juliet sighed. 'Poor Abdy. I think he is more interested in his fishing and shooting than he is in me. He doesn't seem to miss me at all.'

They sat silent for a few minutes while Keith pondered on the enormity of anyone being married to Juliet and not being madly in love.

'I have a little flat in Glasgow,' he said at length. 'It's not much of a place but we could meet there.'

Juliet looked at him speculatively.

'You're a funny boy.'

'Why do you say that?'

'You have a rich father and you'll probably be taking over the business one day. Yet you seem to have so little. Now is the time when you ought to be enjoying yourself. There will be plenty of time for hard work when you're older. What's the matter with your Pop, doesn't he trust you?'

Ever since he had arrived in New York, Keith had been thinking along the same lines.

'You don't know my father,' he said. 'He's never been much of a one for enjoying himself and he does not really see why anyone else should. He thinks because I go sailing a lot and play a little golf that I am on the road to ruin.'

Juliet thought for a moment, then she said, 'I'd like to meet your father. Let's wait a few weeks and I'll have Abdy ask them both out to Ochil for a few days. Do you think they would come?'

Keith who knew of his mother's weakness for the aristocracy was quite sure that they would. That morning he caught the plane and the next night took the train sleeper up to Glasgow unaware that he had become part of a design which was to have far-reaching effects.

5

The installation of the new plant at Greenbank took longer than
expected. There were delays in the delivery of the machinery
and technical difficulties in the laying out of the production
lines. Angus Simpson occupied his men as best he could by
organizing instruction classes in the use of the new machines
but it still made it comparatively easy for a bit of bevying on the
side.

It was a situation which suited Harry Birdsall perfectly. He
brought his weights over from Sol's Gym and installed himself
in an empty equipment shed where he was watched at his
exercises by an admiring group of apprentices.

Billy Caird spent his leisure in a different way, sitting in the
canteen studying new and better systems with which he was
going to win the pools. Such time as he did not devote to the
pools he spent thinking about Betty Brown. For several weeks
now they had been having a regular date and they had got to
the stage of holding hands in the café and having a goodnight
cuddle in the doorway of Inkerman Terrace.

'That young mate of yours is a nutter,' Harry told Chick.
'If I were you I'd tell that Betty to give him the push.' In a way
he was jealous of the friendship between Chick and Billy but
most of all he was annoyed that Billy never came to watch him
while he practised.

Chick mentioned it to Billy one night as they walked to the
bus together.

'Does he still do things? I mean like you told me about that
night.'

'Och, there's nothing to it. It's only when he's had a few
drinks. If you'd just come and watch him at the weight lifting.'

Billy, who had heard some talk amongst the apprentices about
Harry and his habits, was not so sure but to please Chick he went
along the next afternoon. It was unfortunate that he arrived

before any of the daily spectators. He would have ducked out again but Harry, who was setting up his equipment, caught sight of him. Straightening up he gave him a lop-sided grin: 'Well if it isn't young Billy. Come on in, laddie, and give us a hand—if you've got the strength that is.'

Billy came reluctantly into the room and gingerly started to roll one of the heavy bars to the centre of the floor. 'Careful,' Harry sneered. 'You might do yourself an injury.' He took a pace forward and took a grip of Billy's upper arm. 'Christ,' he said. 'You call those biceps? You couldn't pull the skin off a black puddin'.'

'Leave me go.' Billy struggled to get his arm away but Harry pulled him towards him. 'Let's see if you have anything else worth talking about.' He grabbed him by the balls and started to squeeze. Billy lashed backwards with his free arm, his eyes watering with pain. 'You wee bastard,' Harry gasped as Billy's elbow dug into his groin. 'I'll larn you.' He shifted his grip to pinion both Billy's arms behind his back with one hand while the other he plunged inside his overall.

At that moment the door opened and Jim Cantlie stepped into the room.

'What the hell is going on here!' he rasped. 'Birdsall! What are you at!'

Harry released Billy and collected himself quickly. 'Just a bit of fun, Mr Cantlie,' he said. 'He's a cheeky young sod.'

'Never mind about that. I won't stand for bullying in my shop. Are you all right, Caird?' He prided himself in knowing the names of most of his workers.

Billy who was shaking with a mixture of fright and outrage managed to say, 'It was only a bit of fun, sir,' then, unable to contain himself any longer, darted out of the door.

'I don't know what that was all about, Birdsall, but I don't like it,' said Cantlie. 'You had better restrict yourself to your duties or you may find yourself redundant again.' He looked at Harry's equipment spread over the floor. 'You can clear all that out of here this evening. We are supposed to be a factory, not a bloody sports centre.'

When he had gone Harry started to collect up his kit. He was seething with rage. 'If that's the way they want it, that's the way they'll get it,' he said to himself. Filled with righteous indignation he went out that evening to meet his friend Barney Corcoran.

*   *   *

It was after the incident with Harry Birdsall that Chick and Billy started to drift apart.

'I can't understand you,' said Chick. 'Here's Harry trying to be friendly and asking you to help with his equipment and you go all snotty.'

'It wasn't like that,' said Billy desperately. 'He was trying it on. You know what I mean.'

'It's not what I heard. Harry says you cheeked him.'

It was the general opinion in the works. Harry with his own opinion of his chance of becoming an Olympic weight lifter was something of a hero. It lent some glamour to their everyday lives.

Billy was left in no doubt as to how his mates thought one day in the canteen. They were sitting five or six of them at the table drinking their morning mugs of tea. Billy left his half mug while he went to the lavatory. By the time he got back it was filled up again.

'Ta for the tea someone,' he said raising his mug. A moment later he put it down again, spitting with disgust.

'What's wrong?' asked one of the apprentices expressing mock concern.

'It's bloody awful. What's in it?'

'Ought to be hot enough anyway,' leered a spotty youth, leaning his arm over the back of his chair. 'Harry has just been over and pissed in it.'

They all laughed fit to bust. By the time the hooter went for knocking-off time the joke was known all over the factory.

That night Billy had his weekly date with Betty. He was near to tears.

'I think I'll have to pack it up at the works. I don't seem to be getting anywhere.'

Betty was all concern. She was beginning to think of Billy as a possible husband and the thought of him out of work was more than she knew her mother would stand. Mrs Brown understood what poverty was all about and she was not going to see her only daughter married to someone on the dole.

'What's the trouble?' Betty asked. 'I thought you were getting on so well.'

Billy couldn't bring himself to give her an accurate version of what had happened especially with Chick being so friendly with Harry. Instead he said, 'I seem to do everything wrong. All the lads are laughing at me. Even Chick isn't like he used to be.'

'It's since he's taken up with that Harry Birdsall,' Betty declared, hitting the nail more accurately on the head than she knew. 'When I see that big nana I'll give him a piece of my mind, just see if I don't.'

That night Betty asked Billy into the house for the first time. They sat in the front room with Mrs Brown bustling in and out to see that they did not get up to any nonsense.

'It'll be The Fair next month,' Betty said. 'Will you be doing anything special like?'

Billy shook his head. 'Same as usual. Stay at home and watch the telly.' The Fair is the Glasgow holiday when everyone shuts down and all those who can afford it get out of the city. Greenbank were to close for three weeks.

'I thought of going to the berry picking,' said Betty airily as if it was the most natural idea in the world. In fact she had only just heard about it that afternoon from a woman who had come into the shop where she worked.

Billy was silent, not wanting to show his ignorance on such an important subject.

'You have to pay for your train ticket of course,' Betty explained. 'But when you get to the berry fields you get a free bed and they pay you for what you pick. Some folk make a lot of money. I just thought it would be a change.'

'Oh aye,' said Billy cautiously. 'It's out in the country then, is it? You'd have to take a train and everything.' He was already excited about the idea. He had never been out of Glasgow and the thought of actually travelling on a train filled him with awe.

'They start production down at the works after Fairs Week. It would be grand to have a break—if I stay on,' he added hastily.

'Of course you're going to stay on. Once it all gets going it will be different.'

They talked about the idea for a long time until Mrs Brown came in and started to plump up the cushions as an indication that it was time for Billy to go.

54

Two days later they both bought their tickets and started to count the days in an agony of anticipation.

*   *   *

The day of the adventure dawned bright and clear. It was one of those mornings when Glasgow shrugged off its apathy and welcomed its citizens with cheerful good nature. In their bathrooms staid businessmen towelled themselves vigorously after their ablutions and sang little snatches of song. Housewives threw open their windows and breathed in the morning sunshine and when neighbours met on their way to work, they exchanged happy greetings. Even the 'bus conductors seemed to be infected with the general air of gaiety helping young mothers on with their folding prams and making merry quips as they went up and down collecting the fares.

At Inkerman Terrace Betty felt so excited that her legs had gone weak on her and she kept dropping things which she was trying at the last minute to squeeze into her already over-stuffed suitcase.

'Any sign of Billy yet? Ma! Any sign of Billy?' she called for the fourth time to Mrs Brown who was busying herself downstairs cutting an extravagant number of jam sandwiches.

'For goodness' sake haud your whist! He won't be here for an hour yet,' Mrs Brown shouted back but she was almost as excited as her daughter. She was remembering the time Mr Brown had taken her for a day trip down the Clyde and how she had nearly spoiled it all by vomiting with nerves before they had even left the house. Now Betty was going away for a whole week to the country. Just fancy, a whole week, she marvelled to herself. As she worked she issued a stream of instructions and admonitions at the top of her voice. 'Don't forget your clean petticoat, dearie: it's all ironed for you in the kitchen. Remember to send a card. I'll be worried about you. Did you pack those new hankies? Don't miss getting out at the right station.'

When Billy finally arrived a quarter of an hour early, Betty was sure they were going to miss the train. She had not been able to eat any breakfast and the catches of her suitcases had kept bursting open so that in the end it had to be tied around with an old piece of clothes line. The journey to Queen Street Station was an agony of suspense. Every time the 'bus stopped to let

55

passengers off and on, Betty felt it was never going to start again and writhed in her seat with impatience so that Billy had to speak to her sharply. Then she was so downcast that he was immediately sorry.

'When I win the Pools we'll ride everywhere in a bloody great Rolls and I'll chuck money out of the window to folk at the 'bus stops so that they can take taxis,' he promised and kissed his little finger to make it come true.

Of course when they arrived at the station it was still much too early and the train had not yet come in. Billy wanted to go to the station buffet to have a cup of tea but Betty was afraid that the train would come and go without them and insisted that they go to the barrier to wait.

They got there to be faced with a new hazard. The crowd already gathered round the gates to the platform was so dense that it seemed impossible that there would ever be room for them all on the train. They milled around in a disorganized mass and every minute the numbers were getting greater as new parties joined the throng. Men in their best Sunday suits struggled with prams and suitcases while their womenfolk clung to their children, fearful that they would be trampled underfoot. Others with less weighty responsibilities had already been overtaken by the holiday mood. Half bottles of whisky were being passed from hand to hand.

Three middle-aged matrons in paper hats and with enormous rosettes pinned to their heaving bosoms were giving a spirited rendering of 'Knees up Mother Brown' while the men sang lustily and shouted encouragement.

'Swing those tits, missus!'

'I can see you've got a hole in your knickers, lass!'

'They are not all going on our train are they, Billy?' Betty gasped near to tears.

'Looks like it lass. They're all off on their holidays to Aberdeen. Don't worry. We'll manage some road.' But even Billy was beginning to have his doubts as wild shouts of delight continued to announce the arrival of further contingents joining in the mad rush to get out of Glasgow for the joys of a holiday by the seaside.

When the train finally pulled in and the gates were opened, the crowd formed a solid phalanx and poured on to the platform, brushing aside the ticket collector and clambering into the carriages. The more athletic ones dashed on to the refreshment car, packing the bar four deep while the rest scrambled and fought their way indiscriminately into the first- and second-class compartments and overflowed into the corridors.

Billy had to wait until the worst of the stampede was over before he could start off down the platform, his matchstick arms almost breaking under the strain of humping the heavy suitcases. They had nearly reached the end of the train before Betty, skipping ahead impatiently, found a space where they could squeeze aboard.

'What's this then? A honeymoon couple?' shouted a bull-necked man who had obviously appointed himself as the humorist of his party. 'Come on, let's have those bags. Make way for the bride and bridegroom!' The crowd laughed good-naturedly while Betty went pink with embarrassment. Someone opened the door of the toilet and before they knew what was happening their bags were being dumped inside and they were being pushed in behind them.

'There you are sweethearts, the bridal suite!' Red-neck winked at his friends as he pulled the door shut, cutting off the renewed laughter.

'Oooh!' exclaimed Betty, blushing pinker than ever. 'Oooh! He hasna' half got a nerve!'

'Better than standing in the corridor all the way. At least we can sit down.'

'Oh that!' said Betty eyeing the lavatory pedestal. 'How could you be so rude!' But Billy was too occupied examining his novel surroundings to pay much attention to her protests.

'Just look at this. A basin with taps and all. And on a train! It's better than we got at home.' Delightedly he made the water gush out steaming. He peered up at the printed notice above the lavatory, moving his lips as he read carefully: 'Passengers are requested not to use the lavatory while the train is standing in the station.' Underneath someone had written 'Except in Glasgow.'

Then there was a final banging of doors, a whistle blew and the train started to gather speed. For Betty and Billy the novelty of the movement was an incredibly exciting sensation. They clung together, bracing themselves against the swaying of their tiny cabin, as excited as they had ever been in their lives before.

57

Set in the frosted glass of the window there was a small oval of plain glass and through this, by dint of pressing their heads close together, they could both watch the grimy buildings slide by outside. For a while the railway ran alongside a main roadway and they could see with delight that they were going faster than any of the cars heading like them for the unimaginable delights of the country. Then, when the train gave a more than usually violent lurch, Betty lost her balance and, stumbling backwards, was saved from falling to the floor by the fortuitous positioning of the lavatory seat.

'Oooh!' she gasped, horrified at finding herself in such an undignified situation and struggling to regain her feet. Billy wasn't sure whether to laugh at her ludicrous expression or to take advantage of the situation by implanting a kiss on her outraged mouth. He tried to do both with the result that a second later they were tangled together, one moment laughing so much that they could not kiss and the next kissing so much that they could not laugh. Then Billy found himself kneeling on the floor beside her and his hands were somehow right up inside her jersey and fumbling around her back inexpertly trying to disengage the hooks of her bra. It was a manoeuvre which would normally have brought from Betty a flow of 'Ooohs' and admonitions not to be naughty but today, rushing headlong through the bright morning, enclosed in the privacy of their little cubicle, she felt her resistance ebb away and in its place there grew a sudden and fierce determination to lose the virginity she had cherished so uneasily for so long. With a practised movement she undid the last reluctant hook herself and pulled her jersey up round her neck so that her great cantaloupe breasts were exposed in all their voluptuousness. Billy buried his thin face between them, unable to believe his luck and gasping with delight at the spectacle so unexpectedly presented to him. Then there was more hurried fumbling with hooks and zips, both fearful that if there was a moment's delay the mood of wild abandon would pass for ever.

When it was over they stayed glued together in each other's arms, Betty with her eyes tightly closed to shut out the sight of her own nakedness and Billy with his joints aching from kneeling on the hard floor but unwilling to move for fear of breaking the magic of the moment. Then the train started to slow down; brakes squealed and a voice was shouting 'Stirling! Stirling!'

Betty opened her eyes with a jerk and pushed Billy aside to struggle into her skirt. Outside the holiday makers were entertaining Stirling station to a spirited rendering of 'The Bonny Banks o' Clyde'.

> 'When she's starin' at the stars,
> Then I'm pullin' down her dra'rs
> Roamin' in the gloamin'
> By the Bonnie Banks o' Clyde.'

'Oooh!' she gasped, retrieving her knickers from where they had become hooked on the hot tap of the wash hand-basin and modestly turning her back to slip them on. After the train had started again she spent a long time pretending to put on her lipstick but really peering carefully into the mirror to see if she looked any different. One of the girls at work had once told her that you could always tell if a girl had lost it by the look in her eyes. Apart from being rather pinker than usual she decided that she looked much the same and felt a little bit let down. Then they pretended to look out of their peephole again at the green fields and the streams and the cows stampeding with their tails high in the air as the train roared past but they were too pent up with excitement of the thing that had happened to them to register the wonders which were passing before their eyes. They had almost reached their destination before either of them spoke. Then Betty said in a small voice, 'Billy, do you think I'll have a baby?'

No such thought had yet occurred to Billy to mar his happiness. 'I don't know, love,' he said with perfect truth.

'Oh Billy. Ma would kill me if I had a baby. What would I say to her Billy?'

Billy was in far too excited a frame of mind to worry about anything so mundane.

'Just tell her you caught it off the toilet,' he grinned. They both laughed and were happy realizing they had travelled a long way in the last fifty miles.

*   *   *

They climbed out of the train at Perth and then took a 'bus to the little township of Cupar Angus. Cupar Angus is little more than a cluster of houses and shops which, for a brief space, line either side of the main road to and from the north. Heavy goods lorries rumble through in a constant stream, changing gear to take the sharp turn over the level crossing before accelerating again noisily to tackle the last stage of their journey to the important city of Dundee. This Saturday morning, however, there was little traffic and the town dozed sleepily under the warm July sun.

Betty and Billy made their way down the main street, marvelling at the quiet and breathing in the clean air. It now occurred to Billy that he had not the slightest idea in which direction the raspberry fields lay or how to find Mr Ballie whose name they had been given as a likely man who would take them on. If he had thought about it at all he had imagined that somehow they would have stepped off the train to find Mr Ballie waiting for them. The day, however, was too fine and the feeling of happiness too intense for him to worry about such trifles. God was in his Heaven and all was well with the world.

Optimism is an attitude of mind which works its own wonders. They humped their cases into the first café they came to and sat down at a table which was already occupied by a small elf-like man who sat dunking sweet biscuits in his tea and drawing morosely at a rather soggy cigarette.

'Up for the berries, are you?' he asked as soon as they sat down. When Billy admitted that they were, he said, 'You can always tell berry pickers. Have you got a place to go?'

'We are going to Mr Ballie's but we don't know how to get there.'

'Would that be Bob Ballie, Hillside?'

'I think so,' said Billy, feeling very stupid that he had not even found out the name of the farm.

'It'll be Hillside all right. He's a big man in berries, is Bob.'

'Can you tell us how to get there?'

'I'll do better than that. If you sup up your tea and put your bags in my van I'll run you out there. I'm the grieve of Hillside so you'll be working under me.'

Thus it was that they arrived at their destination in fine style in the back of the grieve's van. Willie Henderson was a man not much given to speaking but when he heard that it was their first time at the berries he grew quite communicative.

'You get all sorts coming for the berries,' he told them. 'Some are pretty rough but they are mostly a good lot. I'll put you in a hut with some of the regulars who come up every year. They'll keep you right. Just keep yourselves to yourselves and you'll have no bother.'

They arrived outside a row of wooden huts to find most of the pickers occupied with getting their midday meal. Women were hurrying to and fro from a central hut which served as a communal kitchen, carrying plates of food and pots of tea. Their menfolk squatted on the ground in groups smoking and talking while they waited and everywhere there were children running round in noisy groups, kicking a football or wrestling together in the dust. Beyond the huts and gently sloping up to the horizon were the raspberry canes, set in serried rows and extending in either direction as far as the eye could see. Between the rows could be seen the heads of a few enthusiastic pickers who, anxious to make as much money as possible, had not taken time off for midday dinner. Instead they picked on busily with one hand while munching thick sandwiches of bread and jam in the other.

Willie put his head into one of the huts.

'Any room in here for a couple, Bessie?'

A lady so fat that she found difficulty in walking, her head tied around with a thick scarf in spite of the heat of the day, put down her dinner plate and waddled forward to peer short-sightedly at Betty and Billy.

'They seem clean enough,' she announced brusquely. 'They can bed in the corner there.' She nodded to a space near the door where two palliasses stuffed with straw lay side by side.

'Dump your cases,' said Willie. 'Then come out with me and I'll show you what you have to do before you get changed.'

Betty and Billy, who were so overcome by the strangeness of it all that any thought of eating had quite gone out of their heads, followed Willie out again into the sunshine and over to the edge of the raspberry field where a man stood by a raised platform receiving the little plastic baskets of fruit from the pickers as they came in from the field, weighing them and paying for them from a seemingly inexhaustible box of change which sat by his elbow. Some of the pickers carried up to ten baskets—

'chips' as they soon learnt to call them—hung about their person, suspended halterwise round their necks or tied to their waist bands.

'Just start with two chips 'til you get the hang of it,' Willie advised. 'Only pick ripe fruit, fill your chips full and don't miss any. There are drill walkers to see that you pick clean,' he warned. 'Here Benny!' he shouted to a sunburnt scarecrow of a man who stood watching the baskets as the pickers brought them off the field. 'Give these two a row and watch how they get on.' With a bird-like nod he left them in Benny's care.

Billy, once he had been shown how to hang his baskets, started down his allotted row with a careful concentration. At first it took all his attention to gather the ripe fruit, parting the leaves tc discover hidden clusters. Sometimes he went on to the next cane only to see out of the corner of his eye that he had missed some and had to go back again. After he had filled his baskets two or three times, however, the job came more easily and he could let his mind wander as he worked.

In his imagination he dwelt again with renewed excitement on the pleasure he had so recently experienced. In his innocence he had always imagined women to be hairless all over like alabaster saints. It had been a surprise to him that had. Then his mind went dancing away into the future. When he won the pools the first thing he would do would be to take her to the biggest store in Glasgow and buy her everything she wanted. Evening gowns and expensive furs and wonderful jewellery. It would cost him plenty but he would have the money. They would be married of course and he would buy her a house and have Mrs Brown to live with them. It would be a big wedding in a church and there would be drinks for everybody. Perhaps £100,000 would not be enough. He had better win £150,000 so that after he had bought his car they would have plenty to live on for the rest of their lives. The sun continued to beat down and his dreams grew wilder and more exciting so that he filled his baskets almost without noticing and he floated on a pink cloud of happiness.

Betty's thoughts ran on similar but less extravagant lines. She went over what she would tell her friend Crissie when she got back. She would have to tell her. Such momentous news could not be kept to herself. She could imagine Crissie's envy when she told her how wonderful it had all been. She would not tell her *everything*. Not about it happening in the toilet for example. She began to make up an elaborate story about how she had been wooed and won like the heroine in *Enchanted Nights* which was a book she had bought on impulse in a secondhand bookshop and which had had such a lurid cover that she had had to hide it from her mother.

Then she fell to wondering when Billy would pop the question. Wouldn't it be wonderful if she came back *engaged*! Perhaps if they made enough money between them at the picking they would have sufficient to buy a ring. At the thought of such a terrific happening she picked harder than ever, resisting the impulse to eat any of the berries so that every penny could be made. Almost more than thinking about the marriage which was undoubtedly in store for her, she wondered when they could have it together again. Now that she had done it once, she could not wait for the next time and the next. The week to come shimmered before her eyes like a magic staircase to unutterable bliss.

By knocking off time Billy had had enough of the picking and was remembering that he had had nothing to eat since he had left home years earlier that morning. He had only caught glimpses of Betty during the past few hours. Now he waited impatiently for her to come up to the collecting point. When she arrived he noticed that she had four chips tied round her waist in addition to the two slung around her shoulders.

'Good lass,' said the cashier as he counted out her money. 'If you stick in like that you'll mak' a braw picker.' Billy who had not aspired beyond his original two felt rather put down as much by this display of industry as by the free and easy way the checker spoke to her.

'Come on,' he said. 'It's knocking off time. I haven't seen you for hours. We'll go and get some of your Ma's sandwiches.'

They counted up their money together. Billy had three pounds and Betty nearly four.

'Seven pounds between us. Not bad,' Billy remarked ignoring the disparity in their earnings and, taking her arm, strolled off back to the huts.

Since they had left there had been more arrivals. A travelling van with a flap let into the side to provide a service hatch was doing brisk trade dispensing cups of tea, ham rolls and ice cream. On a piece of ground nearby an encampment had grown out of

63

nowhere. Several small squat tents the shape of Eskimo igloos had already been erected in a rough circle and, as they watched a man and a boy were busy erecting another, bending thin saplings to make a framework over which they were stretching a canvas roof. A wood fire set around with stones blazed merrily in the middle of the circle and, nearby, ponies were tethered grazing with seeming content on the sun-browned grass. A young-old woman, her face burnt the colour of mahogany, sat by the fire, a baby wrapped tightly in a shawl feeding at her breast while the others with the same dark skins and jet black hair moved purposefully about their business.

'That's the tinks come in for the picking,' remarked Willie Henderson who had appeared suddenly at Betty's shoulder. 'Grand workers when the drink is not in them!'

'Where do they come from?' Betty asked, gazing at them as if they were people from another planet. Willie shrugged. 'Who knows? Here today, gone tomorrow, that's the tinker folk. Next week they may be cutting bracken in Glencoe or dealing in horses away on the West Coast. I don't suppose there is any of them who has slept in a bed since the day they were born.'

How wonderful, thought Betty, to wander where you wanted without a care in the world. No catching buses every morning or standing behind a counter telling hideous women how wonderful they looked in hideous hats. Then Billy squeezed her hand and she remembered her own happiness. Slipping her arm under his they made their way over to the travelling van to spend some of their newly earned money on ice cream and cups of sweet, tepid tea.

Although it was quite late before they lay down under their rough blankets, it was very much later before there was any opportunity of sleep. The other occupants of the hut seemed to be disinclined for an early night. The women pulled off their sweaters, massaging their breasts to relieve the tightness of their brassieres. The men in their vests and long woollen pants sat around smoking and talking while two transistor radios competed with each other on different channels of pop music. It was long after midnight before the single naked light which hung from the rafters was extinguished. Then there were more noises from outside as parties returned from the pubs, calling to each other in the darkness. Somebody started up a tune on a mouth organ

64

until there were shouts of 'Shut up' and 'Put a sock in it willya!' There were sounds of a fight in the small hours and the banging of doors as sundry citizens stumbled out to relieve the pressure of beer in their bellies. Billy and Betty lay in the darkness, conscious of each other's nearness and cut off in their own little world until, just before dawn broke, they fell uneasily asleep.

Sunday morning broke as clear and bright as the day before. When Billy and Betty stepped outside their hut the sharp morning air, still unwarmed by the sun, made it almost painful to breathe. Already there was a bustle of activity as families struggled to boil water for the tea on the crowded hot plate provided in the cooking hut. The fat lady who had greeted them so coolly the day before came fussing up to them, suddenly motherly.

'Have you got your kettle, dearie?'

'I never thought to bring one,' Betty confessed feeling thoroughly inadequate.

'You'll get a mug of ours out of the pot then.'

Room was made for them in the circle at the top end of the hut while they drank the scalding, black brew and ate the last of Ma Brown's sandwiches. Everybody was friendly as if spending a night under the same roof had made them part of the family. While the early morning dew dried off the berries, the air was filled with the smell of cooking and wood smoke; in a nearby field a game of football was in progress with jackets piled at either end of the improvised pitch to mark the goalposts; groups gathered together in conversation, there were bursts of laughter and women scurried to and fro seeing to their menfolk's needs. Only the tinkers remained apart, requiring no company but their own, aristocratic in their aloofness.

It was eight o'clock before Mr Ballie, the owner, arrived ready to get the day's work started. He was a short thick-set man with an open face and an air of cheerful friendliness. Willie Henderson darted about behind him as he moved from group to group, greeting the old hands who had been coming to Hillside year after year. When he went over to the tinkers' encampment the men stood up respectfully, touching their caps and smiling.

'Crafty buggers,' said a man standing near to Billy. 'I bet those eggs they are cooking came out of his henhouse. No harm meant, you know. It's just their way.'

65

The way the day had started, so it went on. People who had seemed stand-offish now seemed to be going out of their way to be friendly and helpful. Billy found himself working back-to-back with a little dark fellow called John Menzies who was a fisherman on a North Sea trawler and came from Aberdeen.

'Ah dinna ken fit I'd dae wi'oot the berries to come to ilka year. I like the fishing ye ken but the berries mak a grand change.' At first Billy found his accent difficult to follow but he liked to hear him talk and he was not a little flattered that a man ten years his senior wanted to be pals with him.

'Watch you for thon mannie there wi' the lang neck,' John told him as they passed a tall fellow with a thin hatchet face, who indeed seemed to have a singularly long neck and who stood peering this way and that at everyone who passed him. 'He's one of the drill walkers and a more inquisitive divil o' a fellow you niver did see. Aye peerin' at folk and tryin' to catch them oot daein' something wrong. We ca' him the Periscope for he's aye poppin' his heid up oot o' the rasps to see whi's gaen on twa or three rows awa'. If yer wantin' a wee bit o' slap and tickle wi' that bonnie lass o' yours in amang the berries mak' siccer the Periscope is nae aroon'. He'll fair jump on you and like as not rin' tae Mr Ballie himself wi' his tittle tattle. Not that the boss tak's much notice; he's a guid sport.'

Billy, who had been planning just that thing if he could find the opportunity, promised to be careful. John was a fund of fascinating information about their fellow workers. He knew which of the girls were good for a bit of fun, who was going with whom and which of the men to avoid when they had a drink in them.

'Ma Gawd, nivver work in a row next to that yin,' he warned as an enormous woman with legs like tree trunks waddled past them festooned with baskets. 'They ca' her the Campbeltown Loch and d'ye ken why?' Billy had to confess his ignorance. 'Aye pissin'—that's why. Aye drinkin' tea and aye pissin'. Canna haud her water mair than half an 'oor. She'll be workin' awa an' all of a sudden she'll lift her skirt an' piss awa' all 'oor the ground. Does nae wear any knickers ye ken on account of her affliction. If the Campbeltown Loch pissed whisky we'd a' be drunk oot o' oor minds.'

With so much going on around him Billy found the days slipping past at an alarming speed. On the second evening he

66

and Betty had discovered a little pathway which ran up the hillside above the raspberry fields and petered out by the side of an old ruined cottage. There they made love again as if it was the most natural thing in the world and then they lay for a long time entwined in each other's arms watching the dusk creep gradually down the valley. After that first time they took the path at the end of each day's picking and each time it seemed more blissful than the last.

It was on their fourth visit that Betty could restrain herself no longer. They had finished their love-making and lay on their tummies side by side without speaking. Then she said in a small breathy voice: 'Billy do you think that one day you and I might ... ?' she left the question hanging in the air.

'Might what?' Billy picked a piece of rye grass and started to tickle her nose.

'Well after what's happened and all, I just thought that maybe ...' she couldn't quite bring herself to say the words.

'You mean us get married?' said Billy, comprehension dawning on him slowly.

'You know quite well what I mean, Billy Caird!' she said severely. 'What else could I be meanin'.'

He remained silent for a long time. Then he said, 'I think I'd like that, love.'

So they kissed again to seal the bargain. Then they went down the hill hand-in-hand, Billy wondering just what he had done and Betty's heart beating as if it would burst.

The next day, the day before their last, John Menzies suggested they might go into town. They had not told anybody about their understanding but even Betty, who was anxious to save every penny of their berry money, agreed that they could afford a celebration. They went in early about ten of them packed tightly in the back of somebody's van. To Betty's great delight the shops in Blairgowrie were still open when they arrived and immediately she dragged Billy off.

'It's something private,' she explained to John who had volunteered to show them round. When they met again at the Strath Hotel they were twenty pounds poorer but she had a ring on her finger which she could not stop gazing at. Whenever she moved her hand it caught her eye and she felt that everyone in the pub must notice it immediately.

In fact to her disappointment she had to point it out to John. 'You mean you two are getting spliced,' he exclaimed. 'Ah kent there wis something up. Here lads, come an' meet the happy couple,' he shouted to a bunch of his mates at the bar, holding up Betty's hand.

The effect was gratifying beyond even Betty's hopes. Soon they were the centre of quite a crowd, filled with good will and anxious to buy drinks. Everyone seemed to feel in some way responsible for the romance which had blossomed in their midst.

'You've done it now, lad,' somebody said clapping Billy on the shoulder. 'Na, na, jist keep yer money in your pocket. Yer going to need it, I can tell you!' The berry-picking crowd needed no encouragement to spend their money. With an excuse as good as this one the drinks were being passed over the bar so fast that soon they were piled up in front of Billy and Betty until there was scarcely any room left for another glass on their table.

The pace was so hot that it was fortunate there now occurred a diversion in the person of Michael Higgins. Every head turned as he pushed his way through the swing doors of the pub. He took his entrance like a veteran actor, pausing for a moment and then raising his hand in a sort of benediction before striding across the floor to take his seat at the battered piano which stood against the far wall. He was an immense man. His legs protruded like gnarled trees beneath his ancient kilt. There were silver buckles on his shoes and golden rings glinted in his ears which, with his red beard, gave an impression of piratical ferocity. When he started to play most of the customers gathered round the piano, shouting out requests for this tune or that. Pints of beer started to accumulate on the piano top. Every now and again Higgins would pause to down a pint with a single practised lift of his elbow so that the flow of the music was barely interrupted.

From time to time one of the company would climb unsteadily on to a chair and give a heart-rending version of such favourites as 'Ye Banks and Braes O' Bonnie Doon' or 'Annie Laurie' and each in turn was applauded with an enthusiasm which would have gratified the vainest of professionals. Billy, holding tightly on to Betty's hand, leaned back in his chair and closed his eyes, relieved at last to be no longer the centre of attention. He had no doubt in his mind, now that he had had time to get used to the idea, that he was doing the right thing in getting hitched to Betty. The days of fresh air followed by the beer induced in him a feeling of perfect euphoria and as the music grew wilder and the singing more incoherent, he fell peacefully asleep.

He was awakened by Betty nudging him sharply. As he struggled back to consciousness he was aware of somebody standing over him. Then he opened his eyes sharply. Legs wide apart, gazing down at him with a look of contemptuous amusement, was Harry Birdsall.

'Well, well, look what the tide's brought in,' he sneered as Billy tried to focus his eyes, blurred with sleep. 'What about standing your old friend Harry a drink with all that money you've been earning at the berries.'

'You leave my Billy alone!' Betty was on her feet, her eyes sparking with anger.

'Oh, it's "my" Billy is it?' Harry grinned. 'You engaged or something?'

'Yes, we certainly are,' shouted Betty, showing her ring under Harry's nose. 'You just leave him alone!'

'Then you can buy me a cigar as well for a celebration. Come on, little man.' Harry leaned forward, pushing Betty aside and seizing Billy by the ear, twisted violently so as to bring him to his feet. Betty's reaction was immediate and violent. She swung her handbag, catching Harry full in the face, whereupon it burst open scattering her possessions across the floor.

'You bloody bitch!' Harry brought back his clenched fist but the blow was never delivered. Instead a bar stool crashed down on his head from behind and he crumpled to the floor, his hair matting with blood. Michael Higgins replaced the stool carefully and stood looking down with satisfaction at his handiwork. 'I canna' abide a man who would strike a lady,' he remarked conversationally.

'Shall we put the boot in, Michael?' One of the onlookers stepped forward and stood eagerly over the inert body, his foot raised.

'Na, na. Just sling the bastard oot.' The door was held open while customers grabbed Harry by the arms and legs. 'A-one' the crowd chanted 'a-two, a-three,' and the body beautiful of Harry Birdsall arched through the doorway to land violently on the pavement outside. Others were busy collecting the scattered contents of Betty's handbag. More drinks appeared as Michael returned to thumping the piano as if nothing had happened and soon the whole company was roused again in song.

6

Not ten miles from where Billy and Betty were occupying themselves with berry-picking and other matters, Sir Charles and Lady Puddefant were having a holiday of rather a different kind.

The invitation from the Earl and Countess of Ochil to spend a few days at Ochil Castle had been received by Claire Puddefant with something like ecstasy. In spite of her husband's wealth and position she had always been very conscious of the fact that his being in trade precluded them from being accepted in the highest social circles. Nothing was more calculated to put her out of sorts than to read of shooting parties and Society Balls to which she had not had the entrée. To be asked to stay by the Ochils was a break-through of the highest consequence and she lost no time in making sure that all her friends knew of it.

It is not often that anticipation of an event looked forward to so keenly lives up to the realization but, for Claire, her visit to Ochil Castle proved a notable exception. When Juliet had married her Scottish Earl she had brought with her more than her striking beauty and personality. She had also filled the empty Ochil coffers so that the once austere rooms blossomed under her touch and the power of the American dollar. The antiquated plumbing system which had once kept guests awake half the night was ruthlessly torn out, bathrooms appeared where there had been none before and the great four-poster beds were now hung about with exotic drapes. Even the vast stone-walled hall had been made habitable by the installation of a heating system which was a wonder of ingenuity.

Abdy Ochil had watched the transformation of his ancestral home with some misgivings but being in love with his young wife as much as he was in love with anything except his dogs, had let her have a free hand. The only thing Juliet had been unable to change was Abdy. He was a tall, sandy-haired man who walked with a stoop as if constantly afraid of hitting his head in a doorway. His watery eyes protruded like a spaniel's and he sought to control his soup-strainer moustache by constantly brushing it upwards with his thumb. His speech consisted of a series of grunts and snorts which were only intelligible to his closest friends. At the time of his engagement to Juliet there had been much ribald speculation of how he had actually got around to making a proposal. It was generally considered that it must have been Juliet who had done the asking and that she had taken one of his more articulate grunts as a romantic acceptance. However the improbable alliance had come about it seemed to have turned out happily enough. Abdy showed no inclination to follow Juliet on her frequent trips to the Continent and America and contented himself with running his extensive estates. When she was at Ochil, she filled the castle with guests and entertained the local gentry with a panache which made her one of the favourite topics of conversation in the county but there were few who did not think she was a 'good thing'.

That Claire so readily found herself so much at home at Ochil was a tribute to Juliet's remarkable talents as a hostess. While Sir Charles was taken off every day by Robb, the ghillie, to fish the famous Ochil stretch of the Tay and Abdy strode around his estates with his dogs at his heels, Juliet devoted much of her time to having heart-to-heart chats with her guest. There was nothing Claire enjoyed more than hours of inconsequential chatter over endless cups of tea and Juliet indulged her to the full.

It was on the third day of the visit when Claire had already decided that Juliet was her best friend, that the conversation turned to more weighty matters.

'Claire darling,' said Juliet as they sat over tea and cakes in the small boudoir which opened off the main drawing-room. 'How long do you think Charles will want to go on working at his business?'

Claire was in no way put out by the directness of the question. Indeed Charles was one of her favourite topics of conversation.

'I'm only thinking of you, darling,' Juliet went on. 'It must be so awful for you to be stuck at home day after day while he is away at his silly old office. It's time you had some more fun out of life. You could travel and do all kinds of things while you are still young enough to enjoy them.'

Claire smiled her sad smile and sighed.

'You know what men are. It's not as if I haven't talked to him about it time and time again. He seems to think that everything would go to pieces if he did not go down every day. So ridiculous!'

'It is not as if he had not got Keith.' Juliet leaned forward and laid her hand on Claire's arm. 'I should not tell you this,' she said confidentially, 'but I had a long private talk with Dick Katz just before I left Detroit. We're very close, you know. Well he told me how much he really liked Keith. What is more important he admires him. He'd like to see him handle a bit more responsibility. You know what American businessmen are. They like to give youth its head. If you have not got to the top by the time you are forty you are not going anywhere. Do you think Charles is being quite fair to Keith not giving him his head more?'

Claire sighed again but inside she was glowing with pleasure.

'So typical of Charles. He never thinks of other people. If you only knew what I have to put up with sometimes. I keep telling him he is going to be the ruin of that boy. Of course nothing I say has any effect on him.'

Juliet was silent for a moment or two, gazing out of the window thoughtfully as if weighing up the situation. Then she said, 'Do you think it would be any good if I talked to Charles? Not that I have any influence with him,' she added hastily. 'But sometimes people listen to outsiders when they take no notice of those close to them.'

'I think that would be just wonderful,' said Claire. 'You are such a good friend, dear. You really are.'

The opportunity for Juliet and Claire to get Sir Charles on his own occurred after dinner that same evening. Abdy, it appeared, had to attend a meeting of the local branch of the National Farmers' Union in Blairgowrie and would not be home until late.

'Poor Abdy,' said Juliet as the three of them sat over coffee in the drawing-room. 'He does take his life so seriously. It seems to me all you men are the same. It is just what we were saying this afternoon, isn't it, Claire dear.'

Claire, her pose as the long-suffering little wife forgotten, was quick to pick up her cue.

'Juliet wants to talk to you, Charles,' she said settling herself more comfortably in her chair. 'I hope you will listen carefully.'

73

Charles, who had been looking forward to a quiet evening with a book, recognized that his wife was in one of her I-mean-business moods and composed himself to listen with polite resignation.

* * *

The following morning Sir Charles rose earlier than usual and breakfasted alone in the high panelled dining-room. Then instead of taking the car he decided to walk to the river to keep his appointment with the ghillie, leaving a message for Claire to pick him up at lunchtime.

Robb, the ghillie, accustomed to the eccentricities of Lord Ochil's fishing guests, found his charge less than his usually urbane self that morning. Twice he missed a fish through failing to strike in time and scarcely seemed aware of what was in Robb's eyes a gross misdemeanour. Instead of his usual reluctance to return to lunch Sir Charles seemed almost relieved when Claire and Juliet came bouncing down the rough track to the waterside in the Rover.

'I think I'll give this afternoon a miss, Robb,' he said as he slipped behind the wheel. 'I have some business to attend to.'

Half way back to the house he interrupted a lively conversation between Juliet and Claire.

'You might be interested to know,' he said, aware that he was speaking pompously, 'in connection with what we were talking about last night, that I shall be resigning as Chairman of the Company.'

Claire stopped in mid-speech, her mouth sagging open.

Juliet was the first to recover her equilibrium.

'Why Charles, I did not expect you to take me all that seriously.'

'I didn't,' said Charles bluntly. 'It is something I have been thinking about for a long time. You only helped me finally to make up my mind.'

'What about Keith?' asked Juliet, her practical instincts rapidly asserting themselves. 'Today is Wednesday. Shouldn't you let him know as soon as possible? I mean there will be all sorts of things to talk over between you. I tell you what. Why don't you get him out here for a few days where you can be quiet and get everything put in order?'

Sir Charles was doubtful. 'I expect he will be sailing somewhere up the Clyde. I don't know how to reach him.'

'Don't be so helpless, Charles,' said Claire crossly. 'Somebody is bound to know where he is.' Her head was buzzing with excitement so that she could hardly take in what had happened.

'All right, you find him,' Charles snapped. 'I'll have to spend the afternoon working on some figures.'

It was Juliet who took over the task of finding Keith. It was not very difficult. She suggested to Claire ringing the flat and when Claire volunteered his number Keith answered the phone.

'Have you fixed anything yet?' he asked eagerly when he heard her voice.

With Claire breathing down her neck Juliet pretended not to understand.

'Your parents and I just thought you might like to run up here for the rest of the week. That is if you are not doing anything.' She could not quite keep a certain archness out of her voice.

'Come on Juliet. Spill the beans. What's up?'

'That's settled then,' cooed Juliet. 'We'll expect you in time for dinner.'

Keith replaced the receiver and, in spite of the fact that it was three o'clock in the afternoon, poured himself three fingers of whisky and added a little water.

The leggy blonde who was lounging on the sofa idly beating time to the music coming over the stereo, stretched. 'Was that the call you were waiting for?' she asked, only half interested.

'Maybe. Anyway I have to go out of town. You'd better collect your things.'

'What about that dinner you promised me tonight? And our sailing trip tomorrow?'

'Another time. This is business.'

'Christ,' said the blonde, 'you are an unutterable shit.'

*   *   *

Sir Charles spoke nothing but the truth when he had said to Juliet that he had been thinking of retiring from the board of Greenbank for some time and had already had the advice of his accountants on the value of the shares and the tax complications. Perhaps what had persuaded him more than anything else had been the Camel development. The expansion of the works, the

75

new methods and the unfamiliar problems which they created had made him feel old and out-of-date. Many of the values which had served him and his father before him over so many years seemed to be no longer valid and he missed the old faces which, one by one, had disappeared from amongst those close to him. The future which seemed so bright to Keith and men of his generation like Clancy-Smith had no appeal for him.

Seated with Keith in big leather armchairs in the library at Ochil the following morning he was trying very hard to put into words something of what he felt. He had never found it easy to communicate with his son. Now, when it was important that he should feel he was discussing business affairs with someone who was his equal, he found it difficult to forget the image of the rebellious boy who had caused him so much concern not so very many years ago.

'Of course I am going to miss the office quite a bit,' he found himself saying in his most stilted voice. 'But I know that I am passing everything over into good hands. As a family we have a long tradition of service to the best interests of the Company and I am sure that I can rely on you to carry on these traditions to the utmost of your ability. I am going to propose to the Board that I be retained in the position of a consultant but I do not want to interfere in any way with the day-to-day running of the business. That is your job from now on and I wish you the very best of luck. You will already know that you have a good team around you on whom you can rely so I don't suppose there is much you will want to consult me about.' He smiled rather wryly. As an address to a shareholders' meeting it would have been quite a success.

Now that it was all happening Keith felt suddenly tongue-tied and embarrassed. He was struggling to find something appropriate to say when his father held up his hand.

'Of course I do not expect you to assume so much responsibility without having the power to implement your decisions. I have talked this over with your mother and we have decided that I should make over to you some of my ordinary voting shares in the company. These with the few you already have will give you effective control. I am announcing this at a special Board Meeting I have called for next week and the lawyers will be instructed to register the transfer that afternoon. I think that is all I have to say.' He got up and walked stiffly to the library door. 'I think I may go and try and catch a fish.' Now that the interview was over his smile was almost warm.

Lunch that day was an awkward meal. Keith felt even more tongue-tied than usual with his family and Sir Charles made no effort to join in the conversation. Claire's determined efforts to conduct an intelligible conversation with Abdy resulted in a disastrously one-sided string of platitudes. Only Juliet seemed completely at ease, making a simple action like passing the potatoes into a major social gambit.

After the meal was over she announced firmly that she was taking Keith for a walk. 'Must try and get some of that Glasgow smog out of your lungs,' she declared.

They took the path through the woods which climbed the hillside behind the castle. For some time they walked in silence, each deep in their own thoughts. They had seen a lot of one another since Juliet had got back from Jamaica. Although this was Keith's first visit to Ochil, she had come to Glasgow frequently, often spending the night at Keith's flat in Bearsden. In spite of their closeness Keith still felt uneasy and unsure of himself. She was so self-possessed and she had the knack of puncturing the sophistication he wore so uneasily. It was only in bed that he felt himself to be master of the situation. He made love violently as if to assert his manhood.

It had been Juliet's idea to ask his parents to Ochil and things had worked out exactly as she had planned.

'Somebody has got to do something to get the old buffer to hand over to you and that somebody looks like being me.' Keith had agreed with some misgiving.

'Well don't I even get congratulated,' she said now, taking his hand.

'I haven't really taken it in yet,' said Keith. 'Of course I knew the old man could not go on for ever but I hardly expected him to give in so easily.'

'Hardly put up a struggle,' said Juliet, taking more credit to herself than she was rightfully due.

'I suppose you know that he is making over his voting shares to me as well. I shall have complete control.'

'How does it feel to be a tycoon?'

'No different really. It's not as if it gives me more money. I mean I can't sell the shares or anything. They are just pieces of paper.'

'What nonsense!' Juliet was indignant. 'They are your shares to do what you want with. You don't mean to tell me that you are going to go on living in that crappy little flat. I don't want a lover who lives in a dog kennel.'

Keith considered the matter for a moment. 'I suppose you are right. It's important to have the right image. Dad is bound to see that.'

'Listen, my darling innocent child,' said Juliet squeezing his hand. 'Can't you realize that you don't have to ask for everything any more. You are the big banana. You own Greenbank. If you want a house or a new boat or anything else you just go out and buy it.

Keith laughed. 'I'm afraid it does not quite work like that.'

The sun was warm as they came out from the shadow of the woods at the top of the hill and looked down into the valley beyond. Juliet was making him feel like a little boy again and he reacted as he always did. He pulled her to him and, forcing her head back, covered her mouth with his. For a moment she was rigid and then suddenly relaxed pushing her body against him.

'Not right on top of the hill, darling,' she said breathlessly. 'It would never do for the tenants to see Lady Ochil in the arms of another man.'

He picked her up and carried her back into the trees. When it was over she lay quite naked, the pine needles prickly on her back.

'I like being made love to by a rich man,' she whispered.

'I think you have all the makings of a whore,' Keith said gravely but he felt once more master of the situation.

7

Keith Puddefant found life at Ochil Castle extremely pleasant. Sir Charles, pleading that he had a lot of arrangements to make, left the day after he had announced his decision to give up the Chairmanship. Abdy Ochil was quite put out. 'Damn funny fellow, your friend,' he had protested to Juliet. 'Ask him for a week's fishing and he slopes off in the middle of it. It's not as if he was not catching fish.'

Claire had gone with her husband after much protesting but to Juliet's great relief. She was beginning to find her role as Claire's best friend something of a trial. Besides it left her more time to devote to Keith and Keith was now the main game.

In the days which followed, Keith's attitude to Juliet underwent a considerable change. When he had parted from her after the unplanned and blissful few days in Jamaica he had almost expected never to see her again. It had been like one of those shipboard romances where two people had sworn everlasting devotion only to part forever at the gangway.

It was Juliet who had done all the pursuing. She had come over frequently to Glasgow and they had even managed one long weekend in a small hotel on the West Coast.

Keith did not realize how much he had come to depend on her until he had seen her on her own ground at Ochil. She had always taken a great interest in discussing his affairs. When she had first raised the matter of his father handing over his shares, he had dismissed it as the idle chatter of a woman who neither understood business matters or, more importantly, his family. But she had persisted until even Keith had begun to think there might be something in it. Almost in spite of himself he had got quite excited with the idea of the inviting of his parents to Ochil and subjecting his father to some of Juliet's own particular brand of persuasion.

When it had been so unexpectedly successful he had to accept the fact that Juliet was far more important to him than purely as an eminently satisfactory mistress.

Now as they lay together on the top of the hill above Ochil which had become their favourite place to make love, she stretched her long bare legs in the air and said suddenly, 'Keith darling, I think you ought to buy a yacht. No, not like that little thing you have at the moment,' she silenced his protests. 'A decent boat. Something you can enter for the big races. A lot of important men do it. Apart from the fun it is good publicity—like owning a runner in the Derby.'

To own a big boat had long been one of Keith's ambitions and now with the sun shining and Juliet lying beside him it seemed almost possible but he fell back on his usual arguments.

'I've told you before that my having control of Greenbank does not mean that I have money to burn. Everything is tied up in shares. I mean, of course, I have a big income if we do well but that is all taxed anyway. If I borrow money from the bank the interest is ridiculous. I just can't afford it.'

Juliet made a petulant moue with her mouth.

'Really darling, what is the point of being rich if you can't spend your own money. You might as well not have the beastly shares.'

'If I want to raise that sort of money I would have to put my shares on the open market and go public. Father would die of heart failure.'

'I don't see why you have to go public. Why not sell privately. It would be easy enough to find a buyer.'

'Who, for example.'

'For example,' said Juliet, 'Richard Katz.'

* * *

When Keith arrived back in the office the following week he hesitated at the top of the stairs undecided whether to turn right to his old office or go straight to his father's room which was now to be his. Feeling distinctly self-conscious he turned left and opened the heavy mahogany door without knocking. To his relief his father was not there. He sat down behind the glass-topped desk and rang the bell for Miss Thornton.

She came in clasping her shorthand book.

'Good morning, sir,' she said, her face expressionless.

'So you've heard the news about father?'

'Oh yes, indeed. Sir Charles and I have been working on the details for the past few days. May I offer my congratulations?'

Keith could not trace the faintest trace of irony in her voice.

'Thank you,' he said feeling rather flat and shut out. He had never got over the feeling that Miss Thornton disapproved of him.

'Has everyone been told?'

'I have not mentioned it to anyone,' she said primly. 'There is to be a Board Meeting at three this afternoon when Sir Charles will make an official announcement.'

'Thank you,' said Keith again.

'I have the share transfers which your father has signed. Shall I bring them in?'

Keith nodded. His father had certainly wasted no time.

In many ways the financial structure of Greenbank was remarkable. Generations of Puddefants had pursued a policy of carefully controlled expansion, each taking pride in handing over to his successor a more valuable legacy than he himself had received. No Puddefant had ever succumbed to the temptation to borrow money for expansion, preferring year after year to plough back profits into new plant and buildings. The cumulative effect of this policy had been to raise the turnover of the Company to just over six million pounds while the equity capital had remained unaltered. Non-voting preference shares had been issued from time to time to outlying branches of the family but the number of one-pound ordinary shares—the only shares to carry a vote—had remained at only five thousand. Of these Keith already owned five hundred, his mother owned a thousand and the whole of the balance was held by Sir Charles.

The share transfer certificate which Miss Thornton now laid in front of Keith provided for the handing over to him of three thousand five hundred ordinary shares so that he would now have four thousand against his parents' holding of five hundred each.

He read the document carefully.

'I myself have witnessed your mother and father's signatures.' Miss Thornton sniffed audibly, bristling with disapproval.

'I understand,' said Keith. 'I won't require anything further this morning.'

He resisted the impulse to ring Clancy-Smith. To see his face

81

when the news was announced that afternoon was going to be worth waiting for. Instead he drove down town to the offices of Macgruer, the yacht brokers, and spent a happy morning poring over the specifications of several yachts currently on offer which he was still convinced were far outside his means. There would be plenty of time to get down to work when his appointment as Chairman and Managing Director had been made official.

* * *

Six hours later Keith and Clancy were occupying two stools in the Cavern Bar in Belgrave Place. The Cavern was one of those bar restaurants where business executives like to take their most favoured clients. It was intimate, luxurious and discreet.

'Same again. Large ones.' Clancy pushed his glass across the counter. He still had not got over the shock of the afternoon's meeting.

'Why did he do it, old boy?' he asked. 'I simply don't understand it. Here is the firm never been more prosperous. All plain sailing and him not yet at the retiring age.' He shrugged his shoulders helplessly.

'The point is he has done it,' said Keith. 'What we have to think about now is what we are going to do. I mean now we have a free hand there may be some changes we want to make. New broom sweeping clean and all that sort of thing.'

Clancy noticed with satisfaction the use of the word 'we'. There was no doubt things were going to go his way.

'Let's start with the Board,' he said only half seriously. 'I can do without any of them except you and I.'

'I'm glad you're not thinking of getting rid of me,' Keith grinned. 'Let's leave the Board until things settle down a bit. Shouldn't I issue a statement or something to the men? You know the sort of thing. "I hope you will give me the same loyalty as you gave my father. All pull together. Bright days ahead." Establish communications as Ronnie Motion would put it.'

Clancy shook his head emphatically. 'The less you interfere with the running of the factory the better. Look at it this way. Suppose you tell them everything in the garden is lovely and you're going to make lots of lovely money, what are they going to say? I'll tell you what. They are going to ask for a bigger pay

82

packet. You tell them that things are not so hot and everyone has to tighten their belts and what will they do? Half of them will find jobs somewhere else where the outlook is brighter. You can't win.'

It was Clancy's firm conviction that the workers should be kept in their place and get on with the job while the management got on with theirs.

'I'll tell you somebody who'll be pleased,' Clancy said suddenly.

'Who's that besides you and me?'

'Dick Katz. He'll be delighted. Between you and I, I don't think he was altogether happy with the old man in the chair. He likes a young management. He told me as much when we were over there. He's one of the first people we ought to talk to.'

Keith was doubtful. 'Katz is fine but we must remember that there is much more to Greenbank than the Katz contract. I'll admit it is important and can become much more so, but we managed all those years without it. He's not the be all and end all.'

Clancy was genuinely horrified. 'Listen,' he said, 'Camel Motors is the biggest thing that ever happened to Greenbank. In a few years if things go right we'll be taking in all the work that we sub-contract at the moment and we'll double our total turnover. Isn't that important?'

'O.K., O.K.,' said Keith peaceably. 'I know Camel's a big thing. Just don't let us forget that that is the jam. We still have to take care of the bread and butter.'

Clancy grinned, 'Come on, it's your round. Don't get mean just because you are a millionaire.'

Keith waved his arm in the direction of Bessie, the barmaid, who was in deep conversation with two elderly businessmen at the other end of the counter.

'Talking of that,' he said, 'I was looking at the details of a magnificent boat this morning. Sixty-footer with twin diesel auxiliaries. Spotless condition. Only built three years ago.'

'And sailed by one old lady who never did more than five knots I'll be bound.' Clancy teased him but he was delighted with the turn of the conversation. He was remembering his long talk with Dick Katz in Detroit. It looked like turning out fine.

* * *

83

One person who had not taken advantage of the Fair holiday had been Iggy Salvatori. While Billy Caird and Betty Brown had been planning their future in the berry fields of Blairgowrie and Sir Charles had been coming to far-reaching decisions on the banks of the River Tay, Iggy had remained closeted in his hot little room behind the shop in Dunbarton Road. Among his many callers one of the most frequent had been Joe Kidd, a gaunt giant of a man whose history was written in his blue-scarred face.

Joe Kidd had been a miner for almost thirty years until a fall of rock had put an end to his career. Now when he walked he dragged his left leg, but the scars on his body were not as deep as the scars in his mind. A card-carrying Communist since his very early days, Joe had no comradely feelings for anybody—not even his fellow workers. He had seen his father die, gasping horribly for breath. That had been in the days when the mines had been privately owned and the doctors in the pay of the mine owners. Men did not die of silicosis in those days because it would have meant compensation for their widows. Instead they died of pneumonia. Now that the State owned the mines anyone with a runny nose was diagnosed as a silicosis case. If Joe despised his fellow workers he reserved his particular brand of hatred for what he called 'the Supervision'. Anyone who wore a collar and tie was suspect of being 'supervision' in Joe's book.

Joe's relationship with Iggy was a complicated one. Because Iggy wore smart suits and drove around in a large motor car he belonged among the hated classes but because Iggy was what he was, Joe, with a certain amount of reservation, was prepared to overlook his shortcomings.

When Iggy suggested that Joe try for a job at Greenbank it took all of his powers of persuasion to convince him that was the best thing for the cause. That was what they had in common— a cause, and the cause for which they both strove was the disruption of industry for the sake of disruption.

Joe had gone for an interview at Greenbank and it was all he could do to stay civil long enough to get himself a job. When the interviewer had shown him sympathy over his damaged leg and leant over backwards to find a place for him he had felt the hate welling up inside him but he had said nothing. The result of his forbearance had been that he had found himself taken on as a driver on a fork-lift truck which did not entail any standing about.

With Joe Kidd inside the enemy's citadel another piece in Iggy's jigsaw slotted into place.

Iggy, to give him his due, was not a hater in the same unreasoning way that Joe Kidd was. He was essentially a logical man. He was also a man who liked the good things in life and it seemed to him, when he was released from a slave labour camp near Cracow in Poland after the war, that the logical thing to do was to accept the first offer which looked like giving him a leg up in life.

It happened that the Mayor was looking for someone with a command of languages to help him deal with the polyglot collection of humanity who by their very weight of numbers threatened to clog up the inadequate administrative machine which was required to deal with them. The young Ignatius Salvatori filled the bill admirably. Herr Schneider, the Mayor, showed his gratitude by getting Iggy inducted into the International Socialist Party who arranged for his transfer to the British Zone where it was hoped his talents could be used to greater advantage.

Armed with suitably impressive papers, Iggy found no difficulty in being taken on by the British Control Commission for Germany who found a ready use for his linguistic skills. Perhaps he would have been wise in the light of later events to have stayed in West Germany but Germany was not a very inviting prospect for a stateless person in the immediate post-war years. It was the British and the Americans who appeared to be the conquerors and certainly they could be seen to be enjoying the fruits of conquest. Where most Germans lived little above subsistence level, scrambling for the cigarette ends which even the most junior member of the Occupying Forces could flick casually into the gutter, there was no doubt in Iggy's mind where his future lay.

It took three years of hard work and the influence of an unusually sympathetic officer in the higher echelons of the Control Commission before he managed to get himself shipped over to Britain. It took a further three years of poverty and disillusionment before he found himself a niche as an accredited agitator for the Workers' Revolutionary Party.

Ten years later with a fine record of dedication to the cause he was able to open his shop in Glasgow and settle down to employing his undoubted ability to further the aims of the only people who had shown any interest in his career. To his country of adoption he felt no loyalty at all. Instead he waited and worked for the glorious day of the revolution when the capitalist society would collapse and he would be a real power in the land. Dreams of power ate into his flesh like an acid.

When Barney Corcoran had come to Iggy with the information about the Camel contract which was to be handled by Greenbank, he had managed to conceal his elation. For some time one of the objectives of his carefully laid schemes had been the Camel Company. Not only were Camel large employers of labour which made them an automatic target but they also represented the investment of American capital in Britain and it was a matter of policy to erode any links between the two major capitalist powers, particularly financial ones.

Camel had not proved one of Iggy's most outstanding successes. There had certainly been a series of strikes for higher wages but they were difficult to sustain. Workers showed a deplorable tendency to accept a compromise where wages were concerned, dictated by common sense. It was only where an emotional factor could be introduced into a strike that there could be much hope of delivering a telling blow to the national economy. When the mineworkers went on strike it was more than wages which were at issue. There was a strong tradition of emotionalism amongst the miners and shared by many members of the public. The dangers and the hardships of a miner's life coupled with the memory of starvation wages attracted sympathy and hardened their resolution. The agitator had no such weapons ready to his hand when it came to the highly paid car industry.

It was a subject which Iggy had often discussed with his close collaborator, James Christie, recently elected as a member of the Executive of the Union. Christie, like his father before him, was a life-long disciple of the teachings of Leon Trotsky. Early on in his career he had realized that there were distinct disadvantages in belonging to the Communist Party and had handed in his card. But he had not changed his spots. It was just that he preferred to lead from behind rather than carry the banner.

On one of Christie's regular visits to Glasgow Iggy had explained to him the Greenbank development and Christie had been impressed.

'I've looked up the record of Gaul, the Convenor at Greenbank. He's a sound man but maybe just a little bit too safe. We will have to put some spine in him. On the other hand the management are not experienced. They don't know what industrial relations are all about. We must hit them quickly and we must hit hard. If we can get them on the run there is a chance we may have something big going. It is just a question of getting the right spark.'

They discussed the matter for a long time but they did not realize that in a pub in Blairgowrie the powder trail had already been lit.

8

Billy Caird returned to work after his tremendous holiday with mixed feelings. He had agreed on Betty's insistence that he would not wait until he had won the football pools before leading her to the altar and he was anxious to make as much money as possible so that they could start off in a place of their own. Betty was already talking of fixing a date before Christmas so there was not much time.

On the other hand he was anxious about going back to Greenbank. There was no doubt that Harry would miss no opportunity of taking his revenge for the events in Blairgowrie. What distressed him even more was that Chick took the news of his impending marriage to his sister with indifference if not downright animosity. Perhaps when they both got back to work their friendship might be resumed on its old footing but he rather doubted it. He discussed the matter with Betty.

'If that Harry Birdsall lays a hand on you I'll claw his eyes out, so I will,' she swore, 'and Chick had better mind his step or I'll do him an' all.'

Such militant support made Billy ashamed of his fears but he went back to work on the Monday morning with some trepidation just the same.

For almost three months before the opening of the new plant Chick and Billy had been amongst the squad of men training to take their places on the production line turning out the transmissions. Although there were certain engineering processes carried on in the shop, it had been decided that the main function at Greenbank in the preliminary stages of a three-year development plan would be in the assembly of the units. Such component parts as the forgings, the castings and the valve block itself would be bought in from outside contractors.

It was with a certain amount of pride that Billy was allowed to take his place on the first day after the Fair holiday on the production line. His job was simple enough—fitting 'O' rings to the servo units and placing them in the wire carrier-baskets hanging from an overhead conveyor which carried them on to the next stage.

'You stick in at that for a time,' the shift foreman had said, 'and if you are doing all right I'll see you are moved to something a bit more interesting.'

In fact Billy was perfectly happy with his job. Slipping the rings into the grooves of the servo units was an automatic action which became simpler and more routine with practice so that he had no difficulty in keeping pace with the production line. While his hands worked nimbly he could let his mind wander over the ever exciting prospects of what he was going to do with his Pools winnings and wrestle with some trepidation with the problems of setting up house as a married man. Now that he had finished his apprenticeship his rate of pay was nearly £50 a week. With only £3 a week to pay for his single-end room and the £2 a week he was spending on the Pools as his only luxury he was putting quite a bit each week into his Post Office savings. It was all very satisfactory.

The only flaw in his contentment was that Chick had ceased to be his friend. There had been no actual row between them. It was just that they had stopped walking to the bus together and sitting next to each other in the canteen. If they passed on the shop floor they would exchange greetings but that was all. Instead Chick with several of the other young operators hung around Harry Birdsall. They monopolized one particular table in the canteen for their tea breaks and dinners, defying anyone else to sit there who was not one of their gang. Afterwards they would play endless games of nap, slapping their cards on the table and shouting exultantly when they won. Some of the older hands looked on disapprovingly but they did not interfere.

Harry had returned from holiday with a livid weal across his forehead stretching down to one eye. He gave it out that he had had an accident when he was training and left it at that. He had a job as a charge hand on the casings transfers line and he had managed to get Chick into his section. He affected not to see Billy whenever their paths crossed which would have left Billy feeling relieved were it not that he felt sure that Harry was only biding his time. Sometimes he would look up from his work to see him twenty yards away across the floor just staring at him.

For almost a week everything in the new assembly shop ran smoothly. The men gradually adjusted to the hardness of the concrete floor which at first made their legs ache agonizingly and to the constant noise from the machinery after the months of quiet waiting for it to be installed.

It is an odd thing about the noise which is an inescapable part of working in an engineering factory. For the first few days it seems intolerable, driving every thought from the mind and leaving the senses numbed long after the knocking-off whistle has gone. Then gradually the ears adjust so that men can talk to one another quite easily without raising their voices and the machine operators can anticipate trouble by detecting the slightest change of note of their machine in spite of the surrounding din.

It was during the second week that the first rumblings of trouble to come made themselves felt. At the end of the first shift Joe Kidd came out of the wash-room dragging his twisted left leg behind him and sought out the shift foreman.

He found John Glashan in his glass-enclosed cabin set in the middle of the preliminary assembly lines, just putting on his coat.

'Yes, what is it?' he asked impatiently as Joe Kidd pushed open the door.

'I've got a complaint.'

'What sort of complaint?'

'It's the bleedin' washroom. Not fit for pigs it isn't.'

John Glashan looked at Joe Kidd speculatively. He was an easy-going man who disliked trouble.

'I've just been in the washroom myself. There didn't seem to be much wrong with it to me.'

'Not fit for pigs,' Joe repeated. 'Soap all covered in oil and towels so bloody wet you can't dry your hands on them. I had to use my handkerchief to get my hands dry.'

'For heaven's sake, man, it's the end of the shift. There's a lot of men have just used that washroom. It's bound to get a bit mucky. It'll all be cleared up before the next shift want to use it.'

'Never mind the next bloody shift.' The veins on Joe Kidd's neck were standing out and his voice was strangulated with anger. 'We are entitled to clean soap and dry towels. If you are not prepared to do anything about it I'm going to see the shop steward and we'll see what he has to say.'

John Glashan took a deep breath. He knew the complaint was unreasonable but he knew Joe Kidd's kind. They could make a mountain out of a molehill and this was just the sort of issue to inflame hot heads.

'I don't think there will be any need for that. I'll make a note of your complaint and bring it up with Supervision.'

'Bleedin' Supervision,' Joe snarled. 'What do they care if we have to live like pigs. They don't get their bloody hands dirty. Not bloody likely they don't.'

'I can do without that language,' Glashan said sharply. 'I've told you I'll take the matter up.' He started to button up his raincoat.

'I'm not satisfied,' said Kidd. 'You'll be hearing more of this and don't be surprised if you've got no bloody shift here tomorrow morning.'

'Don't talk daft,' said Glashan as he stepped out on to the floor of the shop and held the door open for Kidd to follow him. Then he turned his back and walked away but he felt uneasy. On his way out of the gates he ran into Willie Jameson, the senior foreman.

'Just had Joe Kidd making a complaint about the washroom,' he said, anxious for assurance that he had acted right.

'The lame fellow who drives a fork-lift.'

'That's him. He was in a hell of a stew. Threatening to take it up with the shop steward.'

'Who is the steward for his section?'

'Harry Birdsall.'

'It would be,' said Jameson. 'I don't go much for either of them. That fellow Kidd is a trouble-maker if I know anything and I don't think Birdsall is much better. You'd better watch it, John.'

'Do you think I should have a word with Sandy Gaul?'

Willie Jameson threw up his hands in horror.

'For God's sake don't start trying to cut corners man! That way they will have a real grievance. Maybe he'll forget the whole thing. Maybe he won't but let's play it the right way. If Birdsall wants to bring it up we'll just have to deal with it.'

'Wet towels for God's sake! Whatever next.'

'I'll tell you the best thing to do. Get some more towels in that washroom.' Willie Jameson grinned cheerfully.

Joe Kidd had no intention of forgetting the incident. He found Harry Birdsall in the Dreadnought, crowding the counter with Chick Brown and one or two others.

'Want a word with you,' said Kidd, jerking his head towards the corner of the room.

Harry took a long swig from his pint and put it back carefully on the counter.

'Something private then?' he asked. He didn't like Kidd's attitude, particularly in front of the lads.

'Business,' said Kidd laconically.

'Business is for business hours.'

'This is a union matter. You are the bloody shop steward.'

Harry shrugged and followed Kidd over to a corner table.

'Well, what's it all about.'

Kidd repeated his story about the state of the washroom.

Harry still unversed in the ways of the hard-liners was not particularly impressed.

'So what do you expect me to do? Wipe your bloody arse for you? I'm not a nursemaid.'

The veins started to stand out again on Joe Kidd's neck but he kept his control.

'It's the attitude of the shift foreman I'm mostly objecting to.'

'What do you mean?'

'I come to him with a legitimate complaint and what does he do? He tells me to go and get stuffed.'

'John Glashan said that?' Harry looked up in surprise.

'When I told him I'd take it up with the Union, he said he didn't give a fuck what I did.'

Harry stood up pushing his chair back from the table. 'We'll soon see about this,' he said. It was a direct affront to his authority and he was white with anger.

* * *

Harry was not able to reach Sandy Gaul that night but the following morning he was waiting for him when he came into the new office which had been created for him in the line of executive offices on the gallery above the shop floor.

He listened carefully to Harry's story, leaning forward with

92

his elbows on his paper-free desk, his fingertips pressed together.

'You're sure you have got your facts right,' he said when Harry was finished. 'This is a very serious matter. Undermining the position of the Union, quite apart from the business of the washroom.'

'Of course I'm sure. Joe Kidd told me himself.'

'But have you heard Glashan's side of the story?'

Harry had to admit that it had not occurred to him to go and see Glashan first.

'You should have done that. We must play these things strictly by the rules.' Sandy Gaul spent a few moments in thought. Then he said, 'I think, seeing the authority of the Union itself seems to have been attacked, it would be all right if I came with you to see what Mr Glashan has to say. If it is not satisfactory I can then take the matter up with the Factory Manager.' Sandy Gaul was a stickler for procedure but he was quite glad to have something to do. Since he had moved into his new office and been relieved of his duties on the shop floor he had felt quite embarrassed at the amount of time he had on his hands.

Heads turned and men looked up from their jobs as Harry Birdsall and Sandy Gaul made their way across the floor to John Glashan's office.

'Something's up,' said one of them.

'Aye, something's up all right. It has to be something to get Sandy out of that new office of his.'

Word passed around causing a mild ripple of excitement and anyone passing the shift foreman's office glanced sideways through the glass windows to try and glean some more information as to what was happening.

John Glashan had half expected a visit from Harry Birdsall but the presence of Sandy Gaul surprised him. 'They must be taking this thing pretty seriously,' he thought with a slight sinking feeling in his stomach. When he heard what it was all about he was deeply shocked. So shocked that for a moment he was left without words. Then he said quietly,

'I think we had better send for Kidd and sort this matter out.'

'Do you intend to deny you used the words complained of?' Sandy Gaul fixed him with the glare of a schoolmaster interrogating a recalcitrant pupil.

'Of course I deny it,' Glashan exploded. 'I may have told him

93

I did not think much of his complaint but I promised to look into it.'

'That's not what the man says.'

'I don't care what Kidd says. He's a liar and what's more I can prove it.'

'You can't prove nothing,' Harry said with a twisted grin. 'It's one man's word against another. Just because you're the bloody shift foreman we've got no reason to take your word.' He was thoroughly enjoying the situation and the feeling of power.

'You are saying that I would not listen to a man with a reasonable complaint.'

'That's about what it comes to,' said Gaul.

Glashan suddenly remembered thankfully his meeting with Willie Jameson on the way home the previous evening.

'It so happens,' he said quietly, 'that I paid so much attention that I mentioned it immediately to the senior foreman. If you care to go over and see him he will tell you the same.'

'What did Jameson have to say?' Gaul was sceptical.

'Told me to order some more towels.' Glashan smiled, now sure of himself. This was certainly his lucky morning.

'Here,' he said, 'is my written request to have the matter rectified.' He shoved a piece of paper across his desk.

Sandy Gaul examined it carefully, reading it twice as if looking for any legal flaws. Then he turned to Harry.

'What have you to say about this, Brother Birdsall?' he asked, his voice far from friendly. Without waiting for an answer, he nodded brusquely at Glashan and strode out of the office.

Harry sat staring at Glashan for a moment. Then he too rose to his feet.

'Think you're bloody clever doncher,' he spat the words out through his teeth. 'Well let me tell you something. I'm going to fix you, you bastard. Just see if I don't.' As he slammed his way out of the office he felt at least he had done something to salve his injured pride.

The matter did not end there for Harry. That night he went down for his usual couple of pints at the Dreadnought and found Barney Corcoran already waiting for him.

'Never mind the drinks,' Barney snapped as Harry tried to attract the barmaid's attention. 'The big man wants to see you and he doesn't like to be kept waiting.'

94

'What the hell are you talking about?'

'You've stepped out of line, laddie, and we're not too pleased with you.' Barney jerked his head towards the door and Harry followed him out obediently. Half an hour later he was having his first confrontation with Iggy Salvatori.

'Joe Kidd has been telling me how you failed to back him up at a meeting with Supervision this morning,' said Iggy conversationally. His tone was bland enough but his little sunken eyes were cold and glittering.

Harry had heard of Iggy but anything he had heard had not prepared him for this meeting. He felt a tingling at the bottom of his spine and the palms of his hands had gone clammy. His usual belligerence had gone out of him like a puff of wind. He struggled for something to say. Finally he blurted out, 'It wisna' my fault. Joe never told me the truth.'

'The truth!' exclaimed Iggy his pudgy hands spreading wide in surprise. 'What concern have you with the truth? Truth my friend is a purely relative thing. We are not concerned with philosophies. We are concerned with facts. Facts, deeds, action! That is what you are there for, Comrade, and this morning you failed. I do not like failure.'

'It wisna' my fault,' said Harry again. 'What could I do?'

'It's what you did do that is bothering me. What you did was go running to the convenor like a little boy who's wet himself. You should have had your men out last night, never mind this morning. The complaint was a serious one and you let the opportunity slip. You've let the management run rings round you. You're a bigger fool than I thought you were.'

'That's no fair,' said Harry sullenly. He felt a sudden welling up of indignation at the unexpected accusations.

Iggy acknowledged the protest with his thin humourless smile. 'I think there are some things we ought to get straight,' he went on. 'One of them is your er ... rather curious personal habits. The authorities do not like men of your age who play around with little boys. They won't let you do your body-building exercises in prison you know.'

Harry's mouth dropped open. Again he struggled to say something but this time no words came.

'I'm sorry,' said Iggy. 'One has to be quite blunt with people of your mental capacity. I hope I have made everything quite clear.'

Harry glanced sideways at Barney to see if he could expect any help from that quarter but Barney was sitting quite still his eyes fixed on the big man in the chair.

'I am prepared to overlook matters this time. Shall we say we will put it down to your inexperience. There will be other occasions when you will be able to demonstrate your qualities. Remember Joe Kidd is not the only one I have who is—how shall I put it—working for the cause.' He nodded his head as a signal that the interview was over.

'Treated you light, I reckon,' said Barney as the two of them made their way down Dunbarton Road, jostled by the crowds hurrying home from work. 'Can be a right bastard when he wants to be.'

'Gave me the creeps,' said Harry, his self-confidence beginning to flood back now that he was out of range of Iggy's powerful presence. 'How about having that pint I never had at the Dreadnought.'

They turned into the public bar at the corner. It was crowded three deep at the counter, the customers jostling each other and waving their hands in the air in an attempt to attract the attention of the two barmaids, who went about their job with an air of stolid indifference, banging the filled glasses down in the puddles of spilt beer.

Barney shoved a five-pound note into Harry's hand. 'There you are. Get them in with that. It's a job for a big bloke.'

Harry eventually managed to struggle back out of the crush with two pints and two nips of whisky.

'I'll gie you yer change in a meinnit,' he said. 'Ah've got it in my pocket.'

'Never mind about the change.' Barney gave him a grin. 'Hang on to it.'

Harry looked at him to see if he was having him on.

'Bloody hell. That wisna' a quid you gave me. It was a fiver.'

'I ken fine it was a fiver. Just call it expenses.'

Harry stared at Barney in blank amazement.

'Iggy's not such a bad bloke if you treat him right. But don't mess him around again like you did this morning.'

The home-going crowd started to thin out rapidly and they had one or two more rounds leaning against the bar.

'They told me you was a good pal to be in with,' said Harry,

96

feeling suddenly warm as the drink worked inside him.

Barney eyed him speculatively.

'You knew fine what you were doing before you ever went to Greenbank. Don't come the innocent wi' me, that's why you came to me in the first place.'

It was not quite true. Harry knew that Barney was a card-carrying Commie and there was talk about there being more behind him than the money he drew each week from the Bureau but that was as far as it went. He had been doing Chick a favour when he had taken him down to meet Barney but he had only the vaguest idea of getting involved himself. His mind worked slowly and he was only just beginning to realize what he had let himself in for. Now that he thought about it he realized that his job at Greenbank was important to him. It was important because it made him feel important and that was what he hankered after more than anything else.

'Do you think he meant that? I mean have me done and all that.'

'There's one thing you can be sure of. Iggy always means what he says.'

'Of course there's no harm in it.' In spite of the drink Harry was embarrassed. 'I mean it's just a bit of fun. Playing around like.'

'Ah'm no carin' what you do. It's naethin' to do wi' me. Nor Iggy neither for that matter. But he'll shop you to the fuzz as soon as look at you if it suits him.' Barney let Harry digest the statement. Then he went on, 'Don't you forget. Iggy's in with the big time. Really big people. There's people in London much bigger than him. Bigger'n the Prime Minister if it comes to that. One day you'll see just how bloody big they are.' Barney licked his lips with relish. 'That's the day Ah'm waiting for. Then we'll see who's the bloody boss in this fuckin' country.' He swallowed his drink at one gulp and ordered another.

Harry felt extraordinarily pleased with himself at having such fine friends.

*   *   *

Harry did not have long to wait before a further opportunity arose for him to prove himself in the eyes of Iggy Salvatori.

Daniel Cooley was one of four coloured men who worked on

97

the main assembly line. At their own request they had stations next door to one another. Willie Jameson had wanted them separated on the grounds that they talked to one another the whole time and slowed up the line but Dan insisted. 'Man, we beautiful people must stand together against you white trash,' he had said flashing his pearly-white grin. Willie had shrugged his shoulders and let them have their way.

Tuesday morning was the first really hot day of the year. Already, when the eight o'clock shift was coming on, the sun had broken through the smog which hung over the city and was riding high and clear in the sky. By the time the mid-morning break was due, it was making its power felt through the opaque glass roof of the assembly shed. Men rolled up their sleeves and unbuttoned the front of their overalls to catch such cool air as was circulating between the open doors at either end of the long building.

'Bejaysus I could go a pint,' observed Joe MacGraw, wiping the imaginary froth from his mouth with his sleeve.

'A pint is no bloody good to me. I could go a bucket.'

'Belt up willya. Me throat is drier than a nun's tit so it is.'

Suddenly the overhead gantry stopped with a jerk setting the carrying baskets swinging and the high-pitched note of the alarm bell rang out urgently.

Up in Jim Cantlie's office the alarm interrupted a meeting he was having with Willie Jameson.

'For God's sake what the hell is this all about?' he snapped but both men were half way out of the room before he had finished his protest. The alarm bell could mean only one thing—trouble.

On the assembly room floor men stood around in groups, shouting at each other to make themselves heard above the noise of the alarm. Strangely they were not all clustered round one spot. Cantlie noted it and thanked God. It could only mean that there had not been a serious accident.

'All right,' Willie Jameson shouted at the nearest group. 'What's the trouble?' One of the men grinned and gestured with his thumb towards the end of the shop where an extra large group of men was gathered, presenting their united backs to the world.

As Cantlie and Jameson pushed their way through the crowd most of the men were laughing.

'All right, all right, stand aside,' Cantlie shouted. 'Who the hell pressed that button?'

Then he saw Daniel Cooley. He was sprawled forward, his black arms in startling contrast to his white T-shirt, spread out for support on a carrier-basket. His head lolled sideways, the whites of his eyeballs seemed to start out of his head and his mouth was opening and shutting as he gasped for breath.

'Turn off that bloody noise somebody.' As the sound suddenly stopped Cantlie stepped forward and took the negro by the shoulder. 'Come on lad,' he said. 'What's up wi' you?'

Cooley groaned loudly and started to roll his eyes.

Winstanley Jackson, a lugubrious-faced Jamaican who worked at the next position to Cooley, stepped forward out of the crowd. 'You best leave that man alone boss. You ain't no doctor. He's took real bad. Maybe he a-goin to die.'

Cantlie turned to Jameson. 'Send for first aid,' he ordered. He was pretty sure that the whole thing was a put-up job but he was taking no chances. 'All right Jackson, what happened?'

'Well man, it was just the heat. You know how it is with we pore nigras. We just can't stand the heat like other folk. No sir. The heat affects us real bad.' Cantlie knew he was being made a fool of. He fought to keep back the anger he felt boiling up inside him.

'You can cut out the comedy,' he said, his voice sounding louder than he had meant. A few of the men who had been standing silently round in a circle started to grin and one or two of them nudged each other.

Jim Cantlie who was never the sweetest-tempered of men felt the last of his control ebbing away. 'All right, you lot,' he shouted. 'Get back to your places. This isn't a bloody sideshow.' He glared angrily round at the circle of faces. A few of the men shuffled their feet and started reluctantly to turn away.

It was at that moment that Harry Birdsall chose to put in an appearance. Men stood aside to make way for him as he came strutting down the line, waving his arms above his head.

'Right, brothers,' he was shouting. 'Pack it up there. We're coming out. All out. Pack it up, brothers.' Behind him Joe Kidd limped along with surprising agility and further back a group of workers straggled out behind. As Harry drew level with the group

99

gathered round the inert figure of Daniel Cooley he stopped and addressed himself to Jim Cantlie.

'That man there might have got himself killed. Men can't work in these conditions. Don't you know your own regulations? The temperature in this shop is eight degrees higher than the top limit. We're coming out before there are any more bleedin' casualties.'

Jim Cantlie stood as still as a statue. The complaint was justified and there was no point in arguing although he felt like landing his fist in Harry's face.

Behind his back Daniel Cooley stopped rolling his eyes and winked broadly at Winstanley Jackson from under his arm.

* * *

Matters were to get a lot worse before they got better. By the time the dinner-hour hooter sounded, the men on the casings transfer line had walked out accompanied by the storeroom staff. Then it spread to the main engineering shop so that by four o'clock the shop stewards were at the front gate to stop the next shifts coming on duty.

At the same time Sandy Gaul called a meeting of the Shop Stewards' Committee. It was held in the front parlour of Jim Anderson's house as the most convenient place for all the members. The business did not take long. Sandy Gaul recounted the events leading up to the walk out of the assembly line operators 'just so that we are all sure what this is all about'. Then Harry confirmed that the account was correct.

'I think we will all agree that Brother Birdsall's prompt action was correct and necessary in the interest of the safety of our members. It is quite clearly laid down that the temperature on the shop floor shall not exceed 68 degrees. I need hardly point out that men working in conditions of excessive heat can easily be suddenly overcome and a dangerous accident occur. Although the whole area of the factory has not yet been subjected to the extreme temperature which occurred in the assembly shop this morning it is right that we should all demonstrate our solidarity with the assembly shop workers by withholding our labour.'

There was a murmur of approval.

'I have already been in touch with the District Office of the Union and their representative is on his way here. I think I can assure you than in a matter of this nature where the safety of men is involved the support of the Union will be automatic.'

Jim Pocock, a thick-set solemn-looking man, who represented the Dispatch Dept, removed his pipe from his mouth before he spoke.

'Do I take it, Brother Gaul, that Supervision have not offered to take any steps in the matter of the temperature of the Assembly Shop?'

'I have not yet had any contact with Supervision,' Gaul spoke sharply. 'There is a matter of principle involved here. We have a right to withhold our labour and I will agree to a meeting with the Management in my time—not theirs. I do not choose to do so until I have had consultation with the area representative.'

Perhaps Gaul might not have taken such an independent line if it were not for some information he had received over the telephone when he had spoke to Area.

'You've hit on a good time to have a walk-out,' Bert Evans the secretary had told him. 'Jimmy Christie is coming up on the Inter City. One of the people he wants to talk to is yourself.'

For a moment Gaul was so surprised that he could find nothing to say. James Christie was really a big wheel in the Union—a member of the National Executive with a reputation for being a hard man when it came to a fight. That he should take the time to have a talk with a mere convenor of a not very important firm struck Gaul as incredible. Just the same it excited him no end.

Sandy Gaul's whole working life had been devoted to the cause of Trade Unionism. No one could have been more assiduous in looking after his members' interests during working hours and most of his spare time was devoted to his duties as secretary of the local branch. For the last three years he had been their delegate to the annual Union Conference and he was generally well regarded higher up the tree.

In fact Sandy Gaul's chief ambition was to become a full-time Union Official and he took every opportunity of displaying his knowledge of the workings of Union affairs wherever he thought it might bear fruit. It was a matter of considerable regret to him that he had never had the opportunity of displaying his talents in a confrontation with the management and he sometimes felt that his militancy might be suspect as a result. While he waited for James Christie to arrive off the train he rehearsed some of the points he wanted to get across to him. To have an ally on the Executive was tantamount to a humble parson knowing a Bishop. The very thought of the coming meeting made him glow with excitement. With a walk-out on his hands where better could he turn for advice as to his attitude to the management?

Confronted with the fact of the sudden strike Ronald Motion experienced quite different feelings. As soon as it had been reported to him he had hurried down to the factory and had spent most of the afternoon in conference with Angus Simpson and Jim Cantlie. Neither of them had proved a great deal of help to him. Simpson, who had resented the disruption of his ordered way of life by the acceptance of the new contract, took every opportunity of telling him that he had known that they were in for trouble. He left no doubt in anyone's mind that it was trouble of which he wanted no part.

Jim Cantlie took a more definite if no less obstructive line.

'I tell you,' he said for the umpteenth time, banging the desk to emphasize his words. 'This was a put-up job. I knew the moment I saw Cooley that he was coming the old soldier. He and his mates had it all fixed up with that trouble-maker Birdsall.'

Motion said wearily. 'It does not alter the fact that the complaint was a justified one. The temperature was almost eight degrees too high.'

'So what. It was a bit warm in the shop. It doesn't mean they can behave like a lot of bloody ballerinas.'

'That's just what it does mean. Regulations are regulations and if they are not observed they can run rings round us if they feel like it.'

'We never had trouble like this before we took on all these new tearaways.' Simpson leaned back in his chair and crossed his arms as if the observation absolved him from making any more constructive contribution to the discussion.

'What's Sandy Gaul doing about the whole thing?'

'He's refused to have a meeting until tomorrow. He says he wants to have consultations first.'

Cantlie snorted impatiently. 'That fellow is getting too big for his boots. I knew we were making a mistake when we took him off the floor and gave him an office.'

Ronnie Motion was acutely aware that he was not impressing his personality on the meeting in the way he should be doing. At the course he had attended at the Manchester School of Business Studies it had all seemed so straightforward. There was nothing a sympathetic forward-looking management team could not achieve in the field of industrial relations. Unfortunately neither Simpson nor Cantlie appeared to be either sympathetic or forward-looking. As for the representatives of the workers with whom he had hoped to establish such good communications, he seemed to have got nowhere.

'Well, gentlemen,' he said clearing his throat and trying to make his voice sound authoritative and decisive, 'The first thing we must do is to attend to the proper ventilation of the assembly shop.'

'You mean you are going to give in to those bastards,' Cantlie interrupted him angrily.

'It's not a question of giving in, Mr Cantlie,' he said coldly. 'It is a matter of getting things put right so that this situation does not arise again. The advantages of having a glass roof to provide as much natural light as possible are obvious. It is only a matter of providing extra ventilation for abnormally warm conditions. After all we do not have so many tropical days in Glasgow,' he essayed a weak joke.

Neither of his audience smiled.

Sandy Gaul called for a meeting with the management the following day at eleven o'clock. He had had an excellent meeting with James Christie. They had dined together late in the four-star Malmaison Restaurant and their conversation had ranged far outside the confines of the Greenbank dispute. Mellowed by an unaccustomed bottle of wine and becoming more comfortable in his surroundings Gaul had found himself talking on terms of easy familiarity with the great man and Christie on his part had appeared to listen attentively to what he had to say. When they had parted on first-name terms well after midnight, Jimmy Christie had gripped him warmly by the hand. 'Remember, Sandy,' he had said, 'we are not living in the dark ages any more. Today the power is in the hands of the workers. Never forget that.'

Sandy was in such high spirits that he stood himself a taxi instead of catching the late night bus. As he drove home in state he resolved that there would be a little less negotiation in the future and a bit more hard hitting. What was it Jimmy Christie had said? 'Remember, you must never come to terms with the bosses. To play it their way is to sup with the devil.'

He looked forward to the confrontation the following morning with a new delight.

*   *   *

Ronnie Motion did not go into the meeting with the Shop Stewards' Committee with a similar feeling of confidence. After his meeting at the factory he had been called into conference with Keith Puddefant and Robert Clancy-Smith. Like everyone else he had been completely taken by surprise by the sudden resignation of Sir Charles. He had always got on well with the old man. They had frequently lunched together and there had been occasions when he and his wife, Rhoda, had been asked out to Cumberland Towers. Keith on the other hand was an unknown quantity. During the time they had both been on the Board their relationship had been purely a business one. In fact he had never been able to take Keith's contribution to the running of the business particularly seriously. He accepted him as the Chairman's son and left it at that. To find him now occupying the seat of authority in the Chairman's office he found a little bit unnerving.

Nor was Keith's attitude calculated to make him any more at ease.

'Whichever way we look at it,' he was saying, 'situations like this should not arise. What do you think our American friends are going to say if we fall down on our deliveries before we have hardly started?'

'If you're looking for a reason for the strike it is bad constructional design of the assembly shop. On a hot day like today it is quite impossible to keep the temperature at the right level.' Ronnie Motion spoke sharply, his temper frayed after the long day.

'I would say it was more a matter of man-management,' said Clancy-Smith drawling his words. 'We give these chaps jobs at a good wage. They should feel jolly grateful instead of trying to rock the boat. It's a question of loyalty and team spirit.'

It was all Ronnie Motion could do to stop himself exploding. Having to answer to Keith was bad enough but to have Clancy-Smith on his back as well was intolerable. He had never liked him from the day he had joined the firm.

He took a deep breath and said quietly, 'Jim Cantlie swears

this was a put-up job. I'm inclined to agree with him. There are some among the new men who are trouble-makers.'

'Well, kick them out,' said Clancy who seemed to be taking charge of the discussion. 'We don't want any bloody Communists in the show.'

'You have to have more against a man than his politics. You start laying off men for no good reason and you are in real trouble.'

'I agree with Clancy,' said Keith. 'We've never had trouble in the factory before and this is no time for it to start. If you are right and this is a put-up job I want whoever is at the back of it out on their ear.'

It was not the end of a bad day for Motion. When he got back to his modest house in Paisley, it was to find that his wife was having one of her temperamental days.

Since their son had left home for a teaching job in London Rhoda's 'bad' days had been coming more and more frequent. Knowing that the long hours she spent alone in the house were getting on her nerves he had formed the habit of trying to telephone her in the middle of the afternoon, suggesting things she might do to pass the time. Sometimes he even invented jobs she could do for him which took her out of the house. When he succeeded she was always in a much sweeter temper when he returned. This afternoon he hadn't been able to make his usual call.

She taxed him with it the moment he came through the door.

'I waited all afternoon for you to ring. It quite ruined my day for me.' Her lips were twisted in the bitter line he was coming to know so well.

Defensively he said, 'I'm sorry, dear. It's been a terrible day. I didn't have time.'

'It doesn't take much time to make one little telephone call. I waited in,' she said again.

'You should not have done that. Was there something you wanted to do?'

'I could have gone over to Mona Booker's for a game of bridge.'

Ronnie knew this wasn't true. The few friends they used to have like Mona Booker had long stopped asking Rhoda to bridge games because she always called off at the last minute.

'I do think it's most inconsiderate of you. I sit here waiting for

105

you all day. Then you come home late without so much as a word of explanation.' She started to sob quietly into her handkerchief.

He put his hand awkwardly on her shoulder. 'Come along, dear,' he coaxed, 'I've had a very bad day too.'

'That's all you think about. Your beastly job. You never give a thought for me.' Her voice was becoming strident with pent-up emotion.

'Come on. It's not as bad as all that. Let's have a glass of sherry and then I'll cook you some supper.' He went over to the neat cocktail cabinet in the corner of the sitting-room and started to get out the glasses.

'I don't want any of your beastly drink. I suppose that's what you've been doing all day. Drinking.' Rhoda flung herself out of the room and he heard her stumbling up the stairs. He decided not to follow her. Instead he poured himself a large whisky.

That night and several unaccustomed whiskies later he went supperless to bed in the spare room.

*   *   *

The meeting between the Shop Stewards' Committee and the Management the following morning turned out to be a rather one-sided affair. It took place round the long table in Angus Simpson's office. Before the shop stewards' representatives were shown into the room Ronnie Motion made an appeal to Simpson and Cantlie.

'Let's keep this on a friendly basis,' he exhorted them. 'They are in a touchy mood and I don't want any of us to say anything we might regret afterwards.' Remembering his training at the business school he added, 'When we sit down, let's try and break them up a bit. I don't want to create an atmosphere of confrontation with all of them on one side of the table and us on the other.'

In fact it did not work out that way. When Sandy Gaul marched in at the head of his party he made straight for the chair at the head of the table and the stewards grabbed the seats on either side of him. The three representatives of Supervision were left to seat themselves together at the bottom end of the table.

Having won the first round Gaul remained in complete control of the meeting.

106

The facts of the case were restated and the management representatives were asked bluntly what they intended to do about the complaint.

'I may add,' said Gaul with evident relish, 'I have had the advice of the Union Executive on this matter. They are taking a most serious view and unless we get satisfaction at this meeting the strike will be declared official.'

Ronnie Motion was regretting the whiskies he had consumed the previous evening. His mouth was dry and he had a headache but he was very conscious of the need not to give in unconditionally.

'Whilst agreeing that the temperature of the assembly shop was above the norm,' he said, 'the Management are very concerned at the lack of consultation in this matter. If the shop steward concerned had shown the good will we have reason to expect this whole affair might have been settled without recourse to such er ... drastic measures.'

'It was no time for consultation,' Birdsall snapped. 'With men fainting all over the place we could have had a serious accident.'

'All over the place?' Motion raised his eyebrows in surprise. Before he could press home his advantage Cantlie said, 'There was nobody fainting. That man Cooley was putting it on.'

Immediately there was an outburst of protest round the table. Gaul rapped sharply with his knuckles. 'I must ask you to withdraw that remark immediately, Mr Cantlie.'

'I'll not withdraw anything.' Cantlie stuck his jaw out and glared around the room.

Gaul at once rose to his feet.

'If this is to be the attitude we must declare the meeting closed. I will not stand for our members being insulted.'

In the ensuing confusion with men pushing back their chairs and talking at the top of their voices, Ronnie Motion had to shout to make himself heard. 'Order, gentlemen, please. Just one moment if you please!' In the sudden silence which followed he spoke quickly. 'Let us not lose our tempers. We have come to this meeting with the best of intentions. We are not denying that there have been reasonable grounds for complaint. We are here to discuss what can be done to put matters right.'

Gaul paused for a moment and then slowly resumed his seat.

'That is a better attitude,' he said magnanimously. 'I think we will be prepared to listen to your proposals.'

The ground thus cut from under his feet Motion had no option but to concede all along the line.

'I have had ventilation specialists in to examine the problem and there is nothing that cannot quite easily be put right. With a number of strategically placed extractor fans I understand that it will be quite possible to achieve a steady temperature at the agreed level. The work is being put in hand straight away.'

After that the meeting became a formality but even then Gaul was not prepared to give an immediate assurance that the strike would be called off.

'The final decision rests with my members,' he declared. 'If after due consideration it is decided to accept your proposals you will be informed.'

It was not quite the end of Motion's tribulations. At three o'clock that afternoon, Gaul intimated that the strike would be called off but not until three o'clock the following day, and only if they were paid for the time they lost.

Ronnie Motion knew what the reaction of the other members of the Board would be to this. The lightning strike was over but he could not help reflecting that it had left in its aftermath a number of barriers and he seemed to be on the wrong side of all of them.

9

The persecution of Billy Caird started the day after the strike was declared over.

When he got back from the fifteen-minute tea break in the canteen it was to discover that the 'O' rings which he kept neatly piled on the left-hand side of his bench had been scattered over the floor. He spent ten minutes gathering them up again. Willie Jameson doing his mid-morning tour of the shop floor found him on his hands and knees.

'Hullo, lad,' he exclaimed, surprised. 'What are you up to? Saying your prayers?'

Embarrassed, Billy scrambled to his feet. 'Someone must have knocked into my bench. I found it like this when I got back from the canteen.'

Willie looked at him shrewdly.

'Having a bit of trouble with the lads, are you then?'

Billy shook his head. He did not want to think that it was anything but an accident.

'Just you come and see me if this happens again. We have quite enough bother without things like this. Go and draw some more rings from the stores. This lot are all covered in muck.' He gave a brisk nod and passed on. Further down the line he came upon Sam McGee. They were old friends and worked side by side in the days before Willie had been promoted to shift foreman. He touched him on the shoulder.

'Listen, Sam. Have you seen any of the boys taking it out on the lad up the end there?' He jerked his head in the direction of Billy's bench.

Sam lifted his cap and scratched his head thoughtfully. 'Young Billy Caird, you mean? Can't say as I have. He's a good worker, that one. Keeps himself to himself.'

'Just keep an eye on him will you. I have a feeling he's being got at.' Then changing the subject he asked, 'How's the wife? We don't ever see her now we've moved.'

Sam grinned. 'Ah, we can't keep up with your style of living. Fancy flats an' all that.' Willie had recently got possession of one of the new council flats out in Cardross.

Willie gave him a playful punch. 'Give over,' he smiled. 'You've no ambition. Remember what I said about the lad.'

Pity there's not more like Sam, Willie thought as he continued his round. Some of this new lot get my goat.

Billy lived on his own since his mother and father had died. He had been accustomed to fend for himself. There was an elderly aunt in Ayr whom he visited about once every two months, but she was too far away to be much of a substitute for his parents. Before Billy had got himself engaged to Betty he used to take his midday dinner each day in the works canteen. Since his return from holiday with an urgent need to save as much money as possible he had taken to bringing a thermos of tea and a jam piece to work, neatly packed in an old canvas gasmask case—a relic of the war which he had inherited from his father. Like everybody else who took their own pieces with them he left it on a peg in the changing room where he put on his overalls.

When he put his hand in the case to get his sandwiches at Monday dinner time he encountered nothing but a squelchy mess. The case had been packed with axle grease and when he opened the thermos flask it was to discover that the glass lining had been smashed into pieces as if it had been dropped on the stone floor.

He did not doubt for a moment who was responsible, and his quick temper boiled up inside him, almost choking him in its intensity. Clutching the case and without really knowing what he intended to do he headed for the canteen. Throwing open the swing doors violently he stopped for a moment to collect himself and glared around. There was a hush as the volume of conversation died and men looked up from their plates, their forks suspended half way to their mouths as they caught sight of the small angry figure.

Intent on their game of cards at a table in the far corner of the room the dozen or so youths gathered round Harry Birdsall were the last to become aware of Billy's dramatic entry. When Harry saw him his face creased in a broad smile. This was far better than he had hoped for.

'Hey lads,' he shouted slapping his next door neighbour on the back. 'Look who's here. It's young lover boy himself.'

There was a burst of laughter from the men at his table. Others, unsure of what the disturbance was all about, grinned uncertainly.

'Did you not enjoy your piece then?' He turned to give an exaggerated wink at the others who greeted the sally with another explosion of mirth.

Billy realized that there was no running away now. He was committed. However much his instinct told him to turn and retreat through the door, it was something he could not do. He knew with certainty that the time had come when he had to make a fight or be utterly destroyed. It was a matter of self-preservation.

Quite slowly and deliberately he started to pick his way through the tables which separated him from where Harry sat. Men pulled their chairs forward to let him pass. One of them noticing his set face, drained of colour and the blind glint in his eye, half rose in his seat. 'Steady on there, lad,' he muttered but Billy, hardly noticing, brushed him aside.

When he came up to the table, Harry sat quite still, nonplussed by the sudden turn of events. The initiative was all Billy's. Nobody moved. Then he lifted his dinner bag and turning it upside down shook its contents out all over the cards, the half eaten plates of food and the mugs of tea. The grease fell in great splodges, covering everything like some well aimed custard pie.

Suddenly the whole room erupted.

Somebody from a next-door table grabbed him by the arm. 'What the hell do you think you're doing, you daft wee bugger!' he shouted.

'That lad's mad.'

'Get that little sod out o' here.'

'Bloody Jesus Christ Almighty!'

Men got to their feet to get a better view of what was going on and pushing and shoving round, while Harry and his companions sat gazing in unbelief at the mess in front of them.

For the first time since the rage had seized him, Billy felt frightened and bewildered. He might have given way to a sudden impulse to burst into tears had not someone grabbed him firmly by the arm and started to propel him towards the door.

'Get back to your seats. Leave the lad alone!' Then to Harry who had risen to his feet, his fists clenched. 'You stay where you are or I'll belt you one, so help me I will!'

'For God's sake, Caird, what got into you?' Sam McGee asked when they were outside. This time Billy's face crumpled up and the tears poured down his cheeks.

It took some time before Sam and Willie Jameson managed to get any sense from Billy about what had led up to the incident in the canteen, but when Billy reluctantly told them about the events in Blairgowrie, Willie shook his head gloomily.

'He's a bad devil, that Birdsall,' said Willie. 'This won't be the end of the trouble. If I have a word with him he'll swear blind he knew nothing about your dinner bag. Best we move you out of Assembly. I'll have a word about getting you fixed up with something in the engineering shop.'

Sam nodded. 'Better make yourself scarce this afternoon. There's no point in asking for trouble.'

But Billy who had now quite recovered his equilibrium would not agree.

'I'm no' scared of Harry,' he said stubbornly. 'I'll just stick in with the same job.'

Willie was doubtful. 'I wouldn't mind so much if it was just Birdsall and his lot we have to worry about. I'll soon see that some of them are moved out of his section. It's the other blokes in the shop as well. They don't know the story. All they know is what you did in the canteen just now. At best they will think you are a bit soft in the head, at worst they will believe any story that Birdsall's lot put out about you. You can be sure that they'll be busy right now. I've seen it before when men get it in for one bloke. They can make his life hell.'

Billy refused to be moved in his resolve. Now that it was all over he felt rather proud of what he had done. He had stood up to Harry and he had come off best. He had done it once and he could do it again. Besides Betty would not think much of him if he ran away.

In the end Willie agreed to his going back to his bench that afternoon but he made up his mind to go and see Jim Cantlie and ask his advice. If there was going to be trouble he did not want to be the one caught in the middle.

Sam walked back with Billy to his bench and then went on to his own station. As he passed down the line young Johnnie

Pritchett, whom he recognized as one of the men who had been sitting with Harry, spoke to him.

'Billy Caird a friend of yours then?'

'What's that got to do with you?'

'Saw you got him out of the canteen pretty fast.' There was a sneer in Pritchett's voice. 'Maybe you haven't heard. He's been sent to Coventry. No one's to speak to him.'

'Because of what he did in the canteen?'

'That's right.'

'Maybe he had a reason for it.'

'Sure he had a reason. Want me to tell you?'

'Fire away.'

'It's on account of his old mate, Chick Brown. He's dead needled at him because he doesn't go with him any more and Chick's taken up with our lot. If you ask me he's a bit of a poof. Acting jealous like a bloody woman.'

So that's to be the story, thought Sam. Just the sort of thing one might expect from Harry Birdsall. Like everything else, Sam had heard rumours of Harry's own habits but he had never taken much notice of them. He was a man who did not believe in taking sides in anything which did not directly concern him. Now he just shrugged his shoulders and passed on but later he sought out Willie Jameson and reported his conversation with Pritchett. He may not have been a man to take sides but he had a sense of justice and liked to see fair play.

* * *

Jim Cantlie was a completely opposite personality to Sam MacGee. He could never shrug his shoulders at the world. He had to get involved. He listened to Jameson's account of the Billy Caird affair with growing indignation. His reaction was not made any less violent by the fact that he already had a couple of scores to settle with Birdsall. Ever since he had told him to clear his weight-lifting equipment off the premises he had marked him down as a trouble-maker and the recent strike had merely confirmed his conviction. Anything which threatened the smooth running of the works he took as a personal affront. Birdsall was a definite threat.

'I'll break that bastard, just see if I don't,' he growled when Jameson had finished. 'Send him up here right away.'

Willie Jameson knew Cantlie's temper and was worried. 'Take it easy, Jim,' he cautioned. 'There's more in this than meets the eye. You know the background and I know the background but the men don't. If they side with Birdsall we may be in for a hell of a lot of trouble. Shouldn't you have a word with Mr Simpson first?'

It was not a very tactful remark. Jim Cantlie's conviction that he should have had the factory manager's job had been growing ever since taking on the new contract. Where he had thrown himself into the challenge with enthusiasm, Angus Simpson had become even more retiring, resenting the added responsibility to the point of becoming almost obstructive. Just lately the relationship between the two men which had never been warm had degenerated into near animosity.

Cantlie now leaned forward across his desk and glared at Willie. 'I'm not asking for your advice,' he almost shouted. 'Get Birdsall up here.'

When Harry received the summons to the works manager's office he took his time. First he went to the locker room and took off his overalls, then he spent ten minutes with a comb in front of the mirror, getting his hair just as he liked it. After that he strolled over to the drinks dispenser and poured himself a leisurely carton of tea. He was enjoying himself immensely. He was already looking forward to reporting the events of the day to Barney Corcoran. Perhaps he would even have another session with Iggy and this time he would have plenty to say for himself.

'I sent for you half an hour ago,' Cantlie snapped, when he finally entered his office. 'Where the hell have you been?'

'Just having a bit of a clean up. You wouldn't like me coming to your office with dirty hands would you?' He remained standing looking down at the man behind the desk. He felt relaxed and confident.

Cantlie controlled his temper with an effort. 'I hear you have given orders that no one is to speak to young Caird in your section.'

Harry's face took on a look of exaggerated amazement. 'Me? Give orders! You must be joking. I'm only an operative like anyone else. I don't give anyone orders.'

'You're the shop steward.'

'This isn't a union matter. What's happened to Billy Caird is a result of a decision taken by my mates. I just go along with it.'

'Don't come the old soldier with me, Birdsall,' Cantlie glared at him. 'I know why Caird acted the way he did in the canteen— and there is a damn sight more I know besides.'

For a moment Harry was disconcerted. 'What are you getting at? It's perfectly obvious the lad is a nutter.' Cantlie could see he was uncomfortable. He leant back in his chair.

'For example you got more than you bargained for in Blair-gowrie didn't you? Got flung on your ear I heard.'

'If that little bastard has been running round telling bloody lies ...'

Cantlie held up his hand, interrupting him.

'There is only one person telling bloody lies around here,' he said beginning to lose his temper again. 'I'm not saying anything about the strike last week and there are a few things I'm not saying anything about at the moment but I'm warning you. I know you are a bully and I know you are a trouble-maker. Just you put one foot out of line again and I'll have you out of this place so fast your feet won't touch the floor. Shop steward or no bloody shop steward. You're a disgrace to the Union.'

Harry swallowed hard and for a moment stood quite still. Then he said, 'Don't you threaten me. You think you can sit there and threaten me. Well you're bloody well mistaken. Don't you come it with me, brother.'

In a moment Cantlie was on his feet. 'Get out of my office!' he yelled. 'Get out. Get out, you bloody Commie.'

For an instant the two men glared at each other; then Harry turned on his heel and walked out of the room leaving the door open behind him. Cantlie strode across the floor and slammed it. Then he sat down heavily in his chair and pressed his hands hard against his temples. He knew he had made a fool of himself.

He drove home early to Paisley, jamming his foot savagely on the brakes at the lights and once almost causing an accident at an intersection by swinging wildly across the line of traffic. When he opened the front door he did not shout his usual greeting to his wife but went straight up to the attic which served as his pigeon loft. It was the only place he knew where he could be sure of being at peace with the world. After a time the anger started to die out of him.

Maybe he should have gone to Angus Simpson as Willie had

advised. But as soon as the thought occurred to him he rejected it. Angus would have washed his hands of the whole incident or passed it all on to higher authority. This had developed into a personal matter between himself and Birdsall. The chips were down. The only thing now was for him to wait for the next move.

*　　*　　*

As Harry pushed his way through the frosted glass doors of the Dreadnought he felt on top of the world. Things could hardly have gone better. What had started off as a bit of fun at Billy's expense had escalated into a situation which was greatly to his advantage. His version of the encounter with Cantlie had lost nothing in the telling. Everyone in the assembly shop knew now that Cantlie had called them a bunch of Commie bastards. Some of the hot heads had been all for having a showdown there and then. Tension was running high and even the moderates who had not been too willing to take sides against Billy Caird were now convinced that the management were taking a downright liberty.

The bar had not yet filled up. Only a few men were leaning against the long counter savouring their first pints. To Harry's disappointment Barney Corcoran was not amongst them. Baldy, the barman, had seen him come in and was already pouring the two bottles of Special Brew into a pint glass, which was always his first drink of the evening. As he felt for his money Baldy waved it aside. 'That's paid for, Harry boy,' he winked. 'You're wanted through in the snug.'

The snug was a little room set apart from the main bar which had its own door into the street. It was used mostly by the few men who took their wives or their birds to the pub and wanted a bit of privacy. As Harry entered he saw it was already half full. Barney Corcoran was there and Joe Kidd with Daniel Cooley and a man he knew only as Andy from the light engineering shop and several others whose faces were vaguely familiar. But in the centre of the group, his presence dominating the room, was the unmistakable figure of Iggy Salvatori.

Taken by surprise Harry stopped in his tracks, almost spilling his drink. Then Iggy caught sight of him and raised a pudgy hand.

'Welcome to our little meeting, Comrade Birdsall. Ah, I see you

116

already have a drink. Find a chair for our Comrade.' He smiled a smile which was nearly welcoming.

Chairs were scraped aside to make room and when Harry was seated, Iggy addressed the room at large.

'I think some of you may not yet have met our new friend Harry Birdsall. He in a manner of speaking is the hero of today's events which we have just been discussing.' Turning to Harry he said, 'Perhaps you are surprised that we already know so much about this morning's affair. Just the same it would be as well if you were to tell us in greater detail of the disgraceful attitude adopted by a responsible member of the management to the quite inexcusable attack made on some of you in one of the canteens this morning.'

There was not much that Harry could add to the account of his interview with Cantlie but he made the most of it. At one point Iggy interrupted him.

'You say the Works Manager threatened to attack you?'

'He would have done,' said Harry greatly enjoying himself. 'He'd have attacked me all right if he had dared but he knew fine who would have come off worst. I don't spend my time and money in the gym for nothing.' He puffed out his chest as several of the company grinned showing their approval of his manliness.

This was really Harry's day.

When he was finished Iggy spoke again.

'It is quite obvious that this is an instance of serious industrial misconduct. Not only have the proper channels of communication been ignored, but a worker has been threatened with physical violence and our right to belong to whatever political party we choose has been attacked. It is an attitude by management which cannot be tolerated and we must now take the first steps in our battle to assert our rights. But be warned, comrades, the time is not yet ripe for militant action. That time will come but first the seeds must be sown. All of you here must spare no effort to see that the disgraceful events of today are known to all your comrades. I have already made sure that our comrades on the back shift will be made aware of the position. Your opportunity will be tomorrow. I think that you will find that your fellow workers will be as shocked as we all are here at the attitude taken up by the management.'

A rustle of approval ran round the room. Iggy's troops were

keen to join battle. By the time a few more rounds of free drinks had circulated there was not a man amongst them who did not see himself a hero in the struggle against oppression.

*   *   *

Sandy Gaul was concerned about events but from a rather different angle. It was Stewart MacGregor, the shop steward who represented the gear cutters, who first made him aware of the current of feeling which was running through the plant. Gaul had worked with MacGregor over Union matters for several years and respected him for his solid and practical approach to such troubles as they had had in the past. He had never seen him more bothered than he was now.

'There is something at the back of this I don't understand.' MacGregor started ticking the points off on his fingers.

'First I don't know what made that boy behave the way he did. There is a story going around that it was jealousy over his pal and that new bloke Birdsall but nobody has bothered about how the grease got into his dinner bag in the first place.

'Second there's this story of Birdsall and Jim Cantlie. Some say Cantlie actually hit him, others say he only threatened him. There is another rumour that Cantlie threatened to fire half the assembly shop for being Commies. I don't have time for the man but I don't believe he could be that stupid.

'Third, there is Birdsall himself. I don't like him. I haven't seen much of him but I think he is the sort who would make trouble for the sake of trouble and I don't want any part of that. He's only been here for a short time yet he is already something of a hero with the young chaps in particular. There's quite a few of them in my shop. Even some of the older men are saying that he is a marked man because he stands up to the management and they don't go along with that.'

Gaul nodded. He had his own reservation about Birdsall especially after he had been made to look a fool in front of John Glashan over the wash-house towels. Yet he had his position to think about. If there was going to be trouble he wanted his actions to meet with the approval of the Executive. Previously all his dealings had been with the area officers of the Union but now he knew that James Christie himself was showing an interest and James Christie was a hard-liner. Whatever else happened

118

he must not appear to be a weak man in the eyes of such a powerful official when it came to dealing with the management. That would not do his chances of becoming a paid Union official himself any good.

After his talk with Stewart MacGregor, Gaul sat in his office for a long time wondering whether or not to seek a meeting with Cantlie or go and talk to Birdsall or both.

In the end he decided to do neither. Nobody had made an official approach to him. It wasn't his job to start chasing after hares. So like Jim Cantlie he sat tight and waited to see what would happen next.

Communications were at a standstill.

* * *

One of the people who was not prepared to sit tight was Harry Birdsall. The day following the meeting in the pub with Iggy was one of the most satisfactory days of his life. Several men he had never seen before came up to him to congratulate him on the stand he had made against Jim Cantlie.

'Is that right he swung a punch at you?' Laurie Green, a charge hand in dispatch asked him.

'Well,' Harry temporized, anxious not to spoil a good story. 'Shall we just say he made a good try at it.'

'Just as well he didn't try a bit harder.' Johnnie Pritchett gave his sycophantic grin, 'Else Harry here might have been had for murder.'

'He's a hard man, is Cantlie.'

'I'll take him any day,' said Harry. 'Just let him try again.'

There was only one small cloud in the blue sky of Harry's admiration of himself. It was something Cantlie had said. There was no doubt now in his mind that he had wiped the floor with the works manager but the remark kept coming back to him. Cantlie had said, 'You got more than you bargained for in Blairgowrie. Got flung on your ear I heard.'

So far as he knew there was nobody had heard the truth about how he came by the damage to his face which was only just beginning to heal. Not even Chick Brown. How then did Cantlie know about it? Certainly Billy Caird could not have told him so he must have heard it from someone else. So who had Billy talked to? Sam MacGee perhaps who had told someone who had told Cantlie, maybe Willie Jameson. They were pretty thick those two. The more he thought about it the more it bugged him. Whoever Billy had told could tell someone else. His whole image of himself as an heroic figure was threatened with disintegration.

Harry's thought processes when he used them at all were not very logical. All that was obvious to him now was that Billy had done him an injury and anyone who did him an injury must be made to suffer for it. It did not do Billy's cause any good in Harry's eyes that he seemed to be quite unaffected by the barrier of silence which had been imposed on him. He still turned up for work, ate his solitary dinner and clocked off again at the end of the shift. Worse, it was not everyone who refused to speak to him. Sam MacGee was the worst offender, seeming to go out of his way to talk to the boy but there were others amongst the older workers on the shift who ignored the embargo.

So day by day Harry Birdsall continued to brood until his hatred of Billy Caird devoured him to such an extent as to blot out his happiness.

Billy Caird on the other hand was quite content with his lot. He did not in the least mind that many of the workers would not speak to him. In fact he liked to be left alone with his dreams. The only aspect of the whole affair which caused him any worry was Chick's attitude. He no longer missed his friendship but he did wonder what would happen on his wedding day. So far he had managed to get by without telling Betty about his being sent to Coventry and Chick had taken good care to be away from the house when he called but it must come out sooner or later.

The ripple of excitement caused by the confrontation between Cantlie and Harry Birdsall would have died a natural death after a few days had Billy not come to work with a bad headache on the Wednesday morning. On such small things big events hang.

By midday the throbbing in his head had become so unbearable that he could not concentrate on his job and there was nothing for it but to report sick and ask John Glashan's permission to knock off for the rest of the day.

Billy never looked robust at the best of times but when Glashan saw him he thought he might be seriously ill. His face was paper white, his pain-filled eyes were sunk in their sockets and his hands shook uncontrollably. Billy tried to explain that he had had

120

these migraines before and that all he needed was to go to bed and sleep it off but Glashan wasn't convinced. Taking him by the arm he led him to the rest room, next door to the canteen and sat him in a chair.

'You just bide there lad until I get someone to come and have a look at you,' he said and went off to his office to ring for the company doctor.

There is little goes on on the shop floor which is not observed and taken note of. When Harry Birdsall heard that Billy had been seen talking to Glashan and that he had taken him to the rest room, his mind at once jumped to the obvious conclusion. The little bugger had been telling tales again. There could be no other explanation. It was still five minutes before the end of the dinner break. Banging down his half finished mug of tea he stamped out of the canteen followed by Johnnie Pritchett, Chick Brown and a couple more of the lads. If there was going to be a bit of fun they did not want to miss it.

When Billy saw them come in he knew it was trouble but his head ached so intolerably that he couldn't really care. Harry seeing the defenceless figure huddled in the chair felt a surge of triumph. It was a situation which was made for him. Now he could even the score once and for all. What was more he could show what a hero he was in front of admiring spectators.

He walked across the room and in one quick movement grabbed Billy by the front of his overalls and pulled him to his feet.

'I'm going to fix you, you bleeding little grass,' he spat between his teeth and hit Billy hard in the stomach. Billy doubled up, gasping for breath and dropped to the floor. Harry picked him up again like a rag doll and threw him against the wall. Then he put the boot in, kicking him in the ribs and about the head. His foot was drawn back for another kick when Chick grabbed him by the arm. 'Hold off,' he shouted. 'He's had enough. You'll kill him!'

Harry turned to shake Chick off and at that moment he saw the figure framed in the doorway. It was Jim Cantlie. For a moment there was complete silence. Then Cantlie walked into the room and up to Harry until he stood face to face with not a foot between them.

When he spoke it was quite softly. 'Right, Birdsall. You can get your cards,' he said. 'I want you off the premises in half an hour.' He looked down at Billy who lay quite still, a trickle of blood starting to ooze from the corner of his mouth. He bent over and felt his pulse. 'What's more,' he said to no one in particular, 'this is a matter for the police,' but when he looked up again the room was empty.

Harry's mind may not have been a very constructive one but there was nothing wrong with his defensive mechanism. In the years he had spent as a teenager with the Tiny Toi gang in Bishopbriggs he had been involved in many fights with rival gangs. Where his mates had done their time in approved schools and Borstal, Harry had always managed to slip out from under. Now his instinct for self-preservation came to his rescue. With the mention of the police his first thought was to fix himself up with a cover story.

In the moment of panic when they had all rushed from the rest room they had stuck together and found refuge in a cleaners' room under the service staircase which they had often used in the past as a place to retire for a quiet smoke.

Of the five of them Chick Brown was the most shaken.

'Do you think you killed him, Harry? Oh my God, do you think he's a goner?' He was almost weeping.

'Shut your gob,' Harry snapped. Then turning to Johnnie Pritchett he said, 'You saw what happened, didn't you, Johnnie?'

'I didn't see nuthin',' Johnnie muttered. He knew the rules. Where the police were likely to be concerned nobody had ever seen anything. Even the victim of an attack could never recognize his assailants. No matter what were the rights of the matter you did not grass to the police. It was the only crime in the book.

'You mean you never saw him fall and hit his head against the radiator. Must have had a fit or something.'

'Oh that,' said Pritchett, relieved to have someone to do the thinking for him. 'I saw that all right. Took a right tumble he did.'

Harry looked at the other two. He hadn't bothered before with who had followed him into the rest room. Now he was relieved to see that they were the Swanson brothers. Jack Swanson and his younger brother Heb both had records for violence dating back to their gang days.

Jack looked doubtful. 'Do you reckon Cantlie saw you putting the boot in?'

'Suppose he did,' said Harry scornfully. 'It's his word against all of ours. It's five to one.'

'We was helping him,' said Heb suddenly struck with inspiration. 'He had this bad fall like and we was helping him when this bloody Cantlie comes in and starts shouting the odds.'

Harry looked belligerently at Chick. 'That's right, Chick. That's how it happened didn't it?'

'That's right, Harry. That's how it happened,' Chick echoed. His first panic had subsided and he was almost convinced now that Harry would see them out of the trouble.

Backed up so solidly, Harry's thoughts now turned in another direction.

'Best get back to work now lads. I've got things to do.'

As they filed out Heb asked, 'Are you going to get your cards then?'

'Not bloody likely I'm not. We'll soon see who's sacked. Just you get back and make sure all the lads know just what happened. There'll be no bloody shift working tonight if I know anything.'

He was already plotting his revenge on Cantlie and his first step was to seek out Joe Kidd.

*   *   *

By two o'clock in the afternoon the whole works knew that one of the shop stewards had been fired by the works manager. Most of them knew Harry Birdsall by name.

'That's the bloke Cantlie had it in for,' explained Sammy Durward, one of the charge hands in the engineering shop. 'Didn't give any reason. Just walks up to him and tells him to get his cards. Plain bloody spite. I reckon Sandy Gaul will call us out.'

'If he doesn't, I'm bloody walking out,' said another. 'I'm not working in a place where blokes can be given their cards for nothing.'

There was a mutter of approval amongst the half-dozen men standing round the tea dispenser.

Others were not so sure.

'There was someone hurt like. Jim Govern saw him being taken away on a stretcher.'

'It was that young chap in assembly. Him that got sent to

123

Coventry. I reckon there was some kind of a punch up.'

'Weren't no punch up. The boy was sick. Fell and hit his head.'

'Is that right?'

'Heard it from a lad who saw the whole thing.'

While the works buzzed with rumours and counter-rumours, Sandy Gaul in his office sought to get to the truth of the matter. On Joe Kidd's advice Harry had taken Andy Stock, the shop steward in light engineering whom he had seen at the meeting with Iggy, to talk to Gaul and between them they had put up a convincing case.

'You know as well as I do that that Cantlie has it in for Brother Birdsall,' said Stock. 'Ever since the lads came out over the temperature in the Assembly shop. He'd have had him out then if he could. Then there was the time he nearly struck him in his office. This is a put-up job and we're not going to stand for it. I'm taking my men out.'

Gaul was cautious. 'There certainly would seem to be a case for investigation. I'll arrange a meeting with Supervision.'

'Bugger Supervision,' said Stock sharply. 'This man has been improperly dismissed. It's our job to protect the interests of the workers. You start letting Supervision push us around and you'll see who's got the power. We're coming out and we're staying out until we get satisfaction.'

Gaul felt he was being pushed into a corner. He was remembering James Christie's words. 'Remember you must never come to terms with the bosses. To play it their way is to sup with the devil.'

He made up his mind abruptly. 'Right we'll come out at the end of the shift. There is a meeting of the District Executive Committee tonight. You can tell the lads we'll put it to a general vote tomorrow morning.'

Most of the men did not wait for the end of the shift. The assembly shop were the first to stop work, then the gear cutting section. By three o'clock all the sheds were silent.

When the back shift came on they were met at the gates by the stewards.

'Don't go through the gates, lads,' they were told. 'There's a dispute. We'll be having a meeting tomorrow morning when you can vote.'

The back shift is always an unpopular shift. Working from

two in the afternoon to ten at night interfered with a man's leisure too much. By chance there was a mid-week football match at Ibrox Park that night and quite a few of the lads had not turned up anyway. The rest were only too glad of the opportunity for release which had suddenly presented itself. There was no trouble.

10

Although Gaul had been almost forced into a decision, when it was made he accepted it as his own. His main concern now was to play it strictly by the rules. Under the procedural agreement which existed at Greenbank he was bound to consult straight away with Supervision.

He telephoned Angus Simpson. No good going to Cantlie, he reasoned. Cantlie was too much involved. Anyway the seriousness of the position warranted his going to the highest level immediately available to him.

Simpson was jerked out of his usual attitude of resigned apathy. He agreed to a meeting with the Shop Stewards' Works Committee at five o'clock the same afternoon. There was not much time to prepare for a confrontation and he had to work fast. First he called Ronnie Motion and then Cantlie. He did not relish a meeting with Cantlie on his own and anyway it was ultimately Motion's responsibility, not his.

When Simpson arrived at the Company's offices in Turk Street he was pleased to see that Cantlie's car was parked outside. 'Let them sort it out between them,' he thought, but he got a shock when he was shown into the meeting. Keith Puddefant and Clancy-Smith were also there and it was obvious that tempers were running high.

'Not to beat about the bush,' said Clancy-Smith when Angus Simpson had taken his seat, 'this whole situation is a first-rate balls-up. Mr Cantlie here has involved us in a situation which should never have occurred. There is a proper procedure to be observed in a case like this and it was not observed. Result, we have the second strike on our hands within ten days.'

Keith nodded his head in agreement. Cantlie remained quite still, his head averted so that he sat staring out of the window. Only the fingers of his left hand beating a tattoo on the table indicated the effort he was making to keep his temper. Then he

126

said, 'You can have my resignation any time you ask for it.'

'That's hardly the point,' said Keith. 'The situation has been created and resignations are not going to help at this stage. Don't you agree?' He looked at Clancy.

'He is in that over-dressed dummy's pocket,' Simpson thought to himself. 'What the hell is he doing in this meeting anyway?' Like most technicians he distrusted salesmen and Clancy-Smith was certainly no exception.

'I sacked Birdsall for the best reason in the book,' Cantlie said, choosing his words carefully. 'He deliberately assaulted a fellow worker. Bloody hell! What am I supposed to do? Pat him on the back and tell him not to be a naughty boy.'

'That's not what Gaul says,' Simpson said mildly. 'Apparently the lad was ill—we know that for a fact—and he hurt himself when he fell in a faint.'

'If you believe that you'll believe the moon is made of cheese.'

'It's not a question of what we believe. It is a question of what the men believe,' observed Ronnie Motion. 'There are four witnesses besides Birdsall who will swear it's true.' He looked at his watch. 'We have the meeting with the Works Committee in three-quarters of an hour. We had better have our policy clear by then.'

'I should have thought the policy was already perfectly clear even to you,' said Clancy offensively.

Motion coloured up at the rebuke. Then he said stiffly, 'I was not aware that we had come to any decision.'

'You can tell your precious Works Committee to go to hell. We won't open any talks until the men go back to work.'

'I would have thought that a decision of this importance is the province of the Managing Director,' Motion said coldly.

'I think I should make it clear,' said Keith, shifting in his seat, 'that with effect from this morning Mr Clancy-Smith is the Managing Director. In my position as Chairman he has my full support.'

'In that case,' said Motion gathering up his papers, 'there would seem to be nothing more to be said.'

*   *   *

Keith had not come to his decision to appoint Clancy-Smith as Managing Director entirely unaided.

The day before the strike he had lunched at Rogano's with Juliet off lobster and a pleasantly cool bottle of Liebfraumilch. Over coffee and brandy he had decided to take the rest of the afternoon off and drive her to Clynder on the Gareloch to look at the latest boat which had been offered to him by James MacGruer, the yacht builders.

She was a real beauty with long slender lines, her newly painted hull gleaming brilliantly white and her proud mast out-topping all the other boats which lay at anchor around her. They had clambered over her like a couple of excited schoolkids admiring the modern equipment in the wheel house, the neat cabins and above all the spacious stateroom with a built-in cocktail bar and teak-panelled walls.

'You have just got to buy it,' Juliet had been ecstatic. 'You run this baby down to the South of France and it will knock everyone's eyes out. Can't you just see it? Why even the Rainiers will have to ask you to dinner.'

Keith was equally enthusiastic but he tried to appear business-like, asking MacGruer's salesman endless questions about fuel consumption, engine capacity and a host of other details, the answers to which were already contained in the list of specifications which he held in his hand.

MacGruer's man could not quite make out what was the relationship between the two but he sensed that he was on the way to making a sale and that Juliet was his ally. He expounded enthusiastically on the superb way the galley was equipped, the comfort of the bunks fitted with continental quilts and the social advantages of having such a grand stateroom.

It was already late by the time they had got ashore and gone to the Yacht Club at Rosneath for drinks. Then there had been an exhilarating drive home in Keith's new convertible and they had arrived back at the flat in a state of exaltation.

It was when Juliet got Keith in this mood that she found him easiest to talk to and there was much she had on her mind. One of them was Clancy-Smith.

If the truth were known she did not much care for Clancy but Dick Katz seemed to have quite taken to him.

'He's the horse I'm backing,' he had told Juliet on one of their frequent transatlantic telephone calls. 'It seems to me that he already has your boy friend where he wants him. It is only going to need a bit of a push to put him on the top of the pile.'

She had raised the matter on one or two occasions previously and now with a bottle of Dom Perignon on the table between them she returned to the attack.

'Don't you see, darling, that you have got to give Clancy more authority for your own good. He is the only one on the Board who talks your language. Sooner or later you are going to have to cut out the old wood like Jock Mackay and Motion. You yourself say they don't fit in with the new scene. If you establish Clancy's authority now you are going to find the job all the easier when the time comes.'

Keith took a sip of champagne and started to speak but Juliet interrupted him. 'I know what you are going to say. Your father was always Chairman and Managing Director and your grandfather before him. What the hell. Times are changing. You leave yourself free to make the big decisions and let Clancy get on with the day-to-day business of running the Company. If he is going to do that, he has to have the power.'

'But Clancy is my Sales Director and a bloody good one. He can't do both jobs.'

'Look, he can be a much more effective salesman if he has the title of Managing Director. You can bring a bright young chap in as sales manager to take the routine work off his shoulders. Good salesmen are ten a penny. Good Managing Directors are not.'

'Meaning I'm not a good one,' Keith remarked wryly.

'Don't be silly, honey. Of course you are a good one. It is just a matter of stacking the cards your way. With you as Chairman and Clancy as Managing Director you would be an irresistible combination. You will have a lot of fights ahead of you and you will need someone you can trust to back you up. With Clancy away on sales trips half the time you would not be able to get the support you need.'

Keith, who knew how much he relied on Clancy, saw the force of the argument.

'Give me a little more time to think about it.'

Juliet knew that what he wanted was an opportunity to clear the idea with his father. There was no doubt in her mind that Sir Charles would be against it. She leaned forward and gave him a light kiss on the forehead.

'There is no time like the present,' she said gaily. 'Why not give Clancy a call now and break the good news.'

Keith hesitated briefly before reaching for the telephone. He was finding it increasingly hard to deny Juliet anything she had set her heart on.

* * *

It was a lucky break for Sandy Gaul that there happened to be a meeting of the District Executive Committee that night. As a convenor of shop stewards he was automatically a member. Since the management had refused consultation until the men went back to work the Executive Committee was now the proper place for him to raise the issue. When the general business had been concluded he rose to address the meeting.

Since his first meeting with Birdsall and Stock, Gaul's attitude to the problem had hardened. Any idea he may have had that the facts were not entirely as they had been presented to him had disappeared into the background. It had now resolved itself into a clear case of job security being threatened. He was conscious that, as Clancy-Smith had pointed out to his colleagues earlier in the day, there was a laid down procedure to be followed when an incident occurred and this had not been done. No serious effort had been made by Supervision to dispute Birdsall's version and he must go on the facts as they had been given to him. As the senior Union official at Greenbank his duty was clear. He had the interests of his workers to protect.

His statement to the Executive Committee was concise and to the point and the vote of the members was a foregone conclusion. All the District Secretary had to do was to put the feelings of the Committee into words.

'It is quite clear on the facts as they have been so ably presented by Brother Gaul that the action of the management in dismissing an employee without proper reason being given and in subsequently refusing consultation is a serious breach of the procedural agreement.

'It is therefore our view that, if the men give a free vote for the continuation of the strike at their meeting tomorrow morning their action will have the full support of this Committee. For my part I will do everything in my power to assist Brother Gaul and his Works Committee in their efforts to find a solution to this extremely disturbing situation.'

There was a murmur of approval round the room as the meeting adjourned.

*   *   *

The meeting of the men took place the following morning in the yard behind the works. It did not last very long. When Sandy Gaul called for a show of hands from those in support of the strike there were only a few who hesitated. Those who did were given a sharp nudge in the ribs by their neighbours until they also raised their hands.

The vote for the strike to continue was unanimous. There was a rush of volunteers to picket the main gate and as if by magic placards appeared bearing slogans like, 'We will not tolerate victimization', and 'We demand job security'. Groups of workers stood around heatedly discussing the situation. Flitting from group to group, his eyebrows bristling and his jaw stuck out, was the pugnacious figure of Barney Corcoran.

In the emotion-charged atmosphere there was nobody who had time to spare a thought for Billy Caird lying in a ward in the Western Infirmary.

II

At the main Camel works at Cumbernauld, ten miles outside Glasgow, there was also considerable unrest.

Only a month previously there had been a short-lived strike by the electricians for higher pay. It had misfired badly. The wages at Camel were higher than the national average and the electricians in their demand for an increase of ten pounds a week had met with little sympathy. Not only had public sympathy been against them but they had failed to gain the wholehearted support of their fellow workers.

'Bit of a bleedin' nerve if you ask me,' Jackie Shearer had said. 'What's so special about sodding electricians anyhow?' and it was the generally held view.

Just the same it had left an aftermath of general dissatisfaction. The hard liners had been quick to point out that the management had emerged victorious from the brief battle and it had set a precedent for the future. It is a long-held tradition of Trade Unionism that no strike should be abandoned without at least some concession being gained. In spite of the faint support for the strike there was a generally held opinion that the management had got away with something and an early opportunity should be found to square the score.

The news that Greenbank had come out accentuated the tension. The first of the new models had only come off the production line that week. Because of the various delays Bill Hamilton had authorized immediate production instead, as he would normally have done, of allowing time to build up a reserve stock of the transmissions.

Men working on a new model, however modest their contribution, feel a sense of pride. For a short time the routine tasks become more bearable with the knowledge that the end product is going to excite public interest. The air of secrecy which surrounds the operation creates excitement and induces a sense of importance. Now it became obvious that unless the problem at Greenbank could be solved quickly production would be halted. Almost worse than the feeling of frustration which this caused was the added fear that it would mean men being laid off. The feeling of insecurity which this generated was not laid at the door of their fellow workers but placed squarely on the shoulders of management in general who, by their refusal to put right a proper grievance, had brought the situation about. It was a climate in which tempers ran high.

While Sandy Gaul held meetings with his works committee to work out a plan of campaign which would end the deadlock, there were others whose aims were quite different.

Iggy Salvatori received reports of the mood of the men at Camel with evident satisfaction. Shortly after he had listened to first-hand reports of the strike meeting he had climbed into his limousine and been driven out to Cumbernauld, taking with him both Barney Corcoran and Joe Kidd.

'We must impress on our friends in the Camel works,' he told them in the car, 'that this is an opportunity which must not be missed. It must be made clear that Greenbank's cause is their cause. If men are laid off, they must demonstrate their solidarity with their fellow workers in their efforts to obtain justice.'

Joe expressed his doubts. 'It's not going to be all that bloody easy. We can't get into the works because we need cards to get past the security check. Camel is not like Greenbank. Most of the lads have their own cars and they drive straight out of the parking lot when the shift is over. What I want to know is how we get to talk to them.'

'I have my contacts,' said Iggy quietly but he was not too sure himself how he was going to go about matters. There were a few men at Camel he could rely on to stir up trouble but it was not the same as getting a mass audience.

In fact it turned out to be Iggy's lucky day. He had timed their arrival for the ending of the day shift and as they turned into the service road which ran past the main gates of the factory, he quickly realized that something was up. Half way down the road there was a car pulled into the side, surrounded by maybe a hundred men. As they stopped at a discreet distance more and more men were joining the crowd. In the centre standing on the bonnet of a car shouting to make himself heard, and punching

133

his fist into his hand as he made his points, was a figure whom Iggy instantly recognized.

'That's Jack Carter. We seem to have come at a very opportune time. Unless I am mistaken Camel are having troubles of their own.' He settled his great bulk comfortably back in the car. 'Just get up the road and find out what it is all about.' Iggy was not a man who liked to expose himself too much to the public gaze, particularly if there was any possibility of trouble.

Ten minutes later Corcoran reported back.

'Had a word with a lad I know in the crowd there. They've got a right row going. Seems they had a crowd of important visitors this morning. When they were going down the pressings line one of them steps on a patch of oil and lands flat on his arse.

'Well somebody had to carry the can for it and some little bloody Hitler from the admin. office picks on the old bloke what's supposed to keep the floor clean. Sacked him on the spot and him due to retire in a couple of months. Wasn't his fault even. Some lad spilled the oil by accident on purpose like just before the big bums were due to arrive. Your pal up there has just got them in the mood for a walk-out.' Barney Corcoran was grinning all over his face and doing a little dance of excitement.

'You can cut out the theatricals,' Iggy snapped. 'Just you get back there and get on top of that car.'

'What me on top of the car! The meeting is bugger-all to do with me.'

'It's everything to do with you, Comrade. You get up there and tell them that their mates at Greenbank are out for the same reason. Job security. Illegal sackings. Christ, do I have to spell it out to you? You get moving before the crowd starts breaking up.'

It was some minutes before Corcoran managed to work himself to the front and catch Jack Carter's eye. When he saw him signalling agitatedly Carter broke off in mid-sentence and bent down to catch what he was saying. A moment later Corcoran was standing up beside him.

'A friend from Greenbank,' he shouted. 'You'll all have heard they are out. I'll tell you why they are out. They are out for the very self-same reason as we are going to come out. We demand freedom from victimization by the management.'

134

There was a rumble of approval as Barney started to speak. Men who were beginning to edge away crowded closer. From somewhere at the back Joe Kidd shouted, 'Quiet lads. Let's be hearing from our brother.' There was complete silence as Barney got into his stride. It was not for nothing that he had once marshalled one of the most prolonged strikes known on Clydebank. Iggy picked his men carefully.

When Barney Corcoran addressed an audience the time-honoured catch phrases rolled off his tongue and took on a new vehemence. 'We must stand together. Brothers, unite now against tyranny or all is lost. Your duty is to your fellow workers. Don't let yourself be trampled underfoot.'

By the time he had finished they were with him to a man.

*   *   *

As Keith Puddefant walked into his office the following morning the telephone was already ringing. It was Roy Brisbane, the Managing Director of Camel (Scotland) Ltd.

'We have more problems,' he told him. 'Looks like far from having to lay off some of my chaps, we'll soon have no work force at all.'

Keith sighed. He had spent the previous evening with his father and the going had been rough. Sir Charles had left him with no doubt in his mind that he considered the strike to be the result of mishandling by the management. He had read Keith a lecture on the qualities of the average British working man.

'If they are kept happy they are not going to deprive themselves of their wages voluntarily. No man likes being out of work and their wives like it even less. I admit there are occasions when men come out for a seemingly trivial reason when the real reason is that they are simply bored with the deadliness of their jobs and any excuse will serve to introduce a little excitement in their lives. But this is not the case here. Good Heavens they have only been on the new contract for a matter of days and you have trouble.'

Keith had tried to argue that the incident had been provoked and that to give in now by reinstating Birdsall would only invite further trouble in the future.

'In that case,' said Sir Charles, 'the young lad who you say was attacked will presumably say the same thing. I suppose some-one has been to see him in hospital.'

Keith had to admit that such a simple way of establishing the facts had been completely overlooked. It was a glaring omission and Keith for the life of him could not understand how he had not thought of it.

'Ronnie Motion should have seen to it,' he mumbled without conviction.

'You're the Managing Director. It's your job to do people's thinking for them.'

He had omitted to tell his father of his sudden decision about Clancy-Smith on the grounds that it would be time enough when a favourable opportunity presented itself. Now it was forced on him. Sir Charles had been even more shocked about that than he had been over the strike.

'Why didn't you consult me? I handed the business over to you and not your friend Smith.'

'It does not affect the ownership of the business. It is purely a matter of spreading the administrative load. The new contract has made running the Company a much more complex business than it was in your day.'

'In my day,' said Sir Charles acidly, 'I did not form the opinion that my sales director had any noticeable aptitude outside his own job. Personally, I wouldn't trust him to run a whelk stall at the seaside.'

If Sir Charles had been a less controlled person than he was, the meeting would have ended in a blazing row. As it was, Keith had left Cumberland Towers in an atmosphere of frigid disap-proval. As he drove back to Glasgow he felt more alone than he had ever done before and fervently hoping against hope that he would find Juliet waiting at the flat for him. She wasn't.

Now dispirited and unsure of himself he felt ill-equipped to deal with the troubles of Roy Brisbane on top of his own.

'You mean your men are coming out on strike as well?' he asked. 'What's it all about?'

'Basically it is nothing we could not have dealt with in the normal course of events. A man was fired perhaps rather hastily. We'd have found a way of reinstating him and everything would have blown over. Unfortunately it has grown rather bigger than that. The shop stewards are taking the stand that your troubles and ours are linked together. They are having a meeting now and it looks as if they are going to call the men out in support of Greenbank. Already half the morning shifts have not signed on.'

'We are having a meeting this morning,' said Keith. 'Not that I think it is going to get us very far. It is my Board's view that we have got to stand firm on this issue. Maybe you would like to come along. At least we would be able to spell out what the issue is better than I can on the telephone.'

'I'll be there,' said Brisbane. 'But for Chrissake try and come up with something between then and now or the balloon will really go up.'

'I only hope we can.' Keith put down the receiver and called Ronnie Motion on the internal phone. There was just a chance that a visit to young Caird in hospital would pull something out of the bag.

Later that day, at the meeting with Brisbane, Motion reported the result of his visit. It was not very satisfactory. He had seen the doctor in charge of the case who had given it as his opinion that the extensive injuries Caird had suffered could not possibly have been caused by a simple fall.

'When a man faints,' the doctor told him, 'it is unusual to do himself any serious damage. His body is relaxed and he falls like a cat. In this case, however, the patient has suffered severe injuries to his ribs and his left arm has been fractured. There are also contusions about the head which looks as if they have been caused by a severe blow, possibly a boot. It looks to me like a typical case of someone who has been mugged.'

When Motion had been allowed in to see Caird, however, it was a different story—or rather no story at all.

'I got the impression that the boy is covering up,' he reported. 'He's either afraid or he is simply living by the code which says that you don't split on your mates. When I told him what the doctor had said he simply shrugged his shoulders. All he is worried about is getting his job back so that he can save money for his marriage. The odd thing about it is that the girl he plans to marry is the sister of one of the lads who claims he saw him fall against the radiator.'

'Surely if you produce a copy of the doctor's evidence to the Works Committee they are bound to take notice of it,' said Keith.

137

Motion was doubtful. 'I don't think they would listen. They are in a position where it is difficult for them to back down without loss of face. We cannot possibly reinstate Birdsall and they are not going to back down from their position without concessions of some sort. It would completely undermine their authority with the men. Besides it would make Jim Cantlie's situation quite impossible.'

'What about the Press?' Brisbane suggested. 'It looks as if Camel will come out this afternoon and that is going to have them all buzzing around. It would give us a platform to put our side of the question. It is my experience that, if you can take away public sympathy for a strike you are half way to breaking it.'

'Will the doctor stick his neck out?' asked Clancy-Smith. 'What he is prepared to say in private and what in public are two different things. What's more, if that young idiot Caird won't come clean we might be in a worse mess than ever. If the men think we are trying to pull a fast one they will be more solid than ever.'

'Besides which,' said Motion, 'it means we are accusing Birdsall and his mates of a criminal offence—assault. Unless we can prove our case beyond all doubt we are on dangerous ground. Remember they are all prepared to swear that black is white and there is no doubt that there is a lot of evidence to support their contention that Cantlie had it in for Birdsall.'

'Something's got to be done,' snapped Brisbane. 'We can't have an irresistible force meeting an immovable rock for ever. I'm already up against it in getting the new model to the dealers on time.'

'Maybe when the matter goes to the National Executive of the Union and our evidence is strong enough, we'll get a different picture. If they refuse to make the strike official we are well on our way.'

'Right, let's start getting our case set out,' said Brisbane. 'It's a pity you have waited this long.'

The meeting broke up in a mood of cautious optimism.

* * *

While the meeting was being held in the boardroom at Greenbank, Danny 'Cowboy' Martin was gunning his truck up the M.6 towards Glasgow. He had started off from Cardiff the day

138

before and stopped overnight to make a delivery in Manchester so that he felt fresh from a good night's sleep and eager to get back to Manchester where he had a girl. As he swung his heavy vehicle into the centre lane to pass the slower moving traffic he sang snatches of song. His favourites were sentimental ballads of the West like 'Ol' Faithful' and to complete his cowboy image he wore high-heeled boots and sported a broad-brimmed stetson.

Just before midday he crossed the Border and pulled into a transport café beyond Gretna for a bacon-and-egg sandwich and a cup of tea. While he waited for his mate, Taffy Jones, to collect the order he stretched his legs under the table and idly cast his eye over a newspaper discarded by a previous customer. Suddenly he sat upright. Taffy returned with the loaded tray to find him absorbed in the front page of the *Daily Express*.

'Blimey. Just listen to this, Taf. Our lot are out on strike. There's pickets and all round the gate.'

'Wotcher mean "our lot"?' asked Taffy, slow in the uptake.

'Greenbank where we are delivering those castings. Listen to this: "Would-be strike breakers were threatened yesterday by militant pickets when they tried to make their way through the main gates of the factory. Two men were slightly injured in an incident and taken to hospital but were later released."'

'Well, looks like we've had our chips,' said Taffy. 'Better turn round and go home.'

Cowboy looked at his mate scornfully. 'Not on yer nellie we don't go back. We'll soon sort this lot out. Any road it only says here that the main gates are picketed. Nothing about the unloading bays.'

Cowboy was by nature a loner. It would be wrong to say that he had a deep hatred of Unions but certainly he resented having to join any organization simply to enable him to get a job. He showed his resentment by always being behind in paying his Union dues and he was quick to take offence when pressure was brought on him to bring his subscription up to date.

He lived in a dream world where life was lived in the raw and a man was only as good as the speed of his gun. Taffy Jones was a few years older than Cowboy but he usually went along with his decisions. This time he just shrugged his shoulders and drained his mug of tea. Cowboy walked taller as he pushed his way through the door of the café and strode across the tarmac to climb

139

into his cab, He was back in the early days of Wells Fargo. A few bad men were not going to stop him getting his cargo through to Dodge City.

As they neared Glasgow he ran over in his mind what he would do if they tried to stop him getting into the factory. Just keep the big truck moving and they will soon get out of the way he thought. High up in his cabin he would have little to fear if anyone did try to start any trouble. Just to reassure himself he felt for the long jack handle which he had by the driver's seat. Once alongside the loading bay he would have done his job. He did not much mind if he got the castings off-loaded or not. It was just a question of pride. Nobody mucked around with Cowboy Martin.

As his truck passed along the front of the Greenbank buildings he could see the pickets by the works' entrance, standing around with their placards. The park usually packed with cars was almost empty. Only a few sightseers hung around the main gates waiting hopefully for something to happen. On an impulse Cowboy pressed the heel of his hand hard down on the horn and then leaned through the window, stabbing the air with a vigorous two-finger gesture. The picket, uncertain whether he was protesting or giving them the V for victory sign, turned to watch his progress down the road. Two hundred yards further on they were left in no doubt. Stamping hard on the air-brakes and with a squealing of tyres he turned sharply right through the open bottom gate which gave access to the delivery yard at the back of the building.

'Bloody fools,' he grinned at Taffy. 'I'll bet they have no one round the back.' But he was wrong. He had to slow as he made a final right turn into the factory yard and someone jumped from behind the pillars on to the step of the truck and hammered on the window.

'You going somewhere, brother?' he shouted. 'Don't you know this place is blacked? Get your truck to hell outta here.'

In his surprise Cowboy stalled the engine. As he pressed the starter other men appeared in front of the truck blocking his way.

'That's it then,' said Taffy. 'We can't get in now.'

'Like to bet,' Cowboy grinned. As the engine fired he engaged bottom gear and gave it full revs as he slowly eased up the clutch.

With the sudden roar most of the men jumped aside but one figure remained right in his path. It was Daniel Cooley. Slipping his clutch Cowboy inched forward but Cooley stood his ground. Arms spread and legs wide apart he started some sort of wild primitive West Indian war dance at the same time shouting his defiance.

'Come on big boy,' he yelled. 'You just go right ahead and run me over. I ain't caring. You just go right ahead.'

The truck was still five yards away from the gesticulating figure when it happened. Danny Martin swore afterwards in Court that he had meant to slip his foot off the accelerator on to the brake and that the man who was still clinging to the side of the cab distracted his attention. Instead he let the clutch up with a bang and the truck took a sudden bound forward. Cooley saw it coming and took a desperate dive sideways but he was not quite quick enough. The nearside wing caught him and he gave a dreadful cry as the heavy duty tyre crushed his rib cage like an eggshell.

They did not take him to hospital. They took him straight to the mortuary.

As he died a martyr was born. Any hope the management may have had of an early settlement of the strike was sunk without a trace.

12

Since the winter of 1976, which had been long and cold, the feeling of discontent which prevailed in the country had been made no better by continued threats of strikes by the coal miners who had long since abandoned any pretence of honouring the Social Contract of which Harold Wilson had spoken with such pride at the hustings of the autumn of 1974.

In the following January and February of 1977 there had been trouble at the power stations. There had been power cuts and while the nation shivered and old age pensioners unable to compete in the black market for fuel had died of cold, the dockers had come out on a handling dispute.

Italy, suffering from the effects of a poor harvest in the south and a decline of productivity in the industrial north, had staged a general strike which had overthrown the Government and brought in a new administration which gave the balance of power to an even more extreme faction of the Left wing. All over Europe the effects of inflation were being felt. Of all the EEC countries only Germany seemed to manage to continue to maintain some semblance of a stable economy in spite of a violent upswing in the cost of living.

Certainly to the British public their own crisis seemed to be worst of all. Whilst those on fixed incomes had found it harder and harder to maintain their standard of living the more militant of the Unions had kept up a constant pressure for higher wages for their members whilst productivity remained at a standstill. It was a case of each Union for itself as they vied with one another on the size of the concessions they could wring from a Government clinging desperately to power.

Nationalization of industries considered vital to the national economy had not proved to be the success which had been hoped. Each new take-over was greeted with cries of anguish from the Right wing whilst the workers of the newly-nationalized industries seemed unimpressed by the thousands of millions of pounds being spent to beat the bogey of unemployment.

The very rich writhed under the wealth tax, selling their heirlooms to keep their heads above water or letting their grouse moors and their salmon fishing to the rich industrialists from Germany and Switzerland who poured across the Channel in an unending stream, taking advantage of one of the last attractions a bankrupt nation had to offer. Even the Americans, the traditional sugar-daddies of Europe, preoccupied with their own problems and concerned about their dwindling domestic economy, were no longer so keen to compete in the luxury market. Only a few predators stalked the country looking for any financial plums to be picked up in the bargain basement.

Richard Katz III was one of them.

The hard-liners on the Left wing were not however having it entirely their own way. Where the sabre-rattling extremists of the Right wing had been freely described as fascists by their political opponents the description had begun to backfire. The meaningless term was now being used to describe the activities of the Trade Union leaders who dictated their terms to the Government with less and less reference to the views of their more moderate members. There had been disquieting evidence at each successive Trade Union Congress that a large body of non-militants were becoming disenchanted with the policy of self-interest which appeared to activate their leaders. Motions calling for a policy of wage restraint were appearing with disconcerting frequency on the agenda and even such outmoded terms as patriotism were being bandied about.

By the summer it had become apparent to all but a handful of dedicated men in the Government that their policy of giving the militants their heads was becoming less and less acceptable to the electorate. Political feeling between the Right and Left was running at a dangerously high level. There was a pent-up emotionalism in the country which only needed the right match to set it alight and the extremist left wing were determined that it was their match which was to be the right one. They had set themselves on a course which could only end in the complete overthrow of capitalism or their own self-destruction.

*   *   *

143

The furore caused by the slaying at Greenbank was immediate and far reaching.

The news reached Camel just as a mass meeting was being held by the shop stewards in the main canteen. When it was announced there was a spontaneous outburst of horror and indignation. If there had been any doubt as to the outcome of the meeting it was now a forgone conclusion. The strike was solid.

In Detroit Richard Katz was informed of the strike just as he was settling in to a meeting on production schedules. His reaction was characteristic. As soon as he had replaced the receiver he flicked the office intercom through to Miss Curtis.

'Call the house and have them send down an overnight bag,' he instructed. 'Call Hank Schum and alert him that we are leaving for Prestwick on the afternoon plane. Call Brisbane and have him book Schum in some place. I have my own arrangements.'

At almost the same time James Christie received two telephone calls. The first was from the Area Secretary of the Union informing him in his capacity as the member of the Union Executive responsible for the Scotland Area of the latest developments. The second was from a Mr Mann.

'I think this may be the big one, James,' said Mr Mann. 'There is all hell to pay at Greenbank and the lads at Camel feel almost as strongly. My boys are ready to press the red button.'

'I'll be on the evening plane,' said James Christie.

Mr Mann was the name used by Ignatius Salvatori when he wanted to preserve his anonymity from prying ears.

*   *   *

Dick Katz always had a reason for what he did but the reason was not always obvious to those who worked for him. It puzzled Roy Brisbane, for instance, that he had been given instructions not to meet him at the airport. Instead a hired car was to be sent. It did not surprise him however that Schum was coming over as well. Hank Schum was both Dick Katz's trouble-shooter and hatchet man. He was the most feared of the close ring of advisers who surrounded the person of the Executive Vice-President. His presence meant trouble for someone.

Now the two men sat in the back of the hired Daimler as they were driven the twenty-five miles into Glasgow and pored over the morning newspapers which they had collected at the airport news-stand. Without exception the death of Daniel Cooley was the headline story. 'Slaughter in the Sun' the *Daily Record* called it. 'Death Drama at Factory Gates' proclaimed the *Daily Express*. It was an otherwise dull day for news and they were making the most of it. *The Times* carried a long feature speculating on whether the incident might not set off a train of industrial action. 'The Left Wing are in the mood for a showdown. This may well prove to be the spark which will set off the keg of dynamite.'

'It's going to be a tough cookie,' Schum observed. 'Any idea which way you want it played?'

For a time Dick Katz continued to stare out of the window as the countryside started to give way to the sprawling outskirts of the city.

'You know what's wrong with this goddam country, Hank?' he asked suddenly. 'Well I'm gonna tell you. Those houses there. That's what wrong.' He stabbed his finger in the direction of a new estate of council houses.

'Yeah?' said Schum encouragingly. He was used to his chief's flights of fancy.

'What happens is the Labour-controlled councils rent those houses out for peanuts. Subsidized rents. Now a guy living in one of those houses comes out on strike so he's getting no money and can't pay his rent so what do the authorities do?'

'Well I guess they sling him out,' Schum ventured.

'That's just what they don't do. They remit his rent until he is good and ready to pay it again. A guy is involved in an action which is against the interests of the country and the country helps him do it.' He shook his head in wonder.

'Now if a guy was buying his house and not renting it where would he be? He'd be out on a limb. No payments and the mortgage company snatch back the house. Make him think twice about coming out.'

'You aiming to sit this strike out until the men starve?' Schum grinned.

'The damn pity of it is you can't starve in the British Welfare State. First thing the men do is get a rebate on their income tax. Then their wives get National Assistance and as likely as not the men get other jobs which they say nothing about and put the money in their pockets.'

The reason Dick Katz won most of his battles was because he took the trouble to know his enemy.

The car dropped Schum at the Central Hotel.

'You just take up your reservation and wait until I call you,' Katz told him.

'You mean you don't want me to contact Roy or anyone?'

'Not Roy nor anyone. This isn't going to be solved in a day. I've got things I want to do before we start talking.'

He waited until Schum had turned to follow the hall porter up the steps with his grip before he leant forward to give the driver his instructions.

'Does your firm do self drives?'

'Certainly sir.'

'Well drive me to your depôt. I'll be needing one of your cars.'

Half an hour later, at the wheel of a Ford Escort, he was heading out of town. He took the road out past Cumbernauld, driving carefully while he got accustomed to keeping to the left-hand lane. He passed the slip road which led to the Camel works but kept right on, taking the new Stirling by-pass and then, doubling back on his tracks, took the road to the village of Bridge of Allan.

The Old Manor House is one of those delightful hotels which one comes across from time to time in Britain which still manages to retain some of the quiet dignity of the days when it was a private home.

Katz went straight to his room. When he entered Juliet Ochil was sitting at the dressing table making some final adjustments to her make-up. She rose and ran quickly across the room to press herself into his arms.

'Darling,' she said, 'it seems to have been such a long time.'

Dick pushed her away gently. 'Honey, before I get back off this trip I'm going to screw you stupid. Meantime we've got some talking to do. What gives with young lover boy?'

Juliet wrinkled her nose. 'Jealous?'

'Not a bit. Just interested.'

'Well, if you're asking me, at this moment he is a very worried guy indeed. What he wants is the quiet life. I got him all keened up to buy this yacht and he's looking round for a house where he can live the gracious life. He's got that creep Clancy-Smith to do the work for him. Then this strike blows up and all the balls are in the air again. A couple of nights ago he had a set-to with the old man and there is no love being lost in that direction. I reckon if you were to talk to him nicely now, he would listen.'

Dick Katz nodded. 'You reckon the family share deal is all sewn up?'

'Of course it is, honey. I've already told you that.'

'Quick work. How much did you have to work on the old boy?'

'Not too much,' said Juliet truthfully. 'Everything seemed to fall together at the right moment. He had the whole thing fixed in a couple of days. I guess he had had it on his mind for some time.'

'I've got Schum over here but I want to get alongside young Keith first before I decide which way to move.'

'Listen, Dick,' said Juliet, 'this strike is serious. When that black got pinned under the truck the thing really took off. On the radio this morning they were saying that Ford and Chrysler may be coming out in sympathy.'

'All the more reason for getting alongside Puddefant fast— what a goddam name that is. If I were him I'd change it.' He leant forward and kissed Juliet on the lips. 'Come on baby. Get on that telephone. The sooner we can get all this fixed, the sooner we can get down to the real business.' He let his hand run briefly over her body.

Juliet got Keith at the office.

'Darling, I've got a friend of ours here.'

'Who's that?'

'None other than Richard Katz III.'

'Like hell you have,' Keith was startled. 'I've already had Roy Brisbane on the phone twice trying to locate him. He's climbing up the wall.'

'Listen, Keith. Dick has something important to say to you. If Roy calls again stall him. Don't let on that you are going to meet.'

'Dick wants to see me? I'd have thought he had more than enough on his hands with Camel.'

'Just do as I say. This is going to be important for you. Trust me, darling, and listen carefully.'

They arranged to meet for a late lunch at the Golden Lion in Stirling. If Keith wondered briefly how Juliet and Dick had got together he quickly put it out of his mind. At least he would be able to discuss with her afterwards whatever it was that Katz

147

had got to say. It gave him a warm feeling to have someone on his side like Juliet Ochil.

They had hardly got through the first course before Katz got down to business.

'Frankly this seems to be one hell of a mess,' he said. 'If we had even three months of production when this happened it might not have been so bad. As it is we have not even got off the ground. My company has already spent a million dollars on promotion, building up to your Motor Show in October and it looks like we are going to have no automobiles. We are committed on our advertising schedule and dealer promotion to another million. We just can't afford the situation.'

Keith toyed nervously with his fork, digging the prongs aimlessly into the table cloth. Katz made him feel very low-powered. The same way he used to feel with his father. In relation to Katz however there was only ten years between them in age which merely served to aggravate his tension.

'We didn't bring the strike about,' he said petulantly. 'Nor are we the only people in the country to be hit by the hard-liners.'

'I guess it was your father said to me some time back that you'd never had a strike in two hundred years. You've picked a fine time to break the record.'

'We've never been this closely involved with a big outfit like Camel before. All the trouble started on the new production lines.'

'You are beginning to get my point,' said Katz quickly. 'Do you reckon your management are equipped to handle this kind of situation?'

Keith swallowed hard, trying to keep his temper. 'Juliet said you wanted to tell me something, not read a lecture. If all you want to do is pick on someone why don't you start over at Camel. They've got eight thousand out. We've only got a thousand.'

Katz smiled his warm smile and put his hand on Keith's arm. 'Sorry,' he said. 'Mebbe I was riding you a bit hard. I'm over here to help. We've had a lot of experience in this field. I've got a feeling that if we can break your problem at Greenbank we can wrap this whole thing up.'

'Any suggestions?' Keith meant to sound sarcastic but it did not quite come off.

'I have this executive of mine, Hank Schum, over here. He's just about the number one trouble-shooter in the automobile industry. I'd like you to let him have a look at the problem.'

Keith looked at Juliet who gave an imperceptible nod.

'I have no objection,' he said. 'Any new ideas would be very welcome.'

It was not until the end of the meal that Katz approached the main object of the clandestine luncheon. The wine waiter had excelled himself by producing a bottle of Hine's 1914 cognac and under its mellowing influence much of Keith's tension had left him.

'Listen, pal,' said Katz, leaning forward with his elbows on the table. 'Whether you like it or not you are in at the deep end of the automobile industry. You can't withdraw without heavy penalty clauses becoming operative and we can't pull out without losing a hell of a lot of money and a hell of a lot of time. Right now we are both on the operating table but Camel are bigger and stronger than you are. We are the more likely to survive major surgery. Now, of course I don't know anything about your share structure except that you are a family business ...'

Juliet held up her hand to interrupt.

'Keith, I think it might be a good idea if you let Dick in on the picture. If he is going to try and help I think you owe him your confidence.'

Keith nodded. 'When my father retired he handed the majority of the stock in the Company over to me. I now out-vote all the rest of the family four to one.'

Dick Katz would have made a fine actor. No one could have detected that his air of surprise was other than completely genuine.

'Well I'll be doggone! That makes what I've got to say a whole lot easier. I'm certainly talking to the right guy.'

Keith felt that his whole status had been raised in Dick's eyes and felt absurdly pleased.

'What I was about to say was that as we are both so heavily committed to one another, it may be that you feel that it would be a good time for you to look at the big picture. Our stock shows a fine investment rate and a long record of growth. You are a family business and you can't get out from under if things start going wrong like they are now. If you want ready capital for anything you can only sell privately to a willing buyer. Now say we were to swop some of our stock. You'd have a stake in a big international corporation and you'd be strengthening your ties with your biggest customer. It would seem to make a hell of a lot of sense from your point of view.'

Keith's first reaction was to say that his father would never agree but he stopped himself in time. As Juliet had so often pointed out to him, it was nothing to do with his father now. It was up to him to make the decisions. He looked across at her but she seemed to be preoccupied in fitting a cigarette into her holder.

'What would your Company get out of it?' Keith asked, playing for time.

'Well I guess it is just a matter of policy. We like to have a stake in anyone who works for us. Maybe have one of our guys on your Board of Directors to look after our interests. Then we like to look at the future. When we get over our present difficulties I'd like to think that Greenbank can take over a hell of a lot more of our outside contracting. This way we can supply some of our expertise over new projects with which we are familiar and maybe your boys don't measure up to yet. Again from your point of view you would have a call on our financial resources so that we can expand Greenbank together.'

Keith swirled the last of his brandy round the bottom of the glass and watched appreciatively the liquid clinging to the sides like a fine malt whisky.

'I'd certainly like to think about it.'

'Why don't you let Clancy-Smith in on your thinking? Juliet tells me that you have gotten him as your Managing Director. From what I've seen of him I'd say that was a smart move.'

Again Keith felt a flush of pleasure.

'I'll have a talk with him this afternoon.'

'That's fine. We won't hang around when we get the go-ahead. No reason why we should not reach agreement on this trip. The formalities can be tied up later. If we can talk eyeball to eyeball it's one hell of a lot quicker and better than trying to communicate across the Pond.'

The conversation ended on a much warmer note than it had begun. As Keith drove back into Glasgow he felt a little heady at the prospects which had opened up before him.

*　　　*　　　*

150

While Keith was seeing visions and dreaming dreams a meeting of a more practical nature was taking place in the office behind the shop in Dunbarton Road.

James Christie, who had flown up the previous afternoon, had already had a series of meetings with area Union Officials. Now he was one of a triumvirate with Iggy Salvatori to discuss the position. The third man present had also flown up from London. In contrast to Iggy he was lean and tall with an unruly shock of black hair and restless eyes. When he walked it was with a light, bouncing step which earned him the nickname amongst his associates of Spring Heel Jack. Nobody called him that to his face. The name on his passport was Shamus O'Donovan and his frequent trips to various capitals in the Western World did not go unnoticed by those whose job it was to look after the security of the State. The C.I.A. and D.I.6 both had bulky files on O'Donovan but neither of them had anything sufficiently concrete to justify restricting his movements.

O'Donovan was also Iggy's boss and it was he who was now doing the talking.

'Let us not forget one thing, Comrades,' he was saying, 'this strike has been brought about for the best of possible reasons—job security. I have no great faith in strikes which are purely about wage claims. They are necessary, of course, but apart from exceptional cases they are difficult to sustain because they generally lack public support. Job security is quite a different matter. It concerns every worker in the country and it is easy for them to identify with their comrades. I know you are both aware of this but I mention it now because I am anxious that it should not be lost sight of in the very understandable emotionalism caused by the murder of Daniel Cooley.'

'That's the way I'm playing it,' Salvatori nodded. 'From the first reports I have had the situation looks good. It is only going to need a slight push to bring out the whole industry. After the Cooley incident I think we have a lot of public sympathy.'

James Christie was leaning back in his chair, gazing at the ceiling almost as if he was not listening. Now he sat up straight, his hands gripping the chair arms so that his knuckles showed white.

'This one has got to succeed,' he said tensely. 'The cause is right and the climate is right. I think I can talk for most of the

151

Unions when I say that we are bloody well fed up with the Government policy. We and the Italians are the poor men of Europe. Everyone else is growing fat at our expense. All this talk of controlled expansion is a load of balls as far as my members are concerned. They want more money and they want it now. If they get that, job security can take care of itself. The Government are scared because they know that we can kick them out whenever we want to. So far as I am concerned that is right now. We need industrial action in every factory in the land ...'

O'Donovan held up his hand, stopping the flow of rhetoric.

'We are not here to make political speeches to one another, comrade.' He spoke with hostility. 'Pardon me. I forget. Of course you are not one of our comrades. You are one of the ones who opted out of the Party.' His lips twisted sarcastically.

'Brother Christie has given us good service.' Iggy spoke quickly, anxious to avoid a rift between the two men.

'Don't be funny with me, pal.' Christie turned to O'Donovan. 'I do as much for the cause as you do. In fact I do a damned sight more. If my Union shows spine over this strike it will be because I put it into them. I'm in there in the front line—not floating round the edges.'

For a moment O'Donovan glared at Christie. Then he shrugged his shoulders. 'I'm not here to pick a quarrel.'

Christie was not so easily appeased.

'I hope you are aware,' he said acidly, 'that I am doing you a favour being here at all. I only agreed to this meeting because I feel the time has come for us all to pull together. If it were known at headquarters that I was having meetings with revolutionary groups my position on the Union Executive would be entirely destroyed.'

O'Donovan nodded curtly. 'Very well. Let's get on with our business. We agree the mood of the workers is favourable to our cause. It is not going to take much to bring out the whole of the automobile industry. If we can spread it to the miners and the transport workers we are well on our way. It will create a national emergency. Once that happens the gloves are off and our task of bringing down the capitalists will be made easy. They will hang themselves.'

'What is going to be the attitude of the T.U.C.?' Iggy asked cautiously. 'They seem to me to have been peddling a soft line with the Government recently.'

Christie snorted impatiently. 'To hell with the T.U.C. The Unions *are* the T.U.C. We have hard men in all the Unions and they will back a General Strike if only to demonstrate their power. Don't you worry about the attitude of the Unions. They've had enough of Social Contracts. What I want to know is how much support we can expect from the International Communist Party and all their brethren. There's too much quarrelling amongst themselves for my liking. The day we get the Trotskyites and the Marxists pulling together I'll feel a lot happier.'

O'Donovan ignored the jibe. 'Italy is already on the verge of a second General Strike. Bring out the dockers and you have the Dutch with you. I'm not sure about the Yanks. The Unions are getting stronger over there but they are not strong enough. It will take something more to tip the scales. It is to our advantage that the automobile industry is one of the vulnerable points. It will help too that Daniel Cooley was a black. His killing made headline news in Detroit.'

Iggy Salvatori pulled his shawl more tightly round his shoulders. 'Richard Katz is over here with his side-kick Hank Schum. It's my guess they are going to make a grab for Greenbank. If they do I think I know how we are going to play it.' Katz was not the only one who prided himself in knowing his enemies.

As Glasgow's traffic ebbed and died and the lights blinked out in the housing estates which ringed the city the three men talked on and on.

*   *   *

Keith lost no time in getting hold of Clancy-Smith to tell him of the discussion he had had with Richard Katz. The more he thought about it the more it appealed to him. His capital would certainly be safe in a big corporation like Camel. What was more important was that if he wanted ready cash it would be immediately available to him. At the same time it would not prejudice his standing at Greenbank. The move might even enhance it. With a sizeable slice of stock in Camel he might get put on their Board and Greenbank itself would benefit. Richard Katz had more or less promised further contracts. It might come as a bit of a shock to his father at first but he would eventually have to admit it was a shrewd move.

If Keith had had any doubts about the decision, his talk with Clancy-Smith would have dispelled them.

'Chance of a lifetime, old boy,' Clancy assured him. 'I wish to hell I was in your shoes. Play your cards right now and you will be a big wheel in Camel before you know it. Just don't forget your old friends, that's all.' He grinned giving Keith a playful punch in the ribs.

Clancy's support for the idea was so warm that Keith, who had been steeling himself for a discussion with his father, decided with relief that it would not be necessary. His father would only put difficulties in the way of something he had already decided upon. He would take that hurdle when he came to it. Meantime he felt for perhaps the first time in his life that he was captain of his ship and master of his fate. He picked up the telephone receiver and rang Dick Katz to tell him of his decision.

13

Katz had shown no particular emotion when Keith had told him that he was prepared to enter into a deal.

'I guess you've come to the right decision,' he said. 'I'd want to get this settled in principle straight away. We have this goddam strike on our hands and the sooner we can take a hand in the negotiations the better. I'll have Hank Schum round at your place at ten tomorrow morning. He has full powers to action everything on my behalf. You sign a provisional agreement with him and we'll have the attorneys fix up the legal aspect afterwards. If you want me you can reach me at the Camel plant.'

When he rang off Keith felt slightly shaken. He wasn't used to things moving so fast. Once again he thought of ringing his father but as soon as the idea occurred he put it out of his mind. Things had gone too far for that. On an impulse he called Juliet. The butler answered the telephone. Lady Ochil was away and not expected home that night. No, the butler had no idea where she could be contacted. He felt too tensed up and restless to drive back to his flat. Instead he walked round to the Cavern. A few stiff whiskies would take his mind off things. He expected he would find Clancy in his usual seat in the corner but he was not there. Instead the bar was crowded with representatives from a sales convention, each with a label announcing their names pinned on the lapels of their jackets. They were loud and jovial and totally involved in one another's company. A couple of large Johnnie Walkers only served to increase his feeling of loneliness and depression.

Then he remembered Susie Blake. She was a girl he used to knock around with before Juliet had started to dominate his life. At least she would be somebody to talk with. She had just finished washing her hair when he called her but she could meet him in a couple of hours. That would give him time for a few more Johnnie Walkers.

By the time they met in the bar at the Central Hotel, Keith was feeling fine. Susie wanted to eat but he had long passed the stage when food was of any interest to him. Instead he took her up to Smokey Joe's, one of the few places in the City where you could drink illegally late. He got her a sandwich while he drank some more and let the words pour out of him in a torrent.

'If that bunch of Commie bastards think they are going to put a spanner in the works they are making one hell of a big mistake. I've taken a decision today which is really going to put the skids under them. I've got them by the short and curlies.' He looked furtively round the room and dropped his voice conspiratorially. 'I can't say too much now but I'm moving into the real big time. You mark my words darling. Now the old man is out of the business things are really going to happen. The trouble with big business in this country is that the men at the top are too damned weak. The workers are getting away with murder. They've got to learn who is the boss and I aim to show them.' As the level of the whisky bottle sank lower his flights of fancy grew wilder and wilder until he stood on a pinnacle of impregnable greatness.

It was after three in the morning before Susie was able to get him back to his flat. She managed to get his shoes off and loosen his tie before he collapsed unconscious on the bed.

He was awakened the following morning at nine o'clock by the insistent ringing of the telephone. It was Susie.

'What the hell do you want at this time in the morning?' he grumbled, his words slurred as he struggled out of a deep sleep.

'I thought I'd better ring you. You said something last night about your important appointment this morning. I wouldn't like you to miss it.'

He rolled off the bed in his crumpled suit, feeling like hell. As he remembered his meeting with Schum in an hour's time he felt his stomach muscles tense up and he struggled for air as he was seized with a fit of the dry heaves. With an effort he made the bathroom, took off his clothes and sponged himself all over with cold water. The Alka Seltzer bottle was empty so he swallowed a couple of Paracetamol tablets to try and clear his head, turned on the electric kettle to make some coffee and started to dress again carefully in fresh clothes. Then he remembered he had left his car at the office and called a cab.

He arrived just before ten. Five minutes later, punctual to the dot, Miss Thornton announced the arrival of Hank Schum.

It was obvious at once that unlike Keith, Schum had had a good night's sleep. He positively exuded well-being and as they shook hands Keith caught the pungent smell of his after-shave lotion.

Schum was all-American. Close-cropped hair, even white teeth and the hearty handshake of an enthusiastic Scoutmaster.

'Glad to know you, Keith,' he said dumping a heavy briefcase on the desk. 'You and I have got a lot of ground to cover. What do you say we cut the formalities and get down to business.'

Keith nodded.

'First thing on the agenda is this stock transfer you and Dick agreed on. It seems to me you pulled one hell of a smart deal there. I guess Dick did not talk figures to you because that's my business. With a private company like yours it is a question of having the accountancy boys assess the value of your shareholding related to the capital value of your company. That's not something which can be done overnight. All I can say is that we are not a lot of penny-pinching bastards. We'll get an independent firm of accountants to assess the real worth of your shares and we'll both stick with what they say. How does that grab you?'

'Seems fair enough to me,' said Keith, fighting back the nausea.

'Point one agreed. Now let us say they figure your ordinary shares are worth two thousand pounds each. Could be more, could be less. You've got a fine business going there so whatever the figure it is going to come to a lot of dough but we'll match you pound for pound. You can take it as you like—cash or stock in the corporation. On top of that we give you a service contract. If we break the service contract you'd be right in line for another pay off. Those are details we can work on later.'

Keith tried to do some mental arithmetic multiplying the number of shares he held by two thousand pounds and came to the conclusion that Schum was right. It was a hell of a lot of money.

'How long do I have to think this over.'

Schum's face took on a look of utter incredulity.

'You want time to think over a deal like this? Why this is making you a real live British millionaire with immediate access to your capital. The way things are going over here I'd want to be as liquid as hell with maybe a stack of money in some Swiss bank. Do you think if your Government decides to take over your business they are going to give you the terms we're giving you? We're taking the risks, you are getting real dough and you want time to think about it!'

Schum reached for his briefcase, extracted a red-ribboned document and shoved it across the desk.

'I had our attorney here draw this up yesterday afternoon. It falls down only if we fail to keep our side of the bargain. You are protected all the way along the line. We are going to need two witnesses. I'll go get my driver while you read it over. He'll do for one. Maybe you'll get one of your staff in.'

When he had left the room, Keith tried to read the legally worded agreement with as much concentration as he could muster. In essence it was an undertaking that he would sell 3,500 ordinary voting shares in Greenbank to a company called the Richard Katz Investment Trust. That left him with a personal holding in Greenbank of 500 shares—the same as his mother and father; it still left the family with a respectable holding. That cheered him up quite a bit. The aching behind his eyes was beginning to disappear. Some of the optimism he had felt the night before started to ebb back. He pressed the intercom buzzer and when Clancy came on the line said, 'Where the hell were you all last night? I was looking for you. Get your ass along here as our American friends would say. We've got business to do.'

*   *   *

Richard Willerby, anchor man in Scotland for the peak hour B.B.C. programme 'Everybody's World', was in many ways the ideal man in a very demanding job. Ever since his early days, twenty years before, as a cub reporter on the *Scottish Daily Express*, the machinations of big business had fascinated him. For a time he had been industrial correspondent on the *Glasgow Echo* and in his spare time had been the author of articles on such diverse subjects as 'The Future of Trade Unionism' and 'The Economic Structure of Modern Society'. Over the years he had earned the respect of all the leading figures on the Scottish industrial scene who admitted him to their confidence. On the other side of the political fence even the more militant Communist leaders had been heard to give it as their opinion that he was a fair man.

If Willerby had a blind spot it was his dislike of internationalism in business. In spite of his English-sounding name he was a chauvinistic Scot. He believed fervently in Scotland for the Scots and frequent hard-hitting articles advocated the investment of Scottish capital in Scottish industry. When the investment of English capital brought employment to Scotland's depressed areas he could be tolerant but the great multi-national corporations were anathema to him. Scottish workers, he claimed, were the finest in the world and they deserved to reap the full benefit of their own industry.

When Greenbank had secured the Camel contract he had been the first to cheer. It was an example of Scottish enterprise winning money from the Americans who, with their heavy investment in Scottish North Sea Oil, had earned for themselves a special place in his gallery of villains.

Willerby was also a man who liked to do his own leg work. While writers of similarly high reputation had others to do their research for them, Willerby worked largely on his own.

Ever since the return of the Labour Party in the October election of 1974 he had found another hobby horse to ride. He had been becoming increasingly concerned with the growing influence of the Left wing of the Party and the dominance of the larger unions over a wide area of policy making. Basically his personal politics were if anything to the left of centre but he had no time for what he considered to be the destructive policies of the hard-liners. The continual flouting of policies agreed between the T.U.C. and the Government in the selfish interest of individual Unions he considered to be body blows against the controlled growth of the national economy as a whole and of Scottish prosperity in particular.

The strike at Greenbank coming so soon after they had been awarded the Camel contract filled him with dismay. He had not been impressed with the bare details of the cause of the strike which had appeared in the national Press. Typically he had immediately set about conducting his own investigations.

He had not found the going easy. If Sir Charles had still been in control at Greenbank he would have had little difficulty in seeing him. They had been friends for many years. As it was, Sir Charles had politely referred him to Keith and Keith had come up with the time-honoured phrase 'no comment'. After that he had begun at the bottom and worked his way up. Birdsall's name had been in the papers as the central figure round whom the whole dispute revolved and Willerby tracked him down to his daily haunt of the bar at the Dreadnought. There was no difficulty whatsoever in getting Harry Birdsall to talk.

In his own estimation Harry had grown immensely in importance since the strike had been declared. Nor was it only in his own eyes. His name had been in the national news and there were any number of complete strangers who liked to boast to their friends that they had met him. There had been a suggestion at the time that he might appear on television but unknown to each other that they had come to the same decision, Sandy Gaul and Iggy Salvatori had squashed the idea.

Harry was also having it good in another way. Where others far less involved in the prime cause of the strike claimed their income tax rebates, Harry suffered no shortage of money. He had received formal notice of his dismissal and his insurance card through the post on the morning following his dismissal—Jim Cantlie had seen to that—so he was able to draw his unemployment money each week. Added to that Barney Corcoran saw to it that he was never short of the ready to buy a pint for whoever cared to listen to the story of how he had been treated by a ruthless management.

When Harry heard that Willerby was from the B.B.C. he excelled himself in retelling his own version of how he had been the victim of a vindictive management.

'Can you tell me what political party you belong to, Mr Birdsall?' Willerby had asked when there had been a break in the flood of words.

'Political party?' said Harry. 'I don't belong to no party. I'm just a working man wanting to do a fair day's work for a fair day's pay if only the bastards would let me.'

'But you are a shop steward.'

'What the hell has that got to do wi' politics? I'm a good Union man. I try to do the best I can for my mates. You've got to fight for your rights. If those fascist bastards at Greenbank had their way there wouldn't be no Unions.'

It was a convincing performance. Harry was learning fast but Willerby was too old a hand to swallow the whole worm. He went to see the Secretary of the local Union Branch but that did not get him much further either.

160

'The situation is causing us a great deal of concern,' he had told Willerby guardedly. 'We have of course followed all the usual procedures in matters of this sort but I cannot say that we are getting the sort of co-operation we would like from the Management. They are refusing to meet the Works Committee until the men go back to work. Under the circumstances it is not a condition we are prepared to accept.'

'How solid are the men behind the Union decision?'

'At the last meeting of the workers the vote to continue the strike was unanimous.'

'By a show of hands?'

'Of course. That is our usual democratic process.'

'What about putting it to a secret ballot?' The question was an old hardy annual and the Secretary treated it as he felt it deserved.

'Our members are not children. If they really believe in a cause they should be prepared to stand up and be counted.'

It was the day after Keith's decisive meeting with Hank Schum that Willerby finally got an interview with Ronald Motion. In the beginning Motion had been most unwilling.

'Really, Mr Willerby,' he protested, 'I have nothing to add to what has already appeared in the daily Press.'

'Why are the Greenbank management playing this so close to their chest? I have already spoken to Birdsall and the Union Secretary and they were both much more communicative. Have you something to hide?'

In the end Motion had agreed to a meeting in his office. He did it with some misgiving. All day long there had been rumours and counter rumours but whenever he had tried to see Clancy-Smith or Keith himself he had been met with a rebuff.

'Just play it with a straight bat, old boy,' Clancy had told him when he had finally managed to run him to earth. 'There are big things going on. We'll be calling a meeting to put you in the picture any time now.'

'On the face of it,' said Willerby when he had settled himself comfortably in a chair in Motion's office, 'this appears to be a straightforward case of lack of communications. Birdsall seems to have some grounds for believing that he is being victimized. The Union officials concerned with the case have backed him up. Contrary to what some diehards seem to think they are neither fools nor knaves. They are not going to give their support to a

161

cause where a man is in the wrong. I agree that there was already trouble brewing in the Camel works before your men came out on strike. They had a similar case of an unjustified sacking but the management are quite ready to climb down on that. They are staying out until you are prepared to do the same in the case of Birdsall.'

Motion shifted in his seat uncomfortably. 'I wish the matter were as simple as that,' he said, desperately wondering how far he could go. Willerby was not a man to fool around with but he himself was being kept in the dark as regards Company policy. 'Can I speak unofficially?'

'No. You are the member of the Board responsible for Industrial relations. So far as I am concerned everything you say is very much on the record.'

Motion swallowed hard and decided to be quite honest.

'It is perfectly true that there has been a history of friction between our Works Manager, Cantlie, and Birdsall. There may have been hastiness on Cantlie's part but there is no doubt that Birdsall is a troublemaker. He also has a lot of influence with a certain section of the workers.'

'That's no reason for firing the man.'

'Agreed but Birdsall finally overstepped the mark. There was some sort of a personal vendetta between Birdsall and one of the young operatives. He had the boy sent to Coventry. I am not going to go into all the details now but matters came to a head and Birdsall and some of his mates beat the lad up. He's still in hospital. Cantlie happened to see the incident and fired Birdsall on the spot.'

'There must be something more to it. The Union would never condone a thing like that.'

'Exactly, but the Union and Sandy Gaul, the Convenor of the Shop Stewards' Committee, don't know or don't want to know the facts. Birdsall has four witness who swear it never happened. They say the boy had a fainting fit and fell against a radiator. Cantlie is not a liar and he is a fair man. A hard man perhaps, but fair. I know he is speaking the truth and he had no option but to act as he did. But it is the word of five men against one.'

'What about the boy himself?' asked Willerby but he knew the answer before he put the question.

'I've just come back from seeing him for the second time. I

162

can't move him. So far as he is concerned no one else was implicated. You know the Glasgow code as well as I do.'

'So if you take Birdsall back you have to fire Cantlie?'

'That's just about what it amounts to.' Motion passed his hand over his eyes wearily.

Willerby did not doubt for a moment the truth of what he had been told. He'd come to a dead end on too many good stories for the same reason before.

'We might have had a chance of convincing Sandy Gaul if there had not been the record of conflict between Cantlie and Birdsall,' said Motion. 'We always found him a reasonable man to deal with in the past. I still have a faint hope that if we have a cooling-off period the Works Committee may have second thoughts. But the hope is very faint. Ever since we took on the Camel contract there has been trouble. Even Gaul's attitude has changed. I have a feeling there is a hell of a lot more to this beneath the surface.'

Willerby was immediately interested but before he could frame his next question the intercom buzzed. Motion flicked the switch to receive.

'I want you in the Chairman's office straight away.' It was Clancy-Smith's voice.

'I have someone with me,' said Motion.

'Well, get rid of him. You have five minutes.' The machine clicked off.

'I'm sorry,' he said to Willerby. He felt acutely embarrassed.

As Willerby stood up to go he came to a sudden decision.

'Look. I've got a feeling there is something big here. Maybe I can help. Why don't we meet outside the office when you're through. Come over to my place and we can talk some more.' He took out a card and scribbled a telephone number on the back. 'I'll wait in for you to call.'

Ronnie Motion hesitated. From the tone of Clancy-Smith's voice he too felt there was something big up but not in the same way as Willerby. Then he held out his hand for the card. Maybe he would want a shoulder to cry on and he could not see that his wife was going to be a big help.

An hour and a half later Ronnie Motion found himself in one of those anonymous street corner bars. At least he could be sure that there was nobody he would be likely to know there and he wanted some more time to himself to think.

It was not until after the third large whisky that he felt himself sufficiently pulled together to ring Rhoda.

She managed to make her voice sound full of self-pity and accusing at the same time.

'Where are you? Why aren't you home? I've been expecting you for the last hour.'

'I've got a man to see. You had better go ahead and have your supper. I may be late.'

'You are the most inconsiderate man I have ever known. You know quite well what the doctor said. I'm not well. Nobody else leaves their wife alone all evening. You are just out having a good time ...' she went on and on while Ronnie held the receiver away from his ear. Then he said, 'I wouldn't wait up if I were you dear. I shall be late and I shall almost certainly be drunk.' He just waited to hear her outraged gasp before he put down the receiver. Then he dialled Richard Willerby.

Half an hour later he rang the bell of the top flat Willerby kept in a tall terraced house along Great Western Road.

'Good God,' said Willerby when he opened the door. 'You look as if you could use a large drink.'

Motion nodded and allowed himself to be led into the comfortable book-lined sitting-room and sank gratefully into a deep leather armchair. In spite of his wife's constant accusations he was not a heavy drinker and the amount he had already consumed was having its effect.

Willerby let him take his time while he fussed with the whisky bottle and the soda syphon.

Ronnie Motion took a long pull at his drink, stretched out his legs, trying to relax in his chair, and said conversationally, 'I've just been fired.'

Dick Willerby would not have been the first class newsman he was if he had not been able to keep a tight control over his reactions. Now he permitted himself no show of surprise. He didn't want to hear a long sob story but he was interested in what was happening at Greenbank and if Motion's misfortunes were part of the story he was prepared to listen.

Now he just said, 'It happens to the best of us. Would you like to tell me about it?'

It was exactly what Motion did want. He was still in a state

164

of shock. All he wanted to do was to unburden himself to a sympathetic audience.

'It's that bastard Clancy-Smith. We've never hit it off. Now he's Managing Director he has it all his own way.'

'Let's hear what happened this afternoon,' said Willerby, heading him off from what threatened to be a diatribe on Clancy-Smith's shortcomings.

'There is not a great deal to tell. I was called into the Chairman's office and told that in view of the critical situation which existed at Greenbank and the Camel factory it had been decided to replace me with someone with a greater experience of dealing with labour problems. They thanked me for my services in the past and all that sort of bullshit. Said they were not really sacking me but asking for my resignation as they felt I would be happier elsewhere. They pointed out that as a member of the Board I was entitled to remain as a director and have the matter put to a vote at a full Board meeting but that the outcome was a foregone conclusion and they hoped I would see it their way and resign gracefully. Of course I refused but I've been relieved of all executive responsibility.'

'Who were "they"? Clancy-Smith and young Puddefant?'

'There was a third. I was introduced to him when I first went in. A guy called Schum. He was an American.'

'An American!' This time Willerby could not conceal his surprise. 'What the hell was he doing there?'

'From what I could gather he's the fireman who is going to take over my job. At least I am supposed to hand over my files to him tomorrow. They didn't spell it out for me but I got the impression that he is a pretty big wheel with Camel.'

'Jesus!' Willerby exploded. He got up from his chair and started to pace up and down the room. 'You say you "got the impression". What gave you the impression that he is a Camel man?'

Motion wrinkled his forehead in thought, trying to sort out the confusion which was in his mind. 'It was something Keith said when we were introduced. Something about him being a new associate who had just flown over from Detroit to sort out some of the problems at Camel.' He shrugged his shoulders. 'I'm sorry. I can't remember the exact words.'

'That'll do to be going on with,' said Willerby. 'Do you by any chance know anything about who owns the Greenbank voting shares?'

Motion shook his head. 'The family hold them all between themselves. The other Directors only hold qualification shares and they are on a blank transfer.'

If Richard Willerby had not been so militantly Scottish the presence of an American at the afternoon's meeting might not have had the same significance. Even if Sir Charles had still been in the saddle he might not have given it further thought—but then in Sir Charles's time such a thing would have been unthinkable. It was more than likely that Sir Charles had made over control to his son and that was a very different matter.

'Do you know young Puddefant's home telephone number?' Motion who had relapsed into silence and was staring sombrely into the fire dragged himself back from thoughts of what he would say when the inevitable time came when he would have to face Rhoda.

'You'll find it in the telephone book. He's the only one with that surname.'

Willerby found it without difficulty. He hesitated briefly before picking up the receiver. There was just a chance he was barking up the wrong tree but the more he thought about it the more certain he became. It was a calculated risk and anyway he had nothing to lose.

When the telephone rang Keith and Clancy were well on their way through the second bottle. They had discussed the events of the past forty-eight hours from every angle and the conclusions they had come to had been wholly satisfactory. There was not a shadow of doubt in their minds that they were a couple of very shrewd operators.

'You answer it,' said Keith. 'If it's a bird tell her to come right over. If it is anyone else tell them to go to hell.'

'Who did you say was speaking?' asked Clancy not catching the name the first time.

'Richard Willerby. B.B.C. You may know my programme, "Everybody's World". Am I speaking to Mr Keith Puddefant?'

'The B.B.C.,' Clancy mouthed, putting his hand over the mouthpiece. Keith made violent gestures indicating that he did not want to take the call.

'I'm afraid Mr Puddefant is rather tied up at the moment. Can

I be any help. My name is Clancy-Smith.' Clancy had a healthy respect for the media. To appear on a television talk programme was one of his ambitions.

Willerby sensed the cordial reception. 'Of course,' he said smoothly. 'I hear you are the new Managing Director at Greenbank. Congratulations.'

'Thank you. What is it I can do for you?'

'It's quite a small matter really. I'm sorry to disturb you at this hour of the evening but I'm working on an idea for a programme and I have rather a tight deadline.'

'Fire away. Ask what you like. I won't guarantee to answer.' Clancy laughed, enjoying his little sally.

'I'm doing one of those surveys on Scottish industry,' Willerby lied. 'Greenbank has for so long enjoyed the reputation of being one of our leading Scottish engineering enterprises. I was just wondering if there are going to be any significant changes of policy now that the Camel Corporation have bought control.' By the sudden silence at the other end Willerby knew that he had struck oil. When Clancy recovered his breath his next words gave Willerby all the confirmation he needed.

'How the devil did you find that out? The decision was only taken yesterday.'

'You know how these things get around,' said Willerby with the utmost affability. 'Feelings are running high, as you know, about foreign investment in our home grown industries and it is not only the Scottish Nationalists who are on the warpath. The Unions don't like it either and with your spot of bother at the moment I thought it only fair to get your side of the question in its proper perspective.'

'Greenbank as you know is a family concern,' said Clancy-Smith, partially recovering himself. 'I'm afraid I cannot speak for them. How about your calling me at midday tomorrow when I have had a chance to consult them?'

Willerby judged it was time to drop the smooth talk.

'I'm afraid that will be too late. Why don't you consult right now and call me back in say half an hour.'

'That's not giving us much time.'

'I haven't got the time. Half an hour.' He gave his number and hung up. Then he called his old friend 'Dinger' Bell, the news editor of the *Glasgow Evening Echo*.

'Get a man over to my place straight away. I've got a big story breaking for tomorrow and it's all yours.'

Willerby realized that what he had come up with so far was not television material but he was riding his favourite hobby horse and he was prepared to ride it into the ground.

It was almost an hour before Clancy-Smith rang back. Once he had got over the initial shock of Willerby's telephone call he had begun to adjust to the idea and realize that perhaps it had happened for the best. Dick Katz had made it clear to him that the handling of Keith was his special assignment. The only real problem with which he had been presented was Keith's anxiety that the details of the share transaction should be kept under wraps for as long as possible. Whilst Clancy was well aware that he was just trying to put off the moment when his father would have to be told, Keith had argued with some justification that they should at least wait until the share transfer had been finalized. For this reason the hurried decision to sack Ronnie Motion and put Hank Schum in his place had made it necessary for them to tread warily. Keith had been persuaded to accept Schum as a negotiator between the Management and the Union but only in the capacity as an outside adviser. Now the gloves were off they could come out in their true colours and Keith felt this would greatly strengthen Schum's authority.

Willerby's telephone call had shocked Keith to the core. He had a great capacity for self-deception and all through the negotiations he had clung on to a feeling that if things went wrong in any way there might still be time to pull out of the deal. Now he was faced with the reality that there was no turning back. He had got Clancy to ring Katz at the Old Manor House in the hope that there was some chance that Katz would agree to a temporary cover-up but he had appeared to be delighted at the turn of events.

'So far as I am concerned you can tell that bum anything he wants to know. If you can get yourself or Hank on a T.V. programme so much the better. It would be a good opportunity to shoot the shit out of the Union case.'

Having delivered himself of this Olympian judgment he put down the telephone and turned to Juliet who was lying alongside him.

'I guess that finally fixes lover boy,' he said. 'I wouldn't like to be in his place when his Pop hears the news.'

'You are a bastard, Dick. I sometimes think you like trampling on people.'

'What! You soft on him or something?'

'I kinda liked the guy.'

'Honey, when you like a guy,' grinned Katz, 'I reckon he ought to take to the hills.' He reached out and pulled her to him under the bedclothes. 'Remember you and I have a working partnership. Let's work at it a little.'

Back in the flat in Great Western Road Richard Willerby and David MacWhirter, chief reporter of the *Evening Echo*, were putting the finishing touches to their article while Ronnie Motion, overcome by strain and whisky, slept it off in his chair under a blanket.

For him the next day was to be a day of reckoning.

14

The story hit the front page of the midday edition of *The Echo* under a banner headline:

STRIKEBOUND FIRM SELLS OUT TO U.S.

'Greenbank Engineering, one of Glasgow's oldest and best known firms this week sold out to the American giant Camel Corporation of Detroit who employ some 8,000 workers at their plant at Cumbernauld.

'Greenbank, a privately-owned Company which has been controlled by the Puddefant family during the whole of their two hundred year history, were recently awarded a contract to supply automatic transmissions to Camel for their "new-look" family saloon whose appearance on the market this autumn is an eagerly awaited event in the motoring world.

'Mr Robert Clancy-Smith, the recently appointed Managing Director of Greenbank, in an exclusive statement to *The Echo* said last night, "This move makes a great deal of sense so far as our Company is concerned. It not only strengthens the ties we already have with Camel but promises a new era of prosperity for us which will benefit every member of the Company down to the workers on the shop floor."

'Questioned about the strike at Greenbank which has also led to the crippling of production at Camel, he said: "We will be immediately seeking to reopen negotiations with the Union with a view to ending the deadlock which appears to exist at the moment. I am confident that this new development will be of the greatest help in enabling us to reach an agreement so that full production can be resumed at the earliest possible moment." '

In an editorial carried in the same issue, *The Echo* did not pull any punches.

'It must be a matter for the greatest regret to all with the interests of Scottish industrial endeavour at heart that yet another firm should come under the sway of the Almighty Dollar. This paper has constantly raised its voice against the action of our own Government in putting such a large sector of industry under public ownership in the belief that this will increase productivity and efficiency. We have even less faith in the belief that policy making on the other side of the Atlantic will have a similar effect. In our opinion it is better by far that the Government should step in in this case—if it is not already too late.'

Within minutes of the story breaking Sir Charles was rung up by the Industrial Correspondent of *The Scotsman* asking for his comments. At first he found it impossible to believe until he had the story read to him word for word over the telephone. When he put down the receiver he was shaking as if he was in the grip of a fever. It was some time before he gained sufficient control of his emotions to tell Claire.

'There must be some mistake, Daddles,' Claire had said soothingly. 'You know what the papers are. Always getting a hold of the wrong end of the stick.' But he knew by sure instinct that there had been no mistake. His first reaction was to drive to the office and confront Keith but he thought better of it. If there had been any misrepresentation of the facts by *The Echo* he knew Keith would already have been on the telephone. Instead he sent him a telegram: 'Require immediate denial today's story in *Evening Echo*. Unless I hear from you personally by five this evening do not try to contact myself or your mother again except through my solicitors who will be authorized to safeguard my interests.'

Keith received the telegram with something like relief. He had been dreading a confrontation with his father and now he felt almost lightheaded at being granted a reprieve from the ordeal.

'What did I tell you,' Clancy gloated. 'You've pulled the old man's teeth. He hasn't power to bite any more. Now perhaps we can get on with the business of making things work our way.'

* * *

The news which had so shocked Sir Charles was greeted by Iggy with unfeigned delight. He was blessed with an almost uncanny instinct of anticipating events and now his hunch that Camel were interested in acquiring Greenbank had proved correct far sooner than he even had foreseen. He picked up the receiver and called Shamus O'Donovan.

'I'm playing this for all it's worth,' he told him. 'American intervention in Greenbank's domestic problems is all we need. With any luck we can escalate this into a national issue. I have already had protest meetings at the shipyards over the sacking of Birdsall. They are pretty edgy out at the Chrysler works as well. If Schum cuts up rough, as I think he will, at his first meeting with the Works Committee we can make a lot of capital out of it. The management is already being blamed for the Cooley killing. The truck driver has been suspended by his Union. If we can drag the Transport Workers into this we have it made. From the tone of the *Echo*'s editorial we are going to have the Press on our side.'

'I'll see what I can do to stir things up at this end,' said O'Donovan flatly. He too was elated but he never showed his feelings. When O'Donovan started to stir things up, he did it at a very high level indeed.

Hank Schum, in his new position as Chairman of Greenbank's Labour Relations Committee, lost no time in getting down to work. He called for a meeting with the Works Committee for the following morning. As Salvatori had prophesied he was in no mood to give concessions. It was unfortunate for him that the morning's Press was hostile to the takeover. The *Echo* story had been picked up by most of the Nationals and the general opinion was that it was not a move calculated to improve labour relations. Out of respect for the feelings of the Works Committee Jim Cantlie was not present but his absence made no difference. So far as Schum was concerned it was a management committee of one and he did all the talking.

Conscious of the attitude of the Press, he opened the proceedings with a pep talk on the benefits which would accrue from belonging to a multi-national corporation. He expanded at length on the fine relationship the Camel Corporation enjoyed with its associated companies and on his own virtues as an open, fair-minded negotiator. Everyone, it appeared, loved good old Hank Schum.

Sandy Gaul and his committee sat through the performance in wooden silence. Then Gaul said: 'We have come to this meeting at your request to discuss the settlement of our present dispute. We are prepared to listen to proposals from any authorized representatives of the management.'

Schum ignored the rebuff. Instead he read them a lecture on

172

the virtues of loyalty, hard work and dedication to the job. 'We are a great organization to work for,' he told them. 'Right here and now I am offering you a good deal for the future. Plenty of work, better communications with the management and a productivity scheme which is going to make you all a hell of a lot more money. In return we require a straight deal from you. We don't stand for being messed around by a handful of troublemakers.'

'So much for better communications,' Stewart MacGregor growled and there was a mutter of approval around the room. Gaul held up his hand for silence. 'I think we would all like that last remark clarified,' he said hostilely.

'This guy Birdsall is a trouble-maker for one. He was fired for a good and proper reason and he stays fired. The same goes for any others like him. You get your men back to work and let's start talking from there.'

Immediately a wave of indignation swept round the room. Several of the Works Committee started to talk at once.

'That will conclude the meeting,' said Gaul standing up. 'We did not come here to be threatened.' One by one the committee followed suit and led by Gaul, filed out in silence.

When they had gone Schum turned angrily to Angus Simpson. 'What the hell is wrong with these guys?' he exploded. 'Don't they want to make more money?'

'Glasgow is not Detroit, Mr Schum,' he said, shaking his overlarge head. 'We are in worse trouble than we were before.'

Simpson was right. The news of the result of the meeting travelled fast. By midday there were new placards being carried by the pickets. 'Hands off our Industries', 'Birdsall for President' and, unoriginally, 'Yanks go Home'.

In the shipyards up and down Clydeside, men gathered together in angry groups to discuss the latest development. Out at Chrysler two hundred men in the press shop walked out, bringing all work virtually to a standstill.

At his office at the B.B.C. Richard Willerby decided to take a hand. He rang Hank Schum to offer him a spot on that night's programme but was abruptly refused. Schum was still smarting over the attitude of the Press to the take-over and had not forgotten the part that Willerby had played.

'We'll make our own statement in our own time,' he had told Clancy and Keith. 'Believe me when we do it will be good. I'll

173

make the charge that Caird was beaten up stick and then we'll see who's left with the egg on their face.'

That night Willerby opened his programme with an interview with Sandy Gaul and James Younghusband of the Transport and General Workers Union. Younghusband had been prominently involved in the threatened transport strike of 1977 and was well known to viewers for his militancy. Willerby had chosen him as much for his strong pro-Scotland views as for his fluency before the microphone. The interview did not however go exactly as Willerby had planned. Although Gaul and Younghusband had only had a couple of hours' notice before they were due to appear on the air both had been well briefed. Gaul had telephoned James Christie direct, cutting out the usual channels of communication.

'Don't allow yourself to be sidetracked, Christie had advised. 'You are out on strike to protect jobs and this effects every Union member in the country. By the way, a friend on the National Executive of the Transport and General Workers Union called me, he tells me he is in favour of coming out in our support. Bear it in mind.' Shamus O'Donovan had been doing his work well.

Willerby had started off the programme with pointed questions on the reaction to the American take-over at Greenbank but Gaul was riding to orders.

'It does not matter to us who the management are,' Gaul declared firmly, 'we are on strike on a fundamental issue which affects every worker in this country. The right to do a fair day's work for a fair day's pay. The sacking of one of our shop stewards, Harry Birdsall, strikes at the very roots of this right.'

'Did your new American bosses give you any hope of a settlement at your meeting today?'

'The management offered no solution whatsoever. Indeed we were threatened with further sackings if they did not approve of a man's political views.'

'Don't you think this is just the American attitude?' Willerby persisted. 'Seeing a Red under every bed?'

'I think it is symptomatic of what is happening in industry throughout this country. No man's job is safe if he can be dismissed because of a whim of the management. Our fight for our rights is the fight of every worker in the land.'

Frustrated in his attempts to make foreign investment in

British industry the main theme of the discussion he turned to Younghusband.

'How far are you in agreement with what Mr Gaul says?'

Younghusband had also been well briefed.

'I'm in complete agreement but what is more important every one of my mates is also in agreement. We see this as just another illustration of unfair domination by the capitalistic classes. Mr Birdsall is one of the martyrs in our cause just as Daniel Cooley, who was murdered in an attempt by the management at Greenbank to break a legitimate strike, is a martyr. We in the working classes are not getting the support from the Government to which we are entitled. It is time we took matters into our own hands.'

'There are many people who say that the Unions in this country already have too much power. After all a Trade Unionist can use his democratic right to vote for the sort of Government he wants. He also has a second vote to vote for the Union leaders he wants and there can be no doubt that the Union leaders exert just as much power if not more than our political leaders.'

'Everyone has the right to join a Union. If they stay outside they only have themselves to blame.'

'If the strike escalates into something bigger a large number of innocent people are going to suffer.'

'The British public are prepared to suffer to defeat tyranny.'

The broadcast had run right off course and was turning into a political platform. Willerby tried to close it up but Younghusband had the last word.

'Make no mistake, the workers of this country have had enough. We are not living in the days of the Tolpuddle Martyrs. Our right to withhold our labour is universally accepted and it is a right we will not hesitate to use to secure justice.'

Willerby smiled weakly and turned with relief to the next interviewee on the programme—a nice old lady who had just celebrated her hundred and fifth birthday.

*   *   *

Lord Ochil, seated in the library at Ochil, at the other side of the fireplace to his old friend Major Patrick Grant, leaned forward and switched off the television set.

'Well?' he asked. 'What do you think of that?'

They were old friends who had served together in the same

175

Regiment of the 51st Highland Division. In the gallant action in the Western Desert where Brigadier Lorne Campbell had won the most coveted of all awards, the Victoria Cross, Pat Grant had been hit in the leg and it had been Abdy Ochil who had carried him back to safety under a hail of German bullets. It had earned Abdy the Military Cross and sealed a lifelong friendship.

Patrick Grant was also a landowner, if not on quite such a grand scale as Abdy. They shared the same interests in looking after their land and had the same hobbies like rearing pheasants in the spring to shoot them in the autumn. But their links went deeper than that. They were both fervent believers in God, Queen and Country and they found it difficult to understand anyone who did not subscribe to their creed.

When during the war a few bombs had started to fall around the dock area in London and the dockers had gone on strike for danger money they had regarded it as tantamount to treason. Ever since then they regarded the activities of the Trade Unions as unpatriotic to a degree of being positively malignant. On the other hand they looked upon anyone who had served with them in the Army from the highest ranks to the lowest as a race apart. To have endured appalling discomfort and been prepared to sacrifice their lives for what the dockers would have regarded as little more than beer money qualified them for membership of a very special circle. Down the years they had kept in close touch with their former comrades, religiously attending Old Comrades Association gatherings, finding jobs for those who needed them and generally fighting their battles for any who fell by the economic wayside.

Abdy Ochil and Patrick Grant were by no means unique. There were many thousands of people throughout the country who thought the same way. If there was any difference between them and their fellows it lay in the fact that they were prepared to do something to preserve what they held sacred.

Ever since a new Government had been elected in 1974 they had watched with dismay as the Left wing had gained greater and greater control of national affairs. Where one section of the community saw the building of a New Jerusalem, they saw in the extravagant pay claims, diminishing productivity and constant crippling strikes nothing but the Gadarene swine rushing headlong over the cliffs into anarchy.

When Abdy in a rare romantic moment, not altogether un-tinged with commercialism, had proposed to the beautiful Juliet and been accepted even he had been mildly surprised. In the first few months following his marriage he had devoted himself industriously to the business of producing an heir. He had even taken her on a honeymoon to Gibraltar where, at intervals of inspecting the fortifications, he had made a real effort to adjust himself to the novelty of married life. Back at Ochil, however, it was not long before the demands made on him in the running of his estate once more assumed their proper importance. Conscious of his shortcomings as a husband he allowed her complete freedom to live her own life, made every effort to be polite to her friends with whom he had little in common and treated her with the affection of a fond uncle for an unpredictable child. If Juliet sometimes could have wished that he would be a bit more articulate in the society with which she liked to surround herself, it was an arrangement which by and large suited them both admirably.

With his own kind, however, Abdy Ochil was far from inarticulate. Indeed it was he who first formulated the plan to combat the forces which were seeking to destroy his way of life.

As long ago as 1972 a retired General in the South of England had issued a rallying cry to like-minded persons to form a private army, the object of which was to take over the running of essential services in the country when the time came, which he believed to be inevitable, when the militants would succeed in bringing about a standstill. Although there were many who were inspired to enlist under his banner, the Press for the most part ridiculed the idea. Those who took it seriously saw in it the genesis of the sort of coup d'état which the Colonels had pulled off in Greece and dubbed him a dangerous fanatic.

Abdy Ochil however adopted the idea with the utmost seriousness. When the first blaze of publicity had died down he had set to work to build up his own organization. His first step had been to appoint Patrick Grant, who had been his Adjutant during the war, as his second-in-command. Together they had pored over old regimental lists, picking out and tracking down individuals who had the specialist skills they anticipated they would require. On his rare visits to London he spent much of his time in the smoking-room at The Whitehall, enlisting the support of land-owners like himself who would set up cells in strategic parts of the country where their local influence could be used to the best effect.

Occasionally news of a secret army would appear in the Press to be treated with an attitude of amused indulgence but the extent of his activities and his own role of Commander-in-Chief remained a well-kept secret. There had been several occasions in the months which followed when a new crisis had tempted him to throw down the gauntlet and disclose his strength but the point had never been quite reached.

There had come a time when it had no longer been possible to keep Juliet out of the picture—not that Abdy deliberately wanted to exclude her from his activities but simply because he felt she would be uninterested and anyway there was no useful function she could perform. When one evening after dinner he had taken her into the little room off his study where he kept his operational maps and explained to her the significance of the many coloured pins which denoted different units under his command he had been surprised by the intelligence she had shown.

Juliet had not only been interested in her husband's plan but found herself looking at him in a new light. Perhaps after all she had not married someone who had just a large castle and an ancient title. The thought that one day he might become a public figure in his own right excited her greatly and she spent many hours familiarizing herself with the intricate details of the great plan. Somebody had once paid her the compliment of telling her that she thought like a man and Abdy came to accept her as an unlikely but valuable ally.

By the Spring of 1977 Abdy Ochil was becoming uneasily aware that all was not well within his organization. The previous winter had been marked by a more than usual number of strikes in support of extravagant pay claims. The T.U.C. continued to pay lip service to their Social Contract with the Government but they had been quite unable to control their more militant members. There had been talk of an autumn election but it had come to nothing. At the same time his private army was becoming restive. Men who had joined were beginning to lose enthusiasm. Local commanders up and down the country were reporting that they were finding increasing difficulty in getting their men to come to the regular talk sessions which were part of the training programme. What they wanted was action and an opportunity to show their patriotism. Now with another winter approaching there was a strong feeling that continued inactivity would result in the whole carefully built up organization disintegrating.

These thoughts were very much in the forefront of the minds of Abdy and Patrick Grant as they watched Willerby's programme. Grant was if anything the keener of the two to press the button which would put into operation what it had been decided to call Exercise Patriot. Now he emphasized his views with his accustomed vigour.

'If there is anything in what that chap said about the transport workers coming out we cannot hold off any longer. The situation is made for us. We have plenty of drivers standing by. We could soon show them that blackmail will not work. Let them have a go and every moderate in the country will be behind us.'

Abdy nodded. 'I know this young fellow, Puddefant. He was up here in the summer. Pal of Juliet's. Struck me as being a bit spineless. I wish like hell Juliet was here. She could mark our card for us. She's also pally with that American Katz. Stays with him in Detroit and all that sort of thing.'

Patrick Grant, himself a model family man, had never been able to understand the relationship between Juliet and Abdy. In his view a woman's place was by her husband's side and her frequent absences from home disturbed him.

'By the way, where is Juliet?' he asked. 'Haven't seen her around for quite a few days.'

By one of those coincidences which happen from time to time, the telephone rang and it was Juliet herself who answered the question.

She wanted to know if Abdy had seen the Willerby programme.

'I have just been talking to Dick Katz,' she told him. 'He's right here in the middle of the situation and the position is pretty grave. I'd like to have him come over and talk to you.'

Abdy had long since ceased being surprised at anything his wife did. Now he just said, 'I've no idea where you are. How long would it take you?'

'We can be with you within the hour. Could you ask Evans to have two guest rooms made ready? I have another American I'd like to bring along and it may be a long session. One other thing, honey. I think you ought to start having a good look at those pins of yours.'

'It looks like this may be it, Pat,' he said as he replaced the receiver. He began to feel the same pleasurable tickle of excitement that he had known during the war just before battle was about to be joined.

* * *

The conference took place in the library at Ochil. It would have been hard to imagine a greater contrast in appearance between the Americans, sharp and alert in their city suits, and Lord Ochil and Patrick Grant in tweed jackets patched at the elbows and cavalry twill trousers, lounging in their arm chairs like prefects in a public school common-room. Yet they got on remarkably well together. Juliet, elegant as ever, perched herself on the leather fire-surround and saw to it that their glasses were kept charged with 'Grouse'—the only whisky Abdy would allow to be served in his house—occasionally intervening to interpret when Abdy seemed nonplussed by the more colourful Americanisms.

At the request of Dick Katz, Hank Schum gave his version of the position at Greenbank.

'It is my opinion,' said Katz, 'that if the Greenbank affair is resolved we will be able to persuade our workers at Camel to call off their action. Which means that Chrysler and the others will follow suit. On the other hand maybe they won't. That negro getting himself killed has upset the cart. One thing I am sure about is that if they stick their toes in at Greenbank this thing is going to spread far outside the automobile industry.'

Schum was in no doubt that there was not going to be any easy solution.

'Back in the States this would be purely a local issue. We don't have the same political climate that you have over here. Sure we have a two party system but there is not a dime of difference between the Republicans and the Democrats. Just depends which part of the country you were born. We don't know the meaning of Socialism, never mind Communism in the way that you know it. In the States if you offer a guy more money it really means something. It seems to me that most of the strikes you have for higher wages are deliberate attempts to break the Social Contract. How else could anyone be so dumb as to ask for more money than his firm can afford to pay? In the end he is just doing himself out of a job.'

'Don't let us get our strings mixed up here,' said Grant, 'I believe that the moderates throughout the country are getting heartily sick of extravagant pay claims by workers who are already highly paid. This is a very different kettle of fish. Everyone is scared stiff of unemployment. For a long time the T.U.C. have been pressing the Government to make sacking illegal. Both Abdy and I believe that the sacking of your man Birdsall can be the flash point which will bring about a national emergency. This is just what the hard-liners are looking for and if they are going to look for trouble we are ready for them.'

Later in the evening Abdy led them through to his operations room and explained how Exercise Patriot would work.

'I just have to pick up that telephone and call one man. He calls ten chaps further down the chain of command and each of them calls ten others. Within a couple of hours I can have upwards of five thousand men standing to, ready to move in wherever they are needed.'

'Five thousand men where there are maybe a million out on strike?' queried Katz. 'How far is that going to get you?'

'It will be enough to man essential services,' said Abdy, waxing almost eloquent in his enthusiasm. 'But that is not the main point. What I believe is that there are a great number of moderates in this country who are just waiting for someone to show the flag. What this country lacks is proper leadership. Look what happened in the last war. We were faced with a national emergency and the country rose to the challenge. Given a proper lead, they will do so again. Give 'em a lead, show 'em we mean business and it will be 1939 all over again.'

Hank Schum in particular was enthusiastic. He was a man who believed in tough action. Moreover he was still smarting over his failure to make an immediate breakthrough with the Greenbank Works Committee. Whilst he was quite ready to lead off about the political situation he was finding himself in unfamiliar waters and his instinct was to strike out first and ask questions afterwards.

Now he said, 'Why wait for the hit? You heard that guy on the box tonight. If the transport workers come out the whole country will be gummed up. The wider the strike spreads the bigger a hero Birdsall becomes. Unless we are careful we will find ourselves in a situation where we cannot afford to back down and at the same time we cannot afford not to.'

Deep inside, Abdy Ochil was afraid that this was just another crisis which was going to fizzle out as had happened so often before. Suppose the transport workers did not come out after all. He could not afford to go on much longer without some sort of action. He warmed towards Schum and his readiness to jump the gun.

'Are you suggesting that we declare ourselves before the transport boys make the move?' he asked. 'Sort of issue a warning that we are not going to stand any nonsense.'

'That's my view,' said Schum, settling back in his chair comfortably.

Dick Katz was more cautious. 'You've got a fine weapon in your hand. There is just the danger that it is going to go off at the wrong time. Maybe you should wait until things get a lot worse before you make a move. That way you are more likely to get the support of the public. If you try and anticipate a crisis it may be that you will only create one.'

They continued to argue but it soon became obvious that the general mood was for action. Even Juliet took sides against Dick Katz so that he found himself in a minority of one in urging the cautious approach.

Finally it was Patrick Grant who summed up the general feeling of the meeting.

'With the labour situation deteriorating the way it has over the past few months it is evident that the time will come when a confrontation will be inescapable. Inactivity on our part means that the extreme Left wing can gain ground bit by bit until they will be in a position of overwhelming strength. We can duck the issue on this occasion but the same situation will arise again and next time we will be just that little bit weaker and they will be that little bit stronger. I do not think we should allow that to happen.'

'I agree,' said Abdy splashing a generous measure of whisky into his glass. 'The best method of defence is attack. We've been sitting on the touchline for too long. Let's join battle.'

15

The Greenbank strike may have seemed of great importance in places as far removed as the little room behind the bookshop in Dunbarton Road and the library of Ochil Castle but the public as a whole were not yet deeply involved. The death of Daniel Cooley had caused a ripple of shock and the more politically aware citizens had paid some attention to the disclosure of the take-over deal with Camel but generally the situation was regarded with apathy. There had been too many strikes over the past eighteen months for anyone to pay much attention to yet another. It was just part of the pattern which a disgruntled public had come to accept.

On the midnight news of 30th September it did not even rate a mention. It was, however, a situation which was not to last.

In the small hours of the morning of 1st October, long after Dick Katz and Hank Schum had retired to bed, Abdy Ochil and Patrick Grant wrestled with the composition of an announcement they intended to issue the following day. Juliet had been charged with the task of setting up a Press conference for three o'clock in the afternoon. Now that the decision to act had been taken, Abdy was in a fever of impatience to fire the first shots. By the time they had finished their task he and his second-in-command stretched themselves out on the big leather sofas on either side of the fire for what was left of the night. They were about to launch their offensive and it had seemed to them inappropriate that they should retire to the comfort of their beds at such a momentous hour.

At nine o'clock on the morning of 1st October—the day when the pheasant shooting season opens—the first telephone call was made ordering a stand-by for Exercise Patriot. As word was passed from person to person in country houses up and down the country, it was received with a certain amount of bewilderment.

'What the hell is this all about?' one choleric old Colonel wanted to know. 'Wasn't aware that we were in a state of emergency. Can't have read the papers properly or something.' Others were equally puzzled but they passed the word on.

'No, you are not to take any action yet.' Patrick Grant snapped down the telephone. 'This is just a warning order. Yes, we do believe there is going to be a national emergency. That's all I can tell you.'

'Give them something to think about anyway,' he said to Juliet. 'Even if it turns out to be a false alarm, it will keep them on their toes.'

Juliet was thoroughly enjoying herself. Since soon after breakfast she had been on her own line to all the newspaper offices she could think of.

The information that Lieutenant-Colonel The Earl of Ochil was going to issue an important statement on national affairs was enough to excite the interest of even the most unimaginative of news editors.

'Who the hell is the Earl of Ochil?' asked David MacWhirter, when he was handed the assignment.

'I have no idea,' said his chief, 'but when obscure Earls start making statements on national affairs from their castles it behoves us lesser mortals to listen carefully. By the way his wife sounds *very* sexy. You'd better take a cameraman with you.'

Richard Willerby also received a telephone call from Juliet and he took the matter rather more seriously. Always looking for the story behind the story he was quick to detect her American accent. Then he took the trouble to look up Abdy Ochil in *Who's Who*. The information that he had married Juliet, the daughter of Mr and Mrs Henry D. Kaplan of Detroit, started off a train of thought which made him decide that it might be very worth while to try and get there early and to have a private word with her ladyship.

Willerby got to the castle shortly after two o'clock to find Juliet superintending the placing of chairs in the main hall.

'Of course I know your name,' she said when he introduced himself, making her voice sound warm. Before her marriage she had worked for a time in a public relations office in New York and knew all about the dangers of alienating journalists. 'I watched your programme last night. How good of you to come.'

'I'm sorry I'm early,' lied Willerby. 'I misjudged the time it would take to get here. Perhaps since I'm here, you could fill me in with a bit of background.'

184

'I wouldn't like to anticipate anything my husband might have to say at the conference.'

'Of course not. Just a few personal details. You come from Detroit.' It was a statement rather than a question.

'Yes I do but that has nothing to do with today's business. I only work here.' She smiled disarmingly.

'So you would know Dick Katz of Camel?'

'Why yes. I guess everybody knows everybody else in little old Detroit. I've known Dick since I was a kid.'

'Have you seen him since he has been over here?'

A warning bell rang in Juliet's mind. The question had been put just a little too quickly.

'That would be telling,' she said pretending coyness. 'I wouldn't like to have my husband being jealous.'

Willerby did not press the point. 'I've been keeping you from your job. Please forgive me.' He moved away and took a seat at the end of the front row of chairs as the room started to fill up.

*　　*　　*

At three o'clock precisely Lord Ochil made his entrance into the hall and took his place behind a green baize-covered table, facing the assembly. He was followed by Patrick Grant and Lilias Proudfoot, his farm secretary, carrying a bundle of duplicated sheets.

It was Major Patrick Grant who opened the proceedings.

He introduced Abdy as 'one of our foremost Scottish landowners' and followed it up with a panegyric of his fine war record. Most of his audience who were too young to remember anything about the war and knew very little about agriculture were beginning to look bored when Grant dropped the first bombshell.

'What few, if any, of you can know is that Lord Ochil some three years ago decided that it was not right that men of goodwill should rest on laurels gained in the field of battle many years ago. For some time he had been deeply disturbed about the state of the country and, being a practical man, he searched about to discover what contribution he could make to restoring the fortunes of the nation which he saw being threatened by the greedy, the unpatriotic and the power hungry. What he decided to do, and what I myself, in my modest way, have been helping him to achieve,

185

was to form a Citizens' Army which could be called upon in time of National emergency. It is our view that that time has now arrived.'

The announcement was marked by a spontaneous outburst of incredulity amongst the thirty-odd journalists present. One or two jumped to their feet anxious to ask questions but Patrick Grant forestalled them.

'There will be plenty of time for questions later on.' He shouted to make himself heard while Abdy brushed frantically at his moustache. 'Our purpose in calling you here today is to make our position absolutely clear so that certain people cannot say that they were not warned of what action the Citizens' Army would take if, as seems likely, a crisis is to be forced on the country. I call on my commander-in-chief now to make a statement after which duplicated copies of the statement will be handed out to you all so that there can be no danger of his words being mis-reported.'

There was complete silence as Abdy rose to his feet, adjusted his half-lens glasses and started to read the carefully prepared statement.

'As Commander-in-Chief of the Citizens' Army, I and my second-in-command, Major Patrick Grant, have made a close study of the political situation as it exists today. We have in particular paid heed to an inflammatory television broadcast which took place as recently as yesterday evening, in which it was made plain that the transport workers in this country are ready to come out on strike in support of the troubles at present being experienced by Greenbank Engineering in particular and the motor car industry in Scotland in general.

'There have been many occasions in the past when I have been on the point of making the aims of the Citizens' Army clear to the general public but for one reason or another I have so far refrained from doing so. In view of this most recent threat to industrial peace I have decided to refrain no longer.

'I am quite sure that the general public in this country, which includes all people of moderate opinion wherever their political affiliations lie, are heartily sick of being held to ransom and of seeing their families suffer because of the action of a few fanatical men. I now say to everyone of goodwill with the future of this country at heart that I am prepared to give them the leadership they have up to now so blatantly lacked.

'If the transport workers carry out their threat to immobilize the country I will immediately call out my forces. There are over five thousand ordinary, decent men ready to take over the manning of essential services. If they are called upon to do so, I am sure that they can rely on receiving the support of every decent man and woman in the country.

'Let the enemies of this country beware. We are resolute men, ready and able to stand against them.' He paused for a moment, then standing to attention, his eyes looking over the heads of his rapt audience, speaking with deep emotion he declared: 'It is a debt we owe to those of my generation who made the supreme sacrifice in order that we should have freedom.'

In the silence which followed as Abdy resumed his seat, Richard Willerby suddenly felt an almost overpowering desire to laugh. The picture of that fine old soldier, Lieutenant-Colonel The Earl of Ochil, defiant and reduced almost to tears by his own eloquence, struck him as a bizarre caricature which could almost have been a music hall turn. Then Patrick Grant and Juliet seated on either side of Abdy started to clap loudly. Nobody took up their lead. Instead most of them were on their feet, waving their note-pads in order to attract attention to ask a question.

It was some time before Willerby managed to get a hearing while his fellow Pressmen demanded to know more about the army which Lord Ochil had so suddenly produced out of a hat.

When he finally managed to catch Abdy's eye he took his time, phrasing his question carefully.

'As you yourself say, there have been many occasions in the past when you could have taken the stand you have elected to take this afternoon. Can you tell me what influenced you to take your decision at this particular moment in time?'

It was Patrick Grant who rose to answer.

'There comes a time when a stand has got to be made. We decided last night that with further threats from the transport workers that time had come.'

Willerby was not to be put off so easily. He asked,

'Was any outside influence brought to bear on you in making your decision?'

'I'm not quite sure that I know what you mean.'

187

'Let me make the question more specific. Did you have discussions with Mr Katz of the Camel Corporation before coming to your decision?'

Patrick Grant was quite unversed in the pitfalls of a Press conference. He took all the questions at their face value. He had nothing to hide.

'Certainly,' he replied, ignoring a warning tug on his sleeve from Juliet. 'Mr Katz and his colleague were very helpful in explaining to us the situation at Greenbank and the Camel factory.'

'So your decision was taken in support of American interests and not from any patriotic motive at all.' Willerby was genuinely outraged at what he took to be yet further evidence of Americans interfering in Scottish domestic affairs.

'That is absolutely untrue!' Grant shouted, but his words were drowned by the uproar which broke out as journalists rose to try and ask supplementary questions or pushed back their chairs to make a dash for the door in order to find a telephone.

When the last of them had departed, clutching their copies of Abdy's statement, Abdy, looking rather dazed, turned to Juliet.

'How d'ye think it went them? Damn funny bunch eh?'

'You were splendid, honey,' Juliet told him without much conviction. 'We'll just have to wait and see what they come out with.'

'They were a pretty Left-wing lot if you ask me,' said Grant. 'Especially that pal of yours on the television programme. He could cause trouble.'

They did not have long to wait. Although Willerby did not have time to set up his own programme, Abdy's statement was carried in full in all newscasts from six o'clock onwards.

Within minutes the telephone at Ochil Castle started to ring. Some of the calls were from genuine seekers after information, some merely abusive, but most were from people anxious to offer their services to the Citizens' Army. Abdy Ochil seated with Patrick Grant in his operations room had Lilias Proudfoot and Juliet bring in notes of each telephone call as it was received while they busied themselves with sticking more pins into their wall map and making an exhaustive analysis of streams of calls which by the ten o'clock news had increased to a flood. By the time they all went to bed it was well after midnight and Abdy

188

Ochil was a happy man. If his analysis of the telephone calls had been correct the next day would see him in command of a force very much larger in numbers than even he had anticipated. The last telephone call of the evening got Hamish MacMurray who kept the paper shop down in the village out of his bed. It was to tell him that His Lordship would require all the daily papers delivered to the Castle an hour earlier than usual the following morning.

*   *   *

On the next day the storm burst.

Every national newspaper carried the story on the front page. For the most part the editorial reaction was far from flattering. The *Daily Mirror* published a large picture of Abdy, his spectacles poised on the end of his nose, with the banner headline: WHO DOES HE THINK HE IS? and described him in their editorial as an 'archaic, backwoods Peer who could be better occupied growing turnips than interfering in matters he does not understand'. The *Sun* was equally scornful. On the front page they called Abdy 'His Lunatic Lordship,' and derided his claim to command a private army. 'A generation ago,' they wrote, 'the Earl of Ochil proved himself a brave soldier and the nation showed its gratitude by making him one of their most highly decorated heroes. Our advice to him now is "stay at home and shut up". The last thing this country needs to solve its problems is a sabre-rattling old bore.' Only the *Daily Telegraph* gave the Citizens' Army some measure of qualified support. 'It is perhaps time that the moderates in this country stood up to be counted. In making a firm stand against the leadership of the extreme Left wing perhaps Lord Ochil may indeed be striking a blow for freedom.'

Everywhere up and down the country the Citizens' Army was the chief topic of conversation and, in spite of the unfavourable Press, there were many who expressed themselves as being in favour of anyone who was prepared to stand up to 'those bloody Commies'. Jack Turnbull, ex-sergeant in The Buffs, spoke for many like him when he dropped in for his regular morning pint in the Bricklayers Arms.

'I reckon he's a good bloke, this Lord Whatsisname. Got the right ideas. What I've always said is if all these long haired louts you see about today had to do a spell in the army we'd have none of this trouble with strikes and suchlike. No, nor none of this hooliganism on the football terraces neither.'

'You got something there, Jackie boy,' said Bill Swaffham the landlord as he pulled him another pint and there were general grunts of agreement round the bar.

There were many others however who held quite a different view. Heavy goods drivers reporting for duty at their depots found their mates angrily discussing the news. Most of them were of the view that Lord Bloody Ochil had taken a diabolical liberty.

'Interfering with our right to withhold our labour. That's what it is. I'd like to see any bloody scab try to take my truck out,' said Buck Taylor, punching his fist into the palm of his hand. 'I'd bloody smash him, so I would.'

'I'm not taking out no shagging truck today. I'm not standing for being threatened by no bugger, not even a bleedin' Earl,' declared another.

In many yards the men never got their coats off. Some of them went straight home again, others stood about in groups letting off steam and waiting to hear what the official verdict of their union would be.

One of the difficulties experienced by officials of the Transport and General Workers Union had always been that their members were dispersed all over the country in relatively small groups. Not only did they not have large centres of labour where communications were easy, but a high percentage of their members were dispersed at any one time delivering their loads. By mid-morning however area officers of the Union were being left in no doubt as to the mood of their members. At headquarters in London a flood of telephone calls was being received from officials reporting that their depots were idle and anxious to get an official ruling.

On the midday news it was stated that already over fifty per cent of the lorry drivers were out, some London bus services had had to be cancelled and that the Executive were expected to make a general statement that afternoon. There had also been demonstrations amongst the coal miners and the dockers and all the Ford plants threatened to come out in support of Greenbank at the end of the day shift.

Ochil Castle was in a state of siege. Newspapers were clamouring for statements on any and every conceivable subject. At first Abdy and Juliet, anxious to try and do something to counteract the bad Press reception, were conciliatory and anxious to co-operate but, as the morning wore on and the demands for intimate details of their lives became more and more outrageous, Juliet ordered that nobody but Lilias Proudfoot would answer the telephone and the Press were to be told that no interviews were to be given. Frustrated in their efforts to get some sort of personal angle on the story editors sent reporters to ring the doorbell and photographers stalked round the castle or hid in the rhododendron bushes hoping that one of the *dramatis personae* would show himself, if only at a window.

Abdy alternated between moods of elation and angry frustration. To have action at last after so many months of waiting stimulated him intensely but the attitude of the Press got him on the raw. Straightforward criticism did not worry him so much as not being taken seriously. For example a cartoon of him as Don Quixote pointing a bent lance in the direction of a windmill labelled Transport House did not amuse him. He was fighting the battle of his life and there was no room for frivolity.

No members of the community, however, were more interested in the revelations about the Citizens' Army than those shadowy figures like Iggy Salvatori and Shamus O'Donovan.

O'Donovan in particular was a man of singularly steadfast views. He came from a deeply religious family and it had been the fervent hope of his impoverished parents that he would one day bring them honour by becoming a priest. Instead, at the age of fifteen he suddenly turned his back on the Church of Rome and espoused the doctrines of Marx and Engels—doctrines which he saw no reason to modify in a changing society. He had early on adopted the Marxist proposition that the destruction of a capitalist society was a desirable end in itself and devoted himself to its achievement with a zeal which would have ensured him high office had he instead entered the Church.

If O'Donovan was capable of any emotion it might be said that he read the morning papers of 2nd October with excitement. Ever since Iggy had drawn his attention to the developing crisis at Greenbank he had had a growing conviction that here at last he was going to be presented with a situation which would bring about all he had worked for. Long before Lord Ochil had dreamed up his Citizens' Army O'Donovan had been marshalling his own forces. In the official records he was described as an International

Socialist but his main role was to co-ordinate the subversive activities of any political body or any individual who could be enlisted in the common cause. His links with the Trotskyist Workers' Revolutionary Party were as close as with the Marxists whilst he also had close connections with many, like James Christie, who held high positions in their own Trade Unions and who did not for tactical reasons identify with any group. They had often proved in the past to be amongst the most effective weapons in O'Donovan's armoury in dealing with the wishy-washy moderates.

O'Donovan did not owe the importance of his position as a Communist agitator only to his position as co-ordinator. He was also the administrator of a considerable budget whose funds were devoted to the maintenance of a body of paid agitators of whom Iggy was one. Others were to be found strategically placed in the industrial areas where the strike weapon could be used most effectively to embarrass the national economy. Thus O'Donovan could make his influence felt not only in the higher echelons of policy making in the Trade Unions but in the pits and power stations, transport depots and steel works, car factories and dockyards—anywhere where discontent could be sown amongst men engaged in tasks where high performance was essential to the general prosperity of the country.

Shamus O'Donovan was a faceless man but he was a very powerful one.

Now while the two senior officers of the Citizens' Army paced up and down their operations room waiting anxiously for the next news flash which might justify their calling out their forces, O'Donovan worked assiduously to bring about that very situation.

*   *   *

The Prime Minister was brought the news that the Transport workers were officially coming out on strike when he returned to 10 Downing Street after a long and gruelling session in the House of Commons.

His first action was to send for the Minister of Labour Relations.

'What the hell is it all about,' he asked testily. 'Surely they have more sense than to get all hot under the collar about that madman Ochil?'

192

'It's a tricky one. I have just come from a meeting with the Secretary of the Union. Reading between the lines I would say that it is a case of the rank and file leading the Executive. They are bloody angry over the Ochil statement. I can't say I blame them. On the other hand the Executive are on weak ground if they give that as the reason for bringing their men out. It would seem a bit like crying before they are hurt. They made it quite clear to me that they are coming out in support of those engineering works in Glasgow where the man got run over.'

'Do you think it is serious?'

'Damn serious. You know the mood of the country better than anyone. It only needs a lunatic like Ochil to bring out his Dad's Army, even just a few of them, and the militants will have an excuse to bring out every Union in the country. If that happens we'll have the next best thing to a civil war.'

The Prime Minister knew better than to ask what steps his Minister proposed to take. It was ground they had been over too often in the past years. All that could be done was to wait for the Union to make up its mind what concessions they wanted to wring out of the Government this time as a condition of their return to work. Instead he said, 'What about Lord Ochil? Has anybody been on to him to find out what he is playing at? If he climbs down it will at least take a lot of the heat out of the situation.'

'I agree. So far it is only the lorry drivers and a few bus depots who have come out. If Ochil climbs down we may stop the strike spreading. I'll have someone get on to him straight away.'

'Do it yourself,' the P.M. snapped. During the past few months he had found himself getting more and more mentally weary and short tempered. 'Put the fear of God into him. There must be something we can threaten him with. Keeping a standing army is treason for a start. Don't try and soft soap him like you do with the unions. He's an old soldier and the only thing he'll understand is a direct order.'

Ten minutes later the Minister for Labour Relations was on the line to Ochil Castle. Lilias Proudfoot took the call and when she heard who was speaking handed the receiver with awe to Abdy.

'We are much concerned here in London,' said the Minister. 'I am calling you personally to urge that you take no further action on the lines of your statement yesterday until we have had an opportunity for consultation.'

'What is there to consult about?'

'I should have thought that would have been perfectly clear. I refer to your threat to call out your so-called Citizens' Army.'

At the other end of the telephone Lord Ochil bristled with indignation. 'Perhaps you are unaware,' he said stiffly, 'that I called out the so-called Citizens' Army just half an hour ago.'

16

The nation first learned of the events of the afternoon on the six o'clock television news. Although the information was still scanty there could be no doubting the seriousness of the situation.

The main news item was the Transport workers' strike and the statement that they were officially supporting the workers at Greenbank and Camel in their fight against the unwarrantable sacking of Harry Birdsall. A member of the Transport and General Workers Union Executive in an interview emphasized the importance of the principles at stake.

'Workers everywhere are already deeply concerned with the steadily rising numbers of unemployed. It only adds to the feeling of insecurity which exists if employers are allowed to dismiss employees at will. It is important that we should demonstrate in unmistakable fashion that we will not tolerate the erosion of the right of every man to do an honest day's work.'

The case of Harry Birdsall had become a cause.

It was only at the very end of the B.B.C. news that the newscaster read a final news flash which had just come in.

'We have just heard,' he said, the surprise showing on his face, 'that Lieutenant-Colonel The Earl of Ochil who yesterday disclosed the existence of his Citizens' Army has ordered his troops to stand by to man public transport services. We expect to bring you further news of this development at nine o'clock this evening.'

If anything further were needed to capture the attention of the nation it was provided by Richard Willerby's programme 'Everybody's World'. Willerby had been disappointed that so little attention had been paid in the Press to the question of how far the Americans had been an influence in persuading Lord Ochil to interfere in the situation and he was determined in his programme to redress the balance.

His first step had been a direct approach to Dick Katz and he had found him only too willing and eager to talk to him.

Sure, Katz told him there had been consultations with Lord Ochil and his aide on the night before the Press conference. Certainly the matter of Greenbank had been discussed and it was agreed that it was a situation on which action should be taken. Finally he turned down a suggestion that he should appear on the programme but saw no reason why Hank Schum should not appear in his stead.

Having secured this prize, Willerby set about picking the other members of his panel with the object of giving Schum a hard time. In addition to Stanley Jackson, a Professor of Economics at the University of Glasgow known for his forthright speaking, he recruited Marcus Irvine, one of the leading lights in the Scottish National Party and J. K. Fendall the well-known freelance broadcaster and Communist intellectual.

The programme was nothing if not lively. Marcus Irvine led off with a bitter denunciation of outsiders interfering in Scottish affairs. Jackson was more objective, naming America as the nation most guilty of profit-grabbing at Scotland's expense.

'As a Vice President of the great American Corporation which has just bought control of one of our old-established businesses, could we have your views on what has been said.' Willerby was as smooth as butter.

Hank Schum was quite at home when the going was tough and prepared to give as good as he got.

'I don't think I've ever listened to more hogwash,' he said blandly. 'There are countries all over the world crying out for foreign investment. What's so different about you Scots? The United States of America has a reputation second to none for constructive investment overseas. I doubt if your oil industry here would have gotten off the ground without American capital and American know-how—certainly it would not have gotten off the ground so quickly. The investment my corporation has made in Greenbank can be nothing but of benefit to the company.'

'And to the country?' Fendall put in quickly. 'It would be unrealistic to imagine that you have made this investment without expecting tangible return. The profits of a company ought to be used for the benefit of the workers not to pay dividends to idle shareholders.'

196

'Listen,' said Schum. 'Where are the idle shareholders? When we buy control of a business we not only spend our money. We take an active part in the running of the business. We earn our corn same as anybody else in the Company. Anybody who does not earn their corn is out on their ear.'

'Or anybody who does not agree with your ideas. Like Harry Birdsall.'

'Birdsall was fired before we came on the scene,' said Schum quickly.

'One might have hoped,' remarked Jackson, 'that your famous American know-how might have come up with some sort of solution in the Birdsall affair. It seems that you are not only unable to solve your own problems but according to today's news you have a problem which is already spreading far outside your own factory.'

It was at this stage that Willerby abandoned his role as anchor man and made his own contribution to the discussion.

'I have been given to understand that you and your fellow countryman, Mr Katz, played an important part in persuading Lord Ochil to issue that extraordinary statement yesterday which has been so widely criticized. If this is so it would seem that far from seeking a solution to your strike problem you are encouraging a confrontation.'

The rest of the panel reacted sharply, all trying to speak at once. Willerby gave Fendall the floor.

'I find it hard to imagine a greater act of folly than to encourage the dangerous clap-trap of which Lord Ochil has been guilty. Such Jingoism may go down well in the States but it simply will not wash in our sort of democracy ...' He wanted to go on but Schum interrupted him.

'You call this a democracy,' he burst out angrily. 'I would not call a country that is being held to ransom by a bunch of Commies a democracy. If a fine man, a real patriot, like Lord Ochil has the courage to stand up to blackmail he can count on me to stand up alongside him ...' The rest of his words were rendered inaudible by the uproar. Fendall jumped to his feet and shook his fist in Schum's face while the other two thumped the table shouting each other down in an effort to make themselves heard. Willerby was desperately trying to restore some order when the programme was faded out.

197

Altogether it had been compulsive viewing. Up and down the country families argued furiously amongst themselves while the rest of the programme flickered on unheeded. Nor did they have to wait long for further news of the developing situation. All networks interrupted their programmes before eight o'clock to announce that trouble had broken out at a Willesden bus depot. A dozen or so men claiming to be members of the Citizens' Army had attempted to force an entry to the depot and take out buses standing idle as a result of the Transport workers' strike. Some of them, the report went on, had been wearing various articles of uniform. They had had to be forcibly restrained by personnel at the depot as a result of which several men had been taken to hospital for treatment.

By the time the nine o'clock news came on the air, the nation was sitting on the edge of its chair with excitement. If people expected dramatic developments they were not disappointed. The Scottish miners and their fellow workers in the north of England and Wales had come out in sympathy with the automobile industry, which had come to a complete standstill. There were warnings to the public that many trains, particularly those taking commuters into London might not be running and there was talk of a go slow among the power station workers. The Prime Minister was having urgent talks with Trade Union leaders and a statement on the situation was expected tomorrow.

Immediately after the Willerby programme Juliet had rung Dick Katz and suggested he come straight over to Ochil. For once in her life she was beginning to feel out of her depth. Abdy had taken on quite a new personality which left her bewildered. Instead of the taciturn, monosyllabic man whom she had become accustomed to as her husband he had become suddenly alert and decisive, issuing orders with an assured authority and dealing with each new situation as it arose with a confidence which Juliet herself was far from feeling. Patrick Grant was exhibiting all the same symptoms as his chief. While the telephone rang continuously and a stream of callers at the door pleaded for an interview however brief, the two men conducted their campaign with all the enthusiasm of boys playing with an elaborate train set. As the strike situation worsened by the hour they seemed to become more and more exhilarated, excitedly moving their coloured pins about on their operations map and sending out a stream of instructions and exhortations to their unit commanders all over the country.

As Dick Katz got out of his car in the forecourt of the castle he was greeted with a barrage of flashes as the cameramen who had kept vigil outside the front door over the past twenty-four hours sprang joyfully into action.

Once inside Abdy greeted him warmly.

'That fellow Schum was absolutely first class tonight,' he enthused. 'Really set about that bunch of long-haired Commies. Make a lot of people sit up and think. Just what the doctor ordered.'

'Couple of good chaps, those Yanks,' Abdy gave his opinion to Patrick Grant after Juliet had carried Dick Katz off for a long chat in the drawing-room. 'If we had a few more of their kind in this country we'd have a lot fewer problems.' Little did he realize that the arrival of Dick Katz at the castle that night was to make the problems for everyone very much greater.

*   *   *

The events of the 2nd October were given the fullest coverage in the Press the following morning. A society beauty involved in a particularly scandalous divorce which was being avidly followed by the nation found to her relief that she had been banished to the inside pages. Even the reports of the midweek clash between league leaders Liverpool and Leeds were severely curtailed to make room for features covering every angle of the national emergency.

Acting on instructions from Hank Schum, Keith Puddefant and Clancy-Smith had refused any interviews but Sandy Gaul, encouraged by the Union Area Organizer had shown no such reticence. Nor had Harry Birdsall. On Iggy's instructions he was accompanied everywhere by Barney Corcoran who drew considerable satisfaction from acting as Birdsall's publicity manager. In one paper there was a photograph of Birdsall gazing wistfully through the gates of the Greenbank factory captioned 'The Man who wants to Work', another of him standing waiting for the door of the Employment Exchange to open and several of him weight-lifting in Solly's Gym. Overnight he had become a celebrity.

Almost equal prominence had been given to the Citizens' Army. On Abdy's instructions local units had turned out on parade to 'show the flag'. There were pictures of ranks of middle-aged men

199

marching down the High Streets of provincial towns, interviews with local commanders and much about the brawl at the Willesden bus depot. All in all it was a reporters' paradise.

Behind the human interest stories, the gimmick photographs and other journalistic tricks, however, Fleet Street was showing a very real concern for the way in which matters were developing. The general theme was criticism of 'a few obstinate men' holding the country to ransom, the identity of the obstinate men varying according to the politics of the paper concerned. A few picked up the theme of the 'Everybody's World' programme but it was only the *Daily Mirror* which made it headline news. On their front page they carried a blown up picture of Dick Katz getting out of his car in front of Ochil Castle while the rest of the page was occupied with the caption, 'IS THIS AN AMERICAN PLOT?'

'There must be grave fears,' declared their editorial, 'that the calamitous strike which is gripping the nation by the throat is inspired by vested interests in America, anxious to bring about a confrontation between employers and workers in this country. American industrialists with substantial investment in industry in Britain have frequently expressed their concern over loss of production due to strike action. Not the least vocal of these has been Mr Richard Katz III whose giant Camel Corporation is at the centre of the present unrest.

'Let us consider the facts. It is now known that Messrs Katz and Schum spent the evening before Lord Ochil made his announcement about the Citizens' Army at Ochil Castle when the matter of the strike at Greenbank was discussed. Richard Katz is a friend of long standing of Lady Ochil who hails from Detroit. Following the remarkable outburst by Mr Schum on the "Everybody's World" programme when he came out in open support of Lord Ochil's private army, Richard Katz hurried to Ochil Castle, presumably for further consultation. So far as can be ascertained Katz is the only outsider who has been invited to Ochil Castle since the announcement was made.

'The conclusion is irresistible that Lord Ochil has been at least strongly influenced to call out his Citizens' Army by his American friends if not in fact at their request. Such interference in our domestic affairs by self-interested outsiders is quite unacceptable and can only exacerbate feelings which are already running dangerously high.'

The point was taken up by speakers at emergency meetings held at factories up and down the country. In many cases it proved to be the final consideration which persuaded yet another section of workers to walk out. With each newscast on the radio there were reports of more and more industries being affected. By midday, with all branches of the Transport Workers' and the National Union of Railwaymen involved, the country was at a standstill.

*   *   *

As industrial Britain ground inexorably to a halt Wallace Fedarb, President of the United Auto Workers' Union in Detroit, was up at his accustomed early hour and was fixing his own breakfast in his downtown apartment when the telephone rang. He answered it quickly so that it would not disturb his wife Effie who slept lightly in the next-door room. It was Marvin Gross, one of the oldest serving members on the Executive and his close friend.

'You read the newspapers yet?' he asked.

'Haven't got around to it yet, Marv. Anything special?'

'You know that trouble over in Glasgow where that coon got killed?'

Wallace had reason to know all about it. Ever since Nelson Edwards, the first black President of the Auto Workers, had got himself shot in a bar-room argument back in 1974 the Union had been particularly sensitive on the colour question. The details of the Daniel Cooley killing had been fully discussed by the Executive at the insistence of some of their more militant members who felt there might be some racial significance out of which capital could be made. They had found none but it had sparked off an interest in the affairs of Greenbank which had become more acute with the involvement of Camel.

'Dick Katz and that sidekick of his, Schum, have gotten themselves into some really deep water. If some of our bright boys want to make something of it at the Executive meeting this morning we may have trouble on our hands.'

'For Chrissake, Marv, we got trouble enough already without worrying about what's happening on the other side of the pond.'

'Just get yourself clued up on the situation, that's all, Wallace. I've a feeling this may be the big one.'

Gross rang off.

At about the same time Spiro Mexas also received a telephone call. Mexas, a first generation American of Greek origin, was a small swarthy man who stood just over five foot in his elevator shoes. What he lacked in inches he made up in volubility. Dedicated to the cause of International Socialism he had talked himself on to the Executive of the Auto Workers' Union where he proved to be a considerable thorn in the flesh of such moderates as Fedarb and Marvin Gross.

Now, however, he listened quietly while the voice of Shamus O'Donovan came clearly over the transatlantic line. O'Donovan gave him a careful résumé of the events leading up to the crisis in Britain, being particularly careful to spell out the part played by Katz and Schum and the violent reaction it had caused amongst certain sections of workers.

'I tell you, Comrade,' O'Donovan summed up, 'this is an opportunity which must not be allowed to slip. It must be made clear to the workers in America and Europe, regardless of nationality, that what we are witnessing here in Britain is a deliberate attempt by the capitalist classes to crush the workers underfoot. They have already demonstrated that they are ready to use force to achieve their aims. We are relying on the support of workers everywhere in our battle against tyranny. If we fail our struggle against capitalism will be put back fifty years.'

'We will not let you down, Comrade,' promised Mexas fervently.

There were some who regarded Spiro Mexas as a bag of hot air but in that they seriously underestimated him. Certainly at times his tongue ran away with him but he was a shrewd operator and his views carried a lot of weight on the Executive. Just lately he had had things going for him better than they had been for some time.

Detroit had always been a sensitive barometer of political feeling in America. The Auto Workers' Union was one of the most powerful in the country and they were quick to use their power at the slightest suggestion that their members were not getting a fair slice of the national cake. Ever since the Watergate affair, however, their interest in the wider political scene had declined, not because they had become any less powerful but because politics itself had become devalued in the eyes of their members. It no

202

longer involved them emotionally. Instead local issues assumed a far greater importance. The trend amongst Union leaders was to view the posturing of politicians in Washington with cynical detachment and to seek to use their influence to wring ever bigger concessions within their own industry for their members.

The main concern of Spiro Mexas and his fellow Left wingers was to make sure that there was no let-up in their battle with the capitalistic system. Dick Katz had been right when he had said that the political differences between the Republicans and the Democrats were becoming increasingly irrevelant but by contrast the feeling between labour and capital had grown steadily more intense.

Galloping inflation was having the effect of eroding the domestic market for consumer goods which had brought in its train a sharp rise in unemployment. Unlike Britain and other European countries where there was a high degree of liaison between the Communist elements of different unions, the Left wing in America tended to be more segmented. There were strong Left wing lobbies amongst such diverse groups as the steel workers of Pittsburgh and the meat packers of Chicago but each tended to be preoccupied with their own problems rather than concerning themselves with a common cause.

The automobile industry in Detroit in particular was obsessed with itself. The workers took the falling sales accentuated by the rocketing price of gasoline which made many of the larger models a drug on the market as a situation for which the management were in some way responsible. The large number of negro workers were especially sensitive. When for example there was a question of redundancies personnel executives had to tread with great care lest they should give some grounds for being accused of racial prejudice. One way and another it was an explosive situation and one which was much to the liking of men like Spiro Mexas.

That same morning he made good use of the information he had received from O'Donovan. He had a strong case and a sympathetic audience. Dick Katz had the reputation in Detroit of being an employer who paid high wages but demanded a higher performance. The constant time and motion probes and the resetting of production targets to achieve an ever higher output resulted in a tension among the Camel work force not found to the same extent in rival organizations. It was generally said that you had to like money an awful lot to work at Camel. Over the past nine months dwindling sales had resulted in savage staff cuts and the threat of redundancies added still further to the feeling of tension.

Perhaps if Camel had had a more benign reputation as an employer of labour the activities of Dick Katz and Hank Schum would not have excited so much indignation or been viewed with such suspicion by the Union Executive. As it was, Spiro Mexas was almost surprised to find how easy it was to persuade his colleagues that the happenings in Glasgow were the thin end of the wedge.

'You can bet your bottom buck that if they get away with it over there we are going to have a heap of trouble over here. Our comrades must not be left to fight the forces of capitalism on their own. We must show the world that we will not be intimidated by a show of force.'

It took only half an hour of general discussion before the Auto Union decided to call their members out and send a telegram to the T.U.C. in London declaring their solid support.

At the same time the senior Union officials in every plant in Detroit sent cables to their sister factories throughout the world demanding that they stand together in the great fight against oppression.

*   *   *

Within hours of the decision of the Automobile Workers' Union in Detroit becoming known there were reactions all over Europe. The Left wing elements were quick to seize their opportunity. With highly coloured reports of physical confrontation in Britain between the workers and the capitalist classes to lend a sense of urgency to the Auto Workers' decision the situation took on the overtones of high drama. Almost at once the workers in all the American-owned automobile manufacturing plants in Europe walked out to be quickly followed by the employees of Italian, French and German manufacturers. By six o'clock in the evening the Dockers' Unions of all the EEC countries had agreed to black British goods and a large sector of Continental road transport was idle.

As the general feeling of tenseness and excitement mounted radio and television services instituted a service of hourly bulletins.

Emergency meetings were called by all the big Unions on both sides of the Atlantic where pent-up feelings were ventilated. Wild statements were made and decisions arrived at in an atmosphere of high emotionalism. It was as if some slow developing boil had suddenly erupted. Moderate opinion was overwhelmed as militants hammered the conference tables and demanded a stand once and for all against capitalism. As the evening wore on it became known that the Teamsters' Union in America had declared to come out in support of the Auto Workers' and the Chairman of the Italian Trades Union Council had issued a statement that his members were in favour of calling a general strike in support of their British comrades.

While the whole of the Western World bubbled with unrest all efforts to cool the temperature in Britain were proving futile.

The Secretary of the Mineworkers' Union whose members had repeatedly held the country to ransom for higher wages in the past few years until they had completely lost whatever sympathy they once may have had from the public, rushed gleefully into the arena.

'This is truly the achievement of a great ideal. At last the workers of the world are uniting. Every time I hear that even one other worker has come out in our support I do a little dance of joy.'

In Parliament a group of Left wing members, most of them sponsored by one Trade Union or another, interrupted an emergency debate by joining hands and singing 'The Red Flag' while their more moderate colleagues sat grim faced and Tory members shook their fists and waved their order papers. It was ten minutes before the Speaker managed to restore order sufficiently to adjourn the House.

The Prime Minister received an anxious telephone call from the President of the United States. The automobile workers and the truck drivers had been joined by the meat packers and there were indications that it would spread further. The French Prime Minister expressed similar anxiety and the German Chancellor angrily demanded that something should be done. There was little the Prime Minister could tell them.

While pickets kept their vigil outside factories up and down the country, all transport came to a standstill and the pits and the docks were deserted, ordinary men and women crowded the

205

streets to listen to orators who appeared as if from nowhere to hold forth on the sacred cause of revolution. Sometimes there were angry scenes but for the most part there was a general air of dazed bewilderment.

Sam McGee in his old tenement flat in Ibrox spent most of the day with his wife, glued to the television set.

'To think all this bloody trouble started out at Greenbank,' he kept saying in bewilderment. 'If they'd let me get on that bloody box I could tell them all a thing or two. Bloody madmen, that's what they all are.'

17

In the middle of all the rumour and counter rumour, the fiction and the reality, Abdy Ochil made an appreciation of the situation with the cool eye of the professional soldier.

He had been quick to realize that the roles open to his Citizens' Army were severely limited. The few experienced train drivers who had enlisted under his banner could not possibly become operative without the backing of other technicians like signalmen and terminus staff and the incident at Willesden had quickly persuaded him that even the bus routes could not be serviced without the co-operation of the civil authorities. It had been a very different matter in the General Strike of 1926 when the strikers were neither so militant nor so highly organized and the Government were prepared to put in the troops.

On the other hand it was essential that his army should be seen to be a reality, that they should be enabled to perform some useful service to strike-bound communities and that the general public should be given an opportunity of demonstrating their opposition to the strikers.

Accordingly he shut himself in his operations room with Patrick Grant and set about drawing up his orders, carefully following the formula which had been drilled into him during his long years of army service. Then he summoned the four motor cyclists enlisted from his estate workers whom he had standing by and charged them with the task of delivering his edict to his unit commanders scattered about the country from the north of Scotland to the south of England.

His orders read:

Information about the enemy. The Communists and other traitors to the country are determined to bring about the fall of the Government in order that they can replace it with their own regime.

Intention. It is the intention of the Citizens' Army to foil them in their endeavours.

Method. 1. It is important that the Citizens' Army should 'show the flag'. Unit Commanders will therefore arrange for the troops under their command to parade daily in military formation at such place and time as will ensure their being noticed by the greatest number of people.

2. Unit Commanders will contact leaders of local industry and offer the services of the force under their command to combat in any way possible the effects of local strike action.

3. The services of private motorists will be enlisted to alleviate distress caused by the transport strike. Cars used for this purpose will be clearly labelled 'Citizens' Army'.

4. The public will be encouraged in every way to demonstrate their support of the Citizens' Army by displaying notices in their windows, joining in the demonstration marches and so on.

5. Troops will not initiate conflict with the enemy but will act vigorously in self defence if attacked, for which purpose they may carry such weapons as heavy walking sticks, policemen's truncheons if available etc.

Administration. All troops will identify themselves at all times by wearing the armbands already issued.

Communications. All units will make a daily situation report by telephone to Headquarters. Telephone number Ochil 215.

*   *   *

The first Monday of October was to go down in history as Black Monday. With commuter trains not running, office workers who owned cars sat for hours in traffic jams only to discover when they arrived at their desks that few of the junior staff essential to the running of their offices had turned up. Frustrated, they crowded into the nearest bars to discuss the situation. Complete strangers bought each other drinks, each anxious to retail his own strike story and describe how he personally would resolve the crisis. Everywhere there was an air of tense excitement and a light-headedness which had not been known in Britain since the darkest days of the wartime Blitz.

It was in this highly charged atmosphere that the unit commanders of the Citizens' Army took the opportunity of showing the flag in accordance with the orders they had received from their Commander-in-Chief.

One of them, Sir James Ballantyne, Alderman of the City of London, chose to assemble his men at Lincoln's Inn and to march them past the Law Courts and down Fleet Street en route for the City. Startled journalists enjoying their lunchtime drinking in such well known rendezvous as the Wig and Pen Club, the Cock Tavern and El Vino's put down their glasses and rushed out to join the crowds lining the roadway to stare at the band of middle-aged men, headed by Sir James himself, as they marched three abreast towards St Paul's. There were stockbrokers, City merchants, insurance brokers and solicitors, some in bowlers, some sporting more dashing soft felt hats, many with their last war medal ribbons pinned to the lapels of their city suits and all wearing the distinctive blue armband of the Citizens' Army.

As they marched by, those who were not carrying walking sticks or umbrellas swung their arms in true military fashion, while the bystanders' cheers were acknowledged by Sir James who every few steps raised his hat and gave a stiff little bow to right and left. Inevitably there were the barrackers who shouted their witticisms for the amusement of their friends. 'Up, Guards, and at 'em.' 'Three cheers for the Old Contemptibles.' 'Mind you keep in step, Grandad.' Quite a few, either inspired by curiosity or a genuine desire to identify with the marchers, joined in with an untidy rabble of followers-on, so that by the time the parade reached Threadneedle Street the procession numbered over two hundred, many of them journalists willing to sacrifice their lunch in the interests of a good story.

It had originally been Sir James's intention to disperse his men when he reached the Bank of England which he regarded as somehow symbolic. Instead he found the response so edifying that on the spur of the moment and with no very clear object in view he decided to carry on. He led his men past the Tower of London and across Tower Bridge Road to plunge into the complex of grey streets in Wapping which lead down to the Docks.

Too late he realized that he was meeting with a very different reaction from the indulgent good humour he had experienced in his progress through Fleet Street and the City. The pubs they passed were also full of men with nothing better to do than fill in their time until three o'clock closing time with drinking but they were in a very different mood. Fists were shaken angrily and there were shouts of 'Scabs' and 'Fascist Bastards'.

If Sir James could have found some way of retreating with dignity he would have done so. As it was he became more and more hopelessly committed. Serious trouble was not very far away. The flash point was reached when a bald headed man with the build of an all-in wrestler broke away from a group of his mates who were marching alongside the procession shouting abuse, and, knocking Sir James's bowler hat from his head, made a grab at him in an attempt to tear his medals from his chest,

The Alderman may have been regarded by many of his contemporaries as a bit of a pompous ass but he did not lack either courage or physical strength. His left hook caught his assailant on the point of the chin and he fell sprawling in the cobbled roadway. At once pandemonium broke out. Burly dockers, their faces red with anger and their bellies full of beer, waded in to swing wildly at anyone wearing an armband while most of the crowd of followers melted away. Middle-aged stockbrokers and their kind are not noted for their physical fitness and they were able to put up little resistance against the fury of their assailants. The few City Police who had accompanied the marchers up to the City boundaries had been forced by regulations to give up their protective role when the procession had passed out of their jurisdiction. Now the few Borough policemen who happened to be on the scene proved to be woefully inadequate in numbers.

The battle only lasted for ten minutes but when the dockers and their friends withdrew victoriously to continue their interrupted drinking they left a battlefield strewn with bodies suffering from a wide variety of injuries to be dealt with by the ambulance men whom someone had had the presence of mind to summon.

As reported in all the papers the following morning there were two baronets, a knight, three colonels and a major among the casualties.

Although, because of the notable names involved, the Battle of Wapping High Street made headline news it was by no means the only incident in which the Citizens' Army was involved in various parts of the country.

In Birmingham there had been a serious outbreak of fighting near the Bull Ring in the city centre where several shop windows had been broken and a respected City Councllor had been injured with a broken bottle; there had been incidents in Newcastle and Sunderland; and in Liverpool a lorry driver had been badly hurt when he had been trampled on by a police horse.

Perhaps the worst outbreak of violence of all had been in Glasgow. There the Citizens' Army parade had passed more or less without incident due to being escorted by a strong contingent of police but it had set off a chain reaction in areas as far apart as the Gorbals and the Easterhouse Estate where gangs of youths had used the opportunity to run amok, smashing windows, breaking up telephone kiosks and beating up anyone unwise enough not to get out of their way.

On the credit side, from Abdy Ochil's point of view, there had been many parts of the country, mostly small market towns, where the Army's show of strength had been enthusiastically, and in some cases even rapturously received. The response to the appeal for private motorists to help out by providing an emergency service had been well supported and, greatest triumph of all, an owner of a boot factory at Leicester had called in the Citizens' Army to keep production moving and they had carried out the job without incident and to the complete satisfaction of the owner.

On the whole, however, the day had been a disaster. Apart from the many instances of militancy, the leaders of the Trade Unions had been unanimous in their condemnation of the activities of the Citizens' Army and the extremists who seemed to hog most of the air time on radio and television were strident in their demands for a demonstration of strength by their supporters. The result was that in the later half of the day incidents of retaliation became more and more frequent. Private citizens who had signified their support of the movement by putting Citizens' Army posters in their windows rapidly took them down when there were reports that windows were being broken, flower beds trampled and shrubs pulled up in front gardens by marauding gangs of youths.

Reports of the civil disturbances were given great prominence by the media overseas. In repeated and urgent broadcasts on the Continent and in America it was stressed that Britain was on the verge of civil war. A wild report that the Prime Minister had called out the army to deal with the situation resulted in the Italian Premier ordering a stand-to of his troops while the whole industrial scene in Italy ground to a halt. In France and Holland the situation was little better. Strikes were widespread and there were demonstrations in most industrial areas including the German Ruhr where, with the rising unemployment contrasted with the great wealth of the industrialists, the theme of job security had a particular significance.

A remarkable feature of the troubles which beset Europe and America was that the militants of each country based their militancy on the same basic propaganda. There were few amongst the demonstrators who had a clear idea of the exact geographical position of Glasgow, fewer still who knew anything about Clydeside and probably none who had ever heard of Greenbank Engineering. Yet the names of Birdsall and Cooley were freely bandied about as the victims of capitalist oppression. The employers were inveighed against as tyrants and murderers against who the working classes must make the final stand. The temperature was raised further when the student population decided to play an active part. Again with a unanimity which could not pass for coincidence they adopted the theme 'Our future free from fear' translated into German, French, Italian and Dutch. Unruly mobs of long-haired youths with their equally untidy looking girl friends assembled outside British embassies and consulates, waving placards and chanting slogans. In Paris the British Ambassador had to be smuggled out of his embassy by the back door to keep an urgent appointment with the French Premier. In Antwerp the British Consul was hit on the side of the head with a stone when he tried to enter his consulate.

It was against this background of high tension that reports of the activity of the Citizens' Army took on the most sinister overtones. Lurid reports of the Battle of Wapping High Street which made much play with the prominent names involved were greeted with particular indignation. Militant leaders everywhere cited it as concrete evidence that the ruling classes were planning to abolish the freedom of the workers by force of arms. 'British Blue Bloods bite the dust' headlined the *Detroit News*. 'A Bas les Aristos' shouted *Le Citoyen*.

The Right wing papers played a straight bat, restricting themselves to trying to give an objective account of events whilst at the same time devoting their editorials to moralizing on the inability of the Government to take strong action without committing themselves to spelling out exactly what action they recommended.

Harry Birdsall, bully boy, homosexual and immature agitator had taken the whole of the Western civilization by the ear, while the scarcely cold ashes of Daniel Cooley exerted a baleful influence far beyond the confines of his lonely grave.

*   *   *

The Tuesday following Black Monday was another day of tension and unrest.

In his operational headquarters in Borough High Street south of the Thames, Shamus O'Donovan had only taken a few hours sleep since Lord Ochil had thrown down the gauntlet. Volunteers manned a telephone switchboard in one room of the shabby first floor flat, receiving reports from agents all over the country of the latest local developments. O'Donovan sat for hours at a stretch on a hard chair behind an eight-foot wooden table examining each report with minute care as it was received. Most of them required a certain amount of editing before they were suitable for reissue to the groups of agitators who eagerly awaited his dispatches throughout the Western world. It was a task for which O'Donovan had a considerable aptitude and it resulted in his fellow propagandists speaking with one voice regardless of nationality. His dispatches may have had a heavy political bias but his service was fast and efficient and provided exactly the sort of ammunition the International Socialists and their allies required to carry the battle into the enemy camp. By contrast the conventional news channels were deplorably ineffective in getting across a more balanced view of events. Where they tried to deal in hard news, O'Donovan imparted an emotion gloss to his reports which found a ready acceptance with his audience. From America's western seaboard to the Berlin Wall a feeling of exhilaration consumed Left wingers of all political shades, inspired by the knowledge that they were standing shoulder to shoulder with their comrades right across the map.

All day the Prime Minister struggled to find some way of coming to grips with the situation. His task was not made any easier by the fact that several of the more Left wing members of his Cabinet were not giving him the support to which he considered he was entitled. The Secretary for Industry, for example, had made a widely reported speech in Sunderland in which he had rather hysterically described the Citizens' Army as 'Gestapo' and indicated that he was emotionally in support of the general strike action. At the same time the T.U.C. called repeated emergency meetings but seemed quite unable to agree on a firm policy to deal with their more radical members. They contented themselves with issuing vague statements which had little more effect than the urgings of an elderly governess to her charges not to be naughty.

On Tuesday evening the Prime Minister went on television to make a statement which was listened to with rapt attention by the whole nation. He appeared before the cameras, pale, tired-looking and unsure of himself. He started off his statement by declaring that he was taking steps to have the Citizens' Army declared an illegal organization and followed this by an assurance to the strikers that he had no intention of calling in the police or the army to restore order. At the same time, trying to look stern and uncompromising, he stated that hooliganism would be dealt with with the utmost firmness. 'No man,' he declared with a show of pugnacity, 'is entitled to consider himself above the law of the land.'

He rolled up an inept performance by urging all men of good-will to show moderation and restraint and expressed the opinion that good sense would eventually prevail to resolve the crisis.

Abdy Ochil waited till the face of the Prime Minister had faded from the screen before giving vent to his feeling of disgust.

'Illegal organization indeed,' he snorted. 'If only that weak-kneed nanny goat would call out the police or the military in our support we could have the whole situation under control in twenty-four hours.'

Ever since his press conference he had resisted all blandishments by the media to make a personal statement of his aims and, by the same token, had refused repeated requests by members of the Government to meet for consultation. Sitting in his operations room, moving his pins about and having urgent conference with Patrick Grant about the situation, he had never been happier in his life.

By contrast with the Prime Minister's performance at six o'clock in the evening, George Mitchell, member of the Executive of the Transport and General Workers' Union and self-confessed Communist, made a much greater impact when he came on the television screen at ten o'clock the same evening.

In clipped venom-packed phrases he lashed the attitude of the capitalistic classes in general and of Lord Ochil and his Citizens' Army in particular but he reserved the most telling part of his speech to launch a bitter attack on the Prime Minister.

'Never has a man in a position of power shown himself to be more weak and incompetent. Not since Lord North lost Britain her American colonies has any Prime Minister shown himself to be more out of touch with the climate of opinion. He has the nerve to brand the ordinary working man who stands up to defend his rights as a hooligan. I say he is not a hooligan but a hero.

'What is the Prime Minister doing to resolve a situation which has roused honest working men throughout the Western world to express their disgust in the only way which is open to them? No power on earth can bring back to life the murdered martyr Daniel Cooley. What can be done is to alleviate the distress caused to the living by oppression. Yet does the Prime Minister say one word about what steps he is taking to stop our industry being raped by the American invader? The American people themselves have shown what they think of such capitalist opportunism. And what above all has the Prime Minister to say about what he proposes to do to ensure that men of principle like Harry Birdsall shall not be victimized? What is being done to ensure that never again will the working man have to endure the tyranny of petty despots? These are the crucial questions. It is not the working man who is holding the Western world to ransom. It is capitalism and all the evil which it brings in its train.

'To the Prime Minister I can only say, "For God's sake go." And in going take with you all your hirelings and lickspittles. Go and leave it to honest men to build on the ruins you will leave behind you.'

The speech had the effect of hardening attitudes on both sides. While the effect of the strike started to bite deeper with shortages of food in the shops, with resultant hardships hitting first at the old and infirm, the rage of the Right wing Tories knew no bounds. Throughout the following day incidents of violence became more and more frequent with Right wingers as often responsible for instigating them as their political opponents. The following day power cuts were announced and one of the most grievously-felt effects was the blacking out of many of the most

215

popular television programmes. If Karl Marx had been alive to see the time of the Glorious Revolution draw nearer he would no doubt have amended his dictum that religion was the opium of the people and substituted instead the television set. Deprived of their opium men and women of all classes flocked into the pubs to find some distraction from their anxieties and a forum where they could express their opinions. Betting shops and bingo halls were crammed to capacity and the gates at football matches and race tracks had to be closed long before the start to keep out the crowds anxious to attend.

In most parts of the country the only television programmes which escaped the effects of the power cuts were those concerned with the dissemination of news and political discussion and, for want of anything more diverting, these were watched avidly by a disenchanted public.

While the Right and Left wing extremists glared balefully at one another, ready at the slightest provocation to grip each other by the throat, the great body of moderates stood by silent and apprehensive.

18

When the doctor did his rounds at the Royal Infirmary the following Saturday morning he had some news for Billy Caird.

'I've had a look at the latest X-Ray plates,' he told him. 'Your ribs are coming along fine. You'll need to keep that arm in a sling for a week or two yet but I reckon we can let you go home tomorrow morning.'

It came as quite a shock to Billy. He suddenly realized how much he had enjoyed being in hospital. The attention he got from the nurses, the menu coming round each morning from which he could choose his meals just like in an hotel and with Betty's evening visits to look forward to he had never had it so good. He had followed the development of the strike with a detached interest. In his comfortable cocoon he had not felt himself to be in any way involved and when Betty came they had been too occupied in making plans for their own future to allow anything else to intrude on their happiness. Now suddenly he was to be pitchforked again into the outside world.

'You will have someone to look after you, won't you,' the doctor asked sensing his dismay.

'I'll be all right. I have my girl,' Billy muttered uncomfortably.

The doctor nodded and passed on to the next bed.

Left to himself, Billy started to worry. Betty had never been to his sparsely furnished room in Ibrox with its gas ring and the lavatory on the half landing shared by four other families. It was something which had been agreed between them without it ever having been mentioned. Betty's father had worked long hours in the bad old days and scrimped and saved to drag his family out of the single-end in the Gorbals where he had started married life. The little house in Inkerman Terrace might not have a bath but it had running water in the kitchen and an inside toilet which was their very own. It was paradise compared with the bleak tenements close to the river bank and had given the Browns a place in society a cut above that of the neighbours they had left behind. It was something of which Mrs Brown never tired of reminding Betty and Chick.

In getting engaged to Billy, Betty was conscious that she was marrying beneath her and Billy who recognized the social gap which divided them would never have thought of asking her down to the rough district where he lived. Instead they devoted all their efforts to finding a council flat with a real bathroom which would enable them to start life on an even higher social plane than that which Betty already enjoyed.

Billy told Betty the news when she looked in that evening.

'I'm getting home in the morning.'

'That's grand,' said Betty uncertainly for she too had enjoyed the hospital visits and the relief they had afforded from making immediate decisions.

Billy hesitated. Then he said, 'Maybe I won't be able to see you for a bit. I mean with this arm and everything.'

'What has that got to do with it?' Betty questioned indignantly. 'What's your arm got to do with it?'

'Well I mean it is going to be a bit difficult getting about, see. Catching buses and all that. I might not be up to it.'

Betty pondered this for a moment, trying to make up her mind whether this was a legitimate excuse. Then she said slowly, 'Suppose I come down to your place.' As the idea took root she became more enthusiastic. 'I could get there first thing in the morning and make it all tidy and warm for you.'

Billy felt a rush of love for her but he was still cautious. 'I don't know about that, hen,' he said. 'It's not much of a place you know. Besides you would never be able to find anything without me there.'

'I'll manage,' said Betty firmly and so it was arranged, although if the truth were known both of them looked upon the experiment with a certain amount of trepidation.

In fact everything turned out far better than either of them had imagined possible. The ambulance delivered Billy to the close and just before midday he climbed the three flights of stone stairs to find Betty had already been there for two hours. The little gas fire was burning. The carpet had been brushed, the few bits of furniture dusted and the table set for a cup of tea. She had even bought a cake to celebrate the homecoming.

218

'Oooh it's just like us being married already,' Betty squeaked, her eyes shining. She put her arms round Billy and gave him a squeeze.

'Hey, lass,' he protested. 'Mind my ribs.' But he felt warm and wanted.

Betty went out for chicken and chips, their favourite meal, and they ate them sitting side by side on the narrow bed. Then they made love for the first time since they had lain together on the hill above the berry fields. It was a tricky business what with Billy's sore ribs and his arm in a sling but they accomplished it with much giggling and joking. As they relaxed they felt more together than they had done during the frustrating weeks in Mrs Brown's front parlour where Betty's sense of what was right and proper would not allow them to go any further than a kiss and a cuddle.

It was while she was tidying up afterwards that Billy let out an agonized cry. As she picked up the newspaper in which the chicken and chips had been wrapped something pricked his memory.

'For Gawd's sake, hen, I've never checked my coupon.' It was something which had never happened before but with the business of getting out of hospital and the excitement of coming home it had been driven right out of his mind. Nothing would satisfy him now but that they should get a newspaper and rectify the omission.

'Where shall we get a paper at this time of the afternoon?' asked Betty in an agony of apprehension that her inability to find a paper would spoil what had been a perfect day.

'Nip over the landing and ask Mr Macbeth. He's sure to have one.'

'Whatever will he think? You with a girl in your room,' Betty's modesty reasserted itself.

'Never mind that. I'd go myself only they'd keep me gossiping all night.'

'You and your football pools,' said Betty scornfully, but she went. When she got back with the sports page of the *Sunday Express*, Billy already had his copy coupon spread out on the table and was waiting in a fever of impatience. The pools were almost a madness with him.

219

'Mr Macbeth says there are only eight scoring draws. You'll be lucky, I don't think.'

Billy almost snatched the paper from her hand and started checking, his lips moving soundlessly, while Betty went on with her tidying. When she next looked at him he was standing up behind the table, swaying slightly on his feet, his face deathly white.

'Billy, what's the matter!'

Billy's lips moved for a moment but no sound came out. Then he said quite distinctly, 'Bloody, fuckin', hell!'

Betty, who had never heard Billy swear before, opened and shut her mouth in amazement.

'Billy love. What's come over you.'

Billy sat down. Then he said quietly. 'I've done it. I've got eight flamin' draws.' His body was convulsed as if in a fit and tears were pouring down his cheeks. 'Here,' he said pushing the coupon over the table. 'You check. See I'm not dreaming.'

He had all eight draws right enough.

'How much will you get?' Betty breathed.

'That'll depend,' said Billy suddenly quite calm. 'Depends how many other people have an all-correct coupon. Won't be many. Whatever it will be a hell of a lot of money.'

'A thousand pounds?'

'A thousand! If you said a hundred thousand you'd be nearer the mark.'

Betty felt weak at the knees and had to sit down. 'A hundred thousand, Billy! Oooh! You'll be able to give up work and we'll be able to get married straight away and have a big wedding and everything just like you've always said.'

'And a car,' said Billy. 'Maybe a Rolls or something.' They chattered on, dreaming aloud and scarcely aware of what the other was saying. They might have sat there for hours but Billy suddenly remembered that by the rules he had to send a telegram to the Pools firm, claiming a first dividend.

'But the Post Offices are all shut,' wailed Betty, feeling that the dream might be suddenly snatched away.

'We can do it over the telephone. Come on. Let's find a box.'

In the end they could not find one which had not been wrecked by vandals and they had to wait until The Athol Arms opened at seven o'clock and ask if they could use their private telephone.

'Wot's up? Nothing serious I hope,' asked the landlord when they had stammered out their request.

'I ... I think I've won the Pools,' said Billy. 'I want to send a telegram.'

'Blimey,' gasped Eck Gillibrand, who had the distinction of being one of the few Cockneys to run a pub in Glasgow. 'Come on into the back, son. Be my guest.'

Eck helped them with the working out of the telegram and then himself read it over to the operator. He would not take any payment.

'Have your celebration party here when you know how much you have won,' he grinned. 'If you've won anything, that is. I've known people think they've won and then found they've forgotten to post the coupon. Once gave a bloke twenty pounds credit 'cos he said he'd won the Pools and never saw a penny of it.'

'Oooh,' said Betty. 'Do you think there might be some mistake?'

Eck, who had checked the coupon, shook his head.

'You'll get something, luv. Mark my words but don't go mad and spend it all tonight. And here's another piece of advice. If you go into my bar and have a drink, don't tell a soul that you think you've won. News travels fast around these parts and they'll be after you like wasps round a honey pot. Now away through and have a drink. The first one is on me but watch how you go.'

Billy and Betty had two or three drinks but they could not enjoy them. They were boiling up too much inside.

Billy, suddenly brave, said, 'Why don't you stay at my place tonight? We can ring next door and have them give a message to your Mum.'

'Oooh, that wouldn't be right. Mum would have a fit.'

'Aw cummon. It's called living in sin and all sorts do it. Pop stars and all. Some of them even have kids and don't bother to get married even. Please Betty.'

Betty was so bewildered by everything that she almost agreed but, in the end, better sense prevailed. They used Eck's telephone again to call a taxi to take her home.

'Just imagine me going home in a taxi.'

'Don't worry, hen. This won't be the last taxi we have.'

They each went their own ways to lie awake tormented with excitement in their separate beds.

*   *   *

While Billy and Betty, taking Mr Gillibrand's advice not to tell anyone of their expectations, floated on a rosy cloud, the majority of their fellow citizens were finding life to be grim and earnest.

New fuel was thrown on the fires of anger and bitterness which burned between Right and Left wing political opinion by the sending of a telegram from the chairman of the Trade Union movement in Russia to the Chairman of the T.U.C., who allowed the text of the message to be published in full. It read: 'We would express our warmest admiration of your great fight. You may rely on us for moral, intellectual and financial support in your struggle against capitalistic oppression.'

It created an immediate uproar in the House of Commons. The Opposition Shadow Minister of Employment led a bitter attack on the T.U.C. He claimed that it was tantamount to treason to accept support from a foreign power dedicated to the destruction of our democracy.

Other members of the Opposition wanted to know what financial support had already been received from Russia and what steps were being taken to make it impossible for politically motivated men to receive aid from any foreign power.

After a relatively quiet weekend in Britain it was made known on Monday that the Italian Government had resigned in the face of mounting pressure from the Communist Party.

In America rumours of food shortages because of the transport drivers' and the meat packers' strikes resulted in near riots in food stores as housewives fought to lay in stocks of whatever they could set their hands on. Canned goods disappeared from the shelves of the supermarkets like melting snow and police had to be called in to control the queues at butchers' shops.

To add to their troubles the police were faced with an upsurge in militant demonstrations by the Black Power movement who took advantage of the national crisis to parade the streets and hold meetings. In Chicago and New York gas bombs had to be used to quell outbreaks of violence between the black and white populations and in Washington a crowd of over five thousand blacks and their white supporters demonstrated in front of the White House. There was a considerable diversity of opinion amongst the demonstrators as to what exactly they were demonstrating about but that did not make the situation any the less menacing.

In the midst of all the chaos on both sides of the Atlantic Dick Katz sent Hank Schum scurrying back to Detroit to exert his talents as a trouble shooter in a more familiar atmosphere while he himself struggled with the problems at Cumbernauld.

Abdy Ochil made a further general announcement that he was offering the services of his Citizens' Army to support the police in their efforts to restrain hooliganism and maintain order in the big city centres where the situation was becoming almost hourly more critical. Few Chief Constables accepted his offer, fearing that the appearance of the Citizens' Army was more likely to inflame feeling than to maintain order.

An official statement was made informing the public that there were sufficient food stocks in the shops to maintain normal supplies providing there was no panic buying which had the effect of sending housewives hurrying to the shops to buy up whatever they could.

Heads of State all over Europe called for urgent consultations with the Trade Unions but the Unions themselves seemed to be finding the greatest difficulty in presenting any sort of a united front. In Britain the Mineworkers were the most vociferous and united. They declared that they would not return to work unless sackings were made illegal throughout industry and added a codicil to the effect that in any event they wanted an unconditional increase of £30 a week in their wages which would bring the coal face worker's pay up to £150 for a thirty-eight hour week, giving them a rather higher income pro rata than that earned by the Prime Minister.

The Engineering Workers Union also demanded that sackings be made illegal as well as insisting on the restriction of investment by foreign powers in British Industry while the Transport workers clamoured for shorter hours and higher overtime rates. Whilst the Unions spoke with different voices each determined to take advantage of the crisis to further their own selfish interests, the Government itself was far from united. There were several amongst the Left wing Ministers who openly advocated surrender to the various demands made by the Unions, pointing to the confrontation with the miners which had brought about the downfall of the Tories in the Spring of 1974. There were others who pointed out in the privacy of the Cabinet Room at 10, Downing Street that conciliation had done nothing to appease

223

Union demands for a greater and greater share of the national cake. They were only united on one point, which was that failure to resolve the situation could only lead to anarchy.

*   *   *

Whilst events were moving rapidly towards a complete economic breakdown throughout Europe the representatives of Gigantic Pools knocked on Billy's door on Wednesday morning.

Billy, who had hardly slept since Sunday and who had been drinking rather more beer than he was normally used to, let his visitor in. Then he had to sit down because he was shaking so much.

'I am happy to tell you that I have got some good news. Some very good news indeed.' The Pools man, who smelled strongly of after shave lotion, smiled genially, exuding bonhomie.

'How ... how much is it?' Billy asked, his excitement almost choking him.

The man held up his hand. 'We won't know that until tomorrow when the cheque will be handed over to you. It will be a nice little ceremony. Miss Penny Fullsome whose record is this week's top of the pops has agreed to make the presentation in a private suite at the Central Hotel. I've just come here to make the arrangements but I can tell you that you are really going to enjoy yourself. You can say it is going to be the greatest day in your life.'

Billy found it difficult to concentrate but he managed to gather that a car would be sent for him so that he would arrive in style and that he could have two guests at the party. He named Betty and Mrs Brown so that a car could be sent for them also.

Then the man was very solicitous about Billy's arm being in a sling and asked him lots of questions. Billy had been careful to follow Eck's advice about not telling anyone about his expected win. Now the relief of being able to talk to someone besides Betty proved too much for him he let the words tumble out of him. The certain knowledge that tomorrow he would be rich made him suddenly reckless. He would never have to return to his bench at Greenbank. Tomorrow he would be able to cock a snook at the world.

He told the man all about his job at Greenbank and having gone that far he could see no reason why he should not tell him the whole story.

'You mean this chap Harry Birdsall who all the fuss is about and some of his friends actually beat you up?' The Pools man was incredulous, hardly able to believe his ears.

'Well yes,' said Billy, suddenly doubtful that he had said too much.

'Why didn't you come out with this before?'

'It didn't seem right like. Not with him once having been a sort of mate of mine.' He was really thinking of Chick Brown. He'd thought a lot about Chick while he had been in hospital and he still did not want him to get into trouble. He did not want to say anything which might come between him and Betty.

When the Pools man came to leave he was more genial than ever.

'We have a really human story here, Mr Caird,' he said, rubbing his hands together with delight. 'Don't be shy when you meet the Press tomorrow. Just be your natural self.'

Billy was horrified. 'You mean there will be people from the papers there and everything?' he asked aghast.

'That's right,' said the man cheerfully. 'You'll have your picture in all the papers. There's nothing to be afraid of. Everybody loves a big winner and that's what you are going to be; a very big winner indeed. Leave it to me to take care of everything. My name is Sam Green. Just you call me Sammy. We'll be seeing a lot of one another in the next few days.' He shook Billy's good arm vigorously and departed, leaving him in an even more anxious state than before.

That night, when Betty called round as usual, Billy told her the whole story of what had happened at Greenbank just as he had told it to the Pools man. It was a matter on which she had had her doubts on, although she had thought it better not to ask questions. So far as she was concerned Billy lived in a man's world and men did not discuss their problems with their wives or sweethearts unless it was something they wanted them to know. As far back as she could remember she had never heard her father talk about his work to her mother even when he had changed jobs or been out of work for a spell and Betty accepted that that was the way things were. Women did not interfere.

Now that Billy had told her, however, her indignation knew no bounds. It was all Billy could do to stop her setting off there and then to have matters out with Chick. As for Harry Birdsall, she was for breaking the unwritten code and going to the police.

Billy was horrified. 'For God's sake, hen, cool down. The whole lot might go to the nick if you start squawking. I only told you because I thought Mr Green might say something. Anyway it's not right for us to have any secrets is it, love.' He pressed her hand awkwardly.

'It's what our Chick's done that gets me,' said Betty. 'I'll have to say something, I will. I can't help myself.'

'As a matter of fact,' said Billy remembering, 'it was Chick tried to stop Harry when he was putting the boot in. He was helping me really.'

Betty eyed him suspiciously. 'Is that right then?'

'Swear to God,' said Billy crossing his heart.

'Chick's been acting funny lately,' Betty said thoughtfully. 'He hasn't said nothing but I don't think he's been seeing much of that Harry Birdsall lately. There was a time when he was with him most nights. Doesn't go out much at all now. Just sits at home watching the telly and saying nothing to nobody.'

'Maybe he don't like Harry no more,' said Billy eagerly. 'Maybe what with my winning at the Pools and so on we might start knocking around together again.'

'He's going to have a piece of my mind first,' said Betty with a glint in her eye as she got up to kiss Billy goodbye.

'See me.'

'See you.'

*   *   *

The day of the presentation dawned bright and sunny. Punctually at eleven o'clock a large silver Rolls-Royce drew up outside Billy's tenement building. Billy was sitting at his window ready and waiting and although he dashed down the stone stairs straight away the car had already attracted quite a little crowd of spectators. He was glad to find that Sammy was sitting in the back seat. As he climbed in beside him and the car drew smoothly away from the kerbside he was aware of curious stares of his neighbours who had appeared as if by magic at their windows. It would certainly give them something to talk about for the rest of the day.

'Not nervous are you, son?' asked Sammy, patting Billy on the

226

shoulder, trying to put him at his ease, but Billy was wishing with all his heart that the ordeal was over and done with. All he wanted was to be told quietly how much he had won and then be alone with Betty so that they could make their plans.

By the time the car drew up outside the Central Hotel and the doorman leaped forward to open the car door Billy was in almost too great a state of funk to move. Then before he knew what was happening he was being ushered into a crowded room, already thick with cigarette smoke.

Sammy steered him through a sea of turned backs to the far end of the long room where a small group of obviously very important people stood around on a raised dais equipped with its own supply of drinks on a table at the back.

Sammy, as the Gigantic Pools Chief publicity officer and the veteran of many similar presentations, was on terms of easy intimacy with everyone. He introduced Billy first to the Managing Director, a thick-set cheery man with many chins who pumped Billy's hand vigorously, making his shoulder ache. Then he introduced Miss Fullsome who in spite of the early hour of the day was wearing a low-cut evening gown which did nothing to conceal that her vital statistics justified her name. She added greatly to Billy's embarrassment by leaning forward and kissing him warmly.

'I do like to meet rich men,' she cooed archly. 'Particularly when they are handsome like you.' Billy blushed to the roots of his hair and looked round frantically to see if he could spot Betty and her mother but they were lost somewhere in the crowd.

'Tell me,' glowed Miss Fullsome, 'how much is your lovely cheque?'

Billy was saved from answering by the Managing Director who wagged a playful finger at Miss Fullsome. 'I'm the only person here who knows that, dear lady. In just a minute it is going to be my great pleasure to give you all a very big surprise.'

'Oh please don't keep us waiting, you naughty man.' Miss Fullsome favoured him with one of her sauciest smiles. 'Mr Caird and I simply can't wait, can we, darling?'

Mercifully, at that moment Sammy Green hammered with a wooden gavel on the table for silence and as the buzz of conversation died away, marshalled the platform party into a rather awkward line facing the audience.

227

'My Lords, ladies and gentlemen,' he announced. Nobody knew if there were any Lords there or not but it sounded good. 'It is my great pleasure to introduce to you our Managing Director, Mr Gordon Williams, who will shortly hand over to that well-known star of stage and screen, Miss Penny Fullsome, the cheque which she has been kind enough to agree to present on our behalf to the lucky winner of this week's first dividend on Gigantic Pools.'

As the scattered applause died away Gordon Williams stepped forward.

'Before asking our honoured guest Miss Fullsome to make the presentation I would like to say that in doing so she will be making history. Without giving away any secrets I would like to say that never in the history of the world has any single person won such a large prize as this young man you see standing by my side. Not only that,' he went on, raising his voice above the outburst of excited chatter, 'I think that when you know the identity of the young man in question and the reason why he has appeared with one arm in a sling, you will agree with me that the gentlemen of the Press who are here today will have a human story which will uplift the hearts of millions of our fellow citizens at a time in our national affairs when such an uplift could hardly be more welcome.'

The silence which followed was so intense that as Miss Fullsome slit open the envelope containing the cheque with a golden paper knife handed to her by the ubiquitous Sammy the noise of the tearing paper could be clearly heard at the back of the room.

'Mr Caird, it is my privilege to present you with this cheque for ...' As she looked down at the amount she did the only genuine double-take of her professional career. 'For one million and eighty-four thousand pounds,' she gasped, her voice rising to a high pitched squeak.

A moment later the whole room was in turmoil as photographers jostled each other for position and journalists sought to climb on to the dais to get some sort of a quote from the winner. Sammy Green tried to protect the platform party from the onslaught but in spite of his efforts they found themselves pushed back against the wall. Billy, crushed between Mr Williams's not inconsiderable stomach and Miss Fullsome's prominent bosom, held on desperately to the cheque which she had pushed hurriedly into his hand while flash bulbs popped and a dozen voices shouted conflicting instructions.

In the midst of it all he suddenly found miraculously that Betty was at his side. Betty had the advantage of weight. 'Just you keep offa my Billy,' she shouted, giving a violent shove which bowled two cameramen off the dais. 'Give over, you great lummock,' she yelled at another, swinging her handbag wildly. Sammy Green took advantage of Betty's intervention to make his voice heard.

'Gentlemen! Gentlemen!' he shouted. 'Just one moment if you please. If you will all stand back, Mr Caird and his fiancée will pose for photographs.'

After some semblance of order was restored, Billy spent an agonizing half-hour posing first with Miss Fullsome and then with Betty, then shaking hands with Mr Williams, then holding the cheque above his head, then kissing it, then kissing Miss Fullsome and Betty again while those journalists who had not already rushed out to file their stories gathered round two of Sammy Green's assistant P.R.O.'s who were handing out roneoed information sheets at the back of the room.

'You're kidding,' said one, 'you can't tell me this is the bloke who all the row is about at Greenbank. This is one of your bloody gimmicks.'

'You public relations guys are all the same. Trying to cash in on something.'

'You expect my news editor to believe this one? You try pulling the other leg.'

Although there was general scepticism, there was one journalist who did not doubt for a moment that the story was a true bill. David MacWhirter had only minutes to catch the last edition of the *Echo* but he had already heard Billy Caird's name in his conversations with Richard Willerby. While his rivals with less pressing deadlines hung around in the conference room waiting for the photographic session to end and get an interview with Billy, MacWhirter fired off his copy from the nearest telephone.

In fact MacWhirter did not miss anything by not holding back. Sammy Green was a very shrewd Public Relations operator. Having issued his press handout with the bare bones of the information about Billy he was not prepared to let him make any further statement. The way he looked at it was that if he could keep

Billy under wraps for the next few days while he extracted more information from him he had a story which he could keep alive for a long time. As soon as the last demands of the photographers had been satisfied he bundled Billy, Betty and Mrs Brown unceremoniously downstairs to where the Rolls-Royce waited to carry them off to a secret hideout.

*   *   *

The news of Billy's staggering win was given out by midday on the radio bulletins without there being any reference to his connection with the Greenbank strike. Just the same it created considerable excitement. All over the country people who had been glued to their sets to hear the latest developments in the crisis were overjoyed to find some other topic to occupy them. For a moment their trials and tribulations were forgotten as everyone speculated what they would do if they had suddenly come into a similar fortune. The general opinion was that it was far too much money for anyone to win but that did not stop it being the principal subject for discussion wherever people met.

'If the bloke wot won all that money says it's not going to make any difference to his life I'll burn my bloody coupon next week,' said Alfie Davidson who had been doing the pools for twenty-odd years and had once won twenty-one shillings.

'They all say that,' said someone else in the circle of regulars having their morning pints in the Queen's Head.

'I reckon even old Nipper there would stand his hand if he won that much,' put in Billy Crisp. 'I might even stand my hand myself come to that.'

'Bloody hell,' said Jack Rawlinson, the landlord. 'It wouldn't be like you lads to go losing your heads over a few bob.'

It was not, however, until David MacWhirter's story in the *Echo*, linking Billy with Greenbank, was picked up on the six o'clock news that the story really took off.

While Sammy Green carefully nursed his ace card in a suite in a private luxury hotel not a mile from the centre of Glasgow Iggy Salvatori took steps to protect his own ace. The six o'clock news was not over before Harry Birdsall, holding court from his usual seat in the corner of the bar of the Dreadnought felt a touch on his elbow. A moment later he was in Iggy's big black limousine heading out of the city. MacWhirter, who prided himself on his quick thinking, pushed open the door of the Dreadnought five minutes later but the bird had already flown.

Keith Puddefant sat alone in his flat in Bearsden. He was only slightly drunk although he had been drinking steadily all afternoon. Mostly he was feeling desperately sorry for himself. Since Schum's precipitate departure for Detroit he had been left without one of his main props. He had not liked the man very much but at least Hank Schum could be relied upon to make decisions and stick by them. He had given Keith confidence that he had done the right thing in agreeing to the share swop. With Schum's sudden disappearance from the scene Clancy-Smith had failed lamentably to live up to his role as Keith's strongest ally. As the crisis deepened Clancy had become more and more distant. He no longer joined him for their usual evening drink sessions. Instead he spent most of his time out at the Camel works, chasing after Dick Katz. Such decisions as were made by them were communicated direct to the departmental heads involved without any consultation with himself.

Worst of all Juliet had deserted him. At a time when he needed her most she had become quite unavailable. Repeated telephone calls to Ochil Castle had drawn a blank although the papers made it clear that she was still in residence. He felt totally discarded.

Just as he had decided to take a drive downtown in search of some diversion the telephone rang. He grabbed it eagerly. It was his father.

'I have been thinking things over,' he told him. 'Matters have become far too serious for us to be quarrelling. Come out to Cumberland tonight for a quiet dinner with your mother and myself. I don't know what I can do to help but at least I can try.'

When Keith replaced the receiver he almost wept with relief.

As the game was reaching its most critical stage, not only had the cards been redealt but there were one or two new players sitting at the table.

19

While the Prime Minister flapped his arms helplessly, making frequent and contradictory speeches aimed at appeasing first one side and then the other, Lord Ochil managed to keep the tension at a high pitch by ordering his troops to continue showing the flag whenever possible. There were some situations where they performed useful services delivering medical supplies in lorries borrowed from private contractors or providing escorts for strike breakers in some of the smaller factories where the vote to come out had not been unanimous, but on the whole the number of incidents of violence which their appearance created in the more solidly Left wing areas outweighed the good they did.

Indeed in one way the very existence of the Citizens' Army militated against the achievement of their objective. There had been strong representations from various quarters that the army should be called out to man essential services but the wave of anger amongst the strikers which the Citizens' Army had provoked had gone a long way to persuading the Prime Minister that such a course might lead to open revolution. The Citizens' Army was in fact a flop as an operational body but that did not prevent the hard liners using the fact of their existence as a powerful propaganda weapon.

Ever since Black Monday there had been strong efforts made on a Ministerial level to persuade Lord Ochil to refrain from indulging in further demonstrations in the hope that it would take some of the heat out of the situation and enable the real issues at stake to be seen more clearly. On one occasion the Prime Minister himself appealed to him on the telephone but His Lordship was not to be deflected. He regarded all politicians as his enemies and took strength from messages of support he received not only from his compatriots but from such diverse bodies overseas as the Daughters of the American Revolution and the German Chamber of Commerce.

On the late news following the announcement of Billy's big win the situation appeared to be graver than ever. There had been student riots both in Britain and the Continent, stirred up and sometimes openly led by cells of Communist teachers. In Italy all form of Government had ceased and speculation was rife as to how long the British Government could last. If the vacillating and ailing Prime Minister were to resign, there was a responsible body of opinion that the Queen would be bound to send for the crypto-Communist Jack Roberts to try and form an administration.

*　　*　　*

In many ways Sammy Green was a remarkable man. Ever since his earliest days as a newspaper reporter he had dreamed of wielding power. He had started out without many advantages in life. His father had been a railway porter with a liking for strong drink and his mother a pillar of the Methodist Church. Their endless quarrels had persuaded Sammy that there was little future in his staying at home. Instead he had got taken on as a message boy with the *Evening Standard* in London and from there had worked his way up through the ranks.

His lucky day had come when he had been given an assignment to cover an art theft from the home of Sir Alfred Brabazon the well-known theatrical impresario. Sir Alfred had made his fortune by his ability to spot talent and he had taken an immediate liking to young Sammy. By the end of the interview Sammy had got a new job as the Press Representative for one of Sir Alfred's touring shows. He had taken to show business like a duck to water and it had not been long before he had become on first name terms with many stars who were internationally famous.

From there he grew rapidly in stature and reputation. He learned to speak with a classless accent and to dress with trendy good taste. With his unmistakable spotted bow ties, his ready smile and his quick wit, an inheritance from his Cockney background, he was soon a familiar figure around the West End of London and a welcome guest of the famous.

Sammy was only thirty when he landed the plum job as Head of the hundred-strong Public Relations Department of Gigantic Pools where his talent as a professional nice chap was rapidly recognized. But all the time he dreamed dreams of greater power.

Now as he sat in his suite in the Beacon Hotel with Billy, Betty and Mrs Brown he listened with great attention to all the news bulletins and rejoiced.

Ever since he had spirited Billy out of the Press conference he had been becoming more and more convinced that he was holding in his hand a card of immense importance. Whereas his first instinct had been to act in a way which would result in the maximum publicity for Gigantic Pools he was gradually beginning to realize that there were much bigger stakes to play for.

Getting information out of Billy had not been easy. He was suffering from shock so that it was some time before he was able to take in the magnitude of his win. The process of bringing him down to earth was not made any easier by Betty or Mrs Brown who were both in a state bordering on hysteria, alternately swamping Billy in an avalanche of words or bursting into tears and throwing their arms round his neck. Fortunately Mrs Brown got so carried away that she forgot her lifelong rule only to have one drink and after half a bottle of sweet sherry collapsed into a chair and sobbed herself to sleep, but it was already halfway through the afternoon before Sammy managed to calm Betty and Billy down sufficiently to have an intelligent conversation.

In the end it was Betty, her down-to-earth common sense coming to her rescue, who proved to be the more coherent of the two.

Sammy got her to tell him again the events leading up to Billy's being committed to hospital. Then he got Billy to go over it again in greater detail. At first he showed all his former reluctance, particularly when it came to naming names, but Sammy persevered.

'Now that you have won all this money,' Sammy told him, 'you are going to need all the help you can get. At Gigantic Pools we are used to the sort of problems which winning big sums can create. Next week I'll get our team of experts in on the act but before I do that I want to get all your personal problems sorted out so that we can start off with a clean slate. Now Betty has already told me that her brother was one of the people who set on you. Let's talk about that for a moment.' Sammy was fatherly and so obviously concerned for their welfare that Billy started to relax.

'I don't think Chick had it in for me,' said Billy. 'It just hap-

234

pened he was with Harry like. It was more him helping me than anything.'

'Listen,' put in Betty. 'After what you told me yesterday I spoke to Chick when I got home. I've not had time to tell you about it what with everything happening at once.'

'What did he say?' asked Billy anxiously.

'Just like you said. He didn't mean no harm. He's sorry Billy. Honest he is. Says he wants to be your friend again and everything. He doesn't go with that Harry no more. Right fed up with him and his ways he is. An' when I was talking to him he didn't know nothing about your winning the Pools or anything.'

'You're not just kidding me on? He said that honest.' Billy found it hard to conceal his sudden joy.

'By the way, where is Chick now?' Sammy asked.

'Oh ma Gawd,' said Betty, putting her hand to her mouth. 'Ma and I left him sitting at home. Didn't tell him where we were going or anything. He'll have heard it all on the wireless. I hope he don't go out an' do anything stupid. Like getting drunk or something I mean.'

Sammy crossed to the writing desk and brought back a sheet of hotel writing paper. 'I'll have my driver take a note round straight away. Ask him to drop everything and come round and tell him not to let on to anyone where he is going.'

Half an hour later Chick was shown into the suite. To Betty's relief he had not been drinking but his face was white with excitement. As he looked round the room uncertainly Sammy stepped forward and putting his hand on his shoulder led him over to where Billy was standing equally nervously.

'What do you say, you lads, shake hands and make up your differences?' he said grinning.

There was only a moment's hesitation, then Chick and Billy were slapping each other on the back and laughing while Betty threatened to dissolve once more into tears.

After that Billy seemed to lose much of his reserve. He showed Chick the wonders of the suite with proprietorial pride and got him a drink from the well-stocked side table while he chattered away happily.

It was several drinks and a lot of laughter later that Sammy picked up the telephone and called his old friend David MacWhirter.

235

'It's you, is it, you crafty bugger,' MacWhirter said when Sammy announced himself. 'What have you done with the boy. The whole of the Press are looking for him.'

'Sitting right beside me,' said Sammy comfortably. 'Want to come over?'

'Me and the rest of the bloody world I suppose.'

'Not at all, Davie boy. Just you.'

'I'll get myself a fast jet.'

'Just one thing, Davie. This meeting is off the record. You are more in the middle of this Greenbank affair than I am. I want your advice.'

MacWhirter groaned. 'I might have known there would be a snag.' But he was up at the Beacon in a time which must stand near to a record.

* * *

It was David MacWhirter who suggested calling in Richard Willerby. He and Sammy had discussed the situation far into the night. Billy, exhausted by the excitement and the drinks he had had with Chick, had gone to bed in the next room and Chick and Betty with some difficulty had managed to get Mrs Brown into Sammy's car and been sent home with instructions that they were to talk to nobody, not even the neighbours, and return to the hotel first thing the following morning. Sammy had wanted them all to stay overnight but when it had been suggested to Mrs Brown she had firmly put her foot down. In her view ladies who stayed the night in strange hotels were not quite respectable.

It was well after midnight when a sleepy Richard Willerby put in an appearance. He confirmed what MacWhirter had already suspected that Birdsall had disappeared and with him Barney Corcoran.

'That piece of yours linking young Caird with Greenbank has put the wind up somebody, Dave,' said Willerby. 'I've been working on this angle for a few days and all that I have come up with is that there is a rather unsavoury character called Salvatori whose name keeps cropping up. I suspect he is a professional agitator but so far I have been unable to get alongside him.'

'Whoever he is and whatever he does is of no importance to the situation as we now know it,' said Sammy Green. 'Dave and I have been over the thing again and again. Here we have a world strike propped up by the indignation fostered over the sacking of one man. There are other factors of course. The death of Daniel Cooley, the inept interference by Katz and the military junketings of Ochil and his merry men. But basically this is a situation which has been manipulated by politically motivated men who have used the common fear of unemployment and redundancies to gain the support of the average non-political worker. We destroy sympathy for Birdsall and we bring down the whole bloody structure. Right?'

'Reduced to its essentials, yes,' said Willerby. 'But I am not sure that it is going to be all that easy to do. You look at it through the other end of the telescope. The other side have created a popular hero and you don't kill off popular heroes that easy. Suppose you get your man to stand up and tell the truth. Who is going to believe it? Remember he has kept silence all this time. Now he becomes a millionaire overnight. He doesn't need a job any more so he stands up and makes a lot of wild accusations about his old mates and then drives off in his Rolls-Royce. People are not going to understand what makes a guy like Caird tick. They are all going to think it is just another capitalist plot and the gap will be wider than ever.'

'Listen,' said Green. 'You talk about the gap. Sure there is a gap as wide as the Atlantic Ocean. The extreme Right and the extreme Left can never be reconciled. But what about those in between. There is a huge body of moderate opinion which both sides try to manipulate. At the moment the Left extremists seem to be having everything their own way. Our job is to pull a stroke which will allow average decent men and women to stand up and be counted. I don't care if they vote Conservative or Socialist, Republican or Democrat. They are the real power in a country if they can only be persuaded to exert it.'

'How?' said Willerby.

'That,' said Sammy, 'is what we are here to talk about.'

*   *   *

Sammy Green had not got to the top of his profession as a Public Relations executive without reason. His contacts in the media were widespread and he knew how to use them.

By three o'clock in the afternoon every evening paper throughout the country had been informed that the million pound pools winner was to appear on the Richard Willerby programme. Many hinted that there was more in store for the viewers than simply an opportunity to identify with the world's biggest money winner. Some were bold enough to forecast that Billy Caird was political dynamite. The millions who tuned in to watch the programme were not to be disappointed.

*   *   *

The interview opened on a predictable note. Billy, who had spent the day quietly with Betty and Chick, appeared surprisingly relaxed. Forty-eight hours of living with the knowledge that he was a rich man had done much for his self-assurance. Most of all he had come to rely on Sammy as his mentor and whatever Sammy said he went along with. It was almost as if it was Sammy who was paying him the money out of his own pocket and might have some mysterious power to withhold it if Billy did not do what he was told.

Richard Willerby only spent as long as was necessary to establish with the viewers the immense amount of money which had been won and he allowed Billy to get used to the unfamiliar atmosphere of the studio before he came to the real meat.

'As most people are aware who read their newspapers,' Willerby said smoothly, 'you were employed by the Greenbank Engineering Company which has been at the centre of the troubles whose repercussions have been felt throughout the whole of the Western world. You were telling me before we went on the air that you had had some kind of an accident which is why you still have your arm in a sling. Would you care to say more about that?'

'I was beaten up,' said Billy bluntly, just as Sammy had schooled him.

Willerby's eyebrows shot up in well-simulated astonishment.

'Beaten up?'

'Harry Birdsall done it. Him that all the fuss is about. That's why the Works Manager fired him.'

Shamus O'Donovan, watching the programme in his office with group of voluntary helpers, gave a short bark of mirthless laughter. 'Who's going to believe that lot of baloney,' he said to no one in particular. But he never took his eyes off the screen.

Willerby took Billy through his paces with professional expertise. Betty, sitting above the studio floor with the cameraman and surrounded by monitor sets—a special privilege for her arranged by Willerby, found her lips moving to make the well-rehearsed answers and glowed with pride.

As question followed inexorable question the image of Billy, the lucky millionaire, vanished and in its place there grew a feeling of sympathy for the underdog—a feeling not unmixed with dismay.

'It's a bleeding trick,' exploded Johnny Cripps, a coal-face worker in Alloa.

'You just shut your gob and pin your ears back,' snapped his wife.

'The puir wee bugger,' said Granny Reid, looking angrily at her four hefty sons. 'You should be ashamed of yerselves,'—as if they had been guilty of violence against someone unable to defend themselves.

'Well, Mr Caird,' said Willerby, winding up the interview. 'I am sure you have given everyone a great deal of food for thought. I have just one more question which I am sure will interest everyone looking in tonight. You have won over a million pounds. You are going to get married right away to your fiancée and the world is your oyster. Could you tell the viewers what plans you have got for the future?'

Billy took his time. Then he said, 'On Monday morning I'm reporting back at work at Greenbank.'

*   *   *

The timing of Billy Caird's appearance on 'Everybody's World' for Friday evening had been dictated by circumstances but it could hardly have been bettered to achieve the maximum impact. Every paper in the country was desperate to cash in by finding some exclusive angle to the new development.

Sammy Green, his commercial instincts in no way blunted by the excitements of the morning, sold an exclusive interview with Billy Caird to the *Sunday Mirror* for a record sum for a single shot. Other Sunday papers clamoured to sign up anyone remotely concerned with the events. The *Sunday Express* pulled off a considerable journalistic coup with another exclusive arranged by the ubiquitous Sammy with Chick Brown which was banner headlined as 'The Man who really knows the Facts' in which independent evidence was given for the first time in support of Billy's statement. A police guard was provided outside Inkerman Terrace to keep at bay the photographers and reporters who wanted interviews. Sammy provided Betty and Mrs Brown with their own publicity man from the Public Relations resources of Gigantic Pools to arrange picture sessions and guide them through the intricacies of Press interviews. Press agencies were given special facilities to feed the overseas media, and any journalist who could not get his foot in any door filed highly imaginative stories which added to the general excitement. On Shamus O'Donovan's orders only Harry Birdsall remained out of reach while he himself worked feverishly to find spokesmen who would declare that the whole thing was a gigantic capitalist plot.

In the midst of all the frenzy Sir Charles Puddefant quietly took a hand in the game. First he drove to Jim Cantlie's house and had a long talk as a result of which the two men paid a series of visits to the homes of some of the older Greenbank employees. Then he drove on his own out to Ochil Towers.

At five o'clock on Sunday evening he made the first appearance of his life on television.

'I have decided,' he said, 'after consultation with my son, who had succeeded me as Chairman of Greenbank, to take back the reins of office which I have held for so long. I have only taken this step after long and serious thought. I have talked to Mr Katz whose Company now has a controlling interest in the business. He has agreed that I shall have complete control over the future policy and I have this pledge to give to all my employees. Your grievances will be looked into as a matter of urgency. I will approach the whole question with an open mind. I will appoint a committee to be drawn from the shop floor to enquire into the questions which you are all now debating. I have also seen Lord Ochil and he has given me his solemn assurance that all activity of the Citizens' Army will cease forthwith to give us time to find a solution which will be acceptable to the majority. In the meantime I urge you all to keep cool heads. Tomorrow when the afternoon shift is due to begin at Greenbank you will all have an opportunity to demonstrate your belief in the democratic processes which exist between men of good will in the Trade Union movement and Management to resolve our differences. Have a good night's sleep and let us all face our problems tomorrow in a spirit of goodwill and comradeship.'

Within an hour the bones of Sir Charles's speech were being quoted on newscasts throughout Europe and shortly after midday in America the President went on the record as saying, 'At last there seems to be some sanity prevailing where it is needed most.'

20

Billy awoke on the Monday morning with a feeling of sickening dread in the pit of his stomach. The floor waiter came in with his breakfast and pulled the curtains to reveal that the bright sunny weather of the past few days had changed. Now the sky was overcast with scudding cloud and the wind whipped occasional spatterings of rain against the windows.

He switched on the radio just as the announcer was beginning to read the nine o'clock news.

'... Glasgow's Police chief Mr John Stevens said last night that he is ordering an unprecedented turn out of the City Force to ensure that there will be no civil disturbance if Mr Caird attempts to carry out his challenge to the strike picket by reporting for work at the Greenbank factory at four o'clock this afternoon. During the weekend extensive arrangements have been made to give the fullest news coverage to the story which has excited the imagination of the world. It will be relayed live through Europe and transmitted by satellite to the United States. Crowds are already beginning to line the approaches to the factory but the strike picket is standing firm. One of them told our reporter "He'll get a bloody nose if he tries anything here. He may be a millionaire but he is still a scab so far as we are concerned." '

Billy, listening to himself being discussed on the radio, had a feeling of detached unreality. The strangeness of his surroundings, being the centre of attention where nobody had taken any notice of him before except Betty, and the constant reminders that he was a rich man made the role that Sammy was insisting he played that afternoon all part of the dream. Although there were moments when he felt appalled at the prospect before him it never occurred to him not to go through with it. It was all part of winning the Pools and merely a variation on the fantasies he had lived with for as long as he could remember.

Billy was not the only person to wake up that morning with

a feeling that something momentous was about to happen. Apart from such diverse personalities as Mr Shamus O'Donovan and Sir Charles Puddefant whose aspirations differed so widely, there were millions of ordinary men and women who had been built up to a state of excitement by the media during the previous two days. For many people the vicarious thrill they had experienced at the news of the big win had been short lived; or rather it had only served to make the image of Billy Caird, the underdog and the victim of a gross injustice, much more vivid. Women of all ages from the elderly and maternal to the young and romantic readily identified with the frail figure of the boy gladiator about to step into the arena.

Feelings amongst the male population were rather more mixed. There were many who supported those who sought to make out that it was a capitalistic manoeuvre to undermine their entrenched position but for the most part they kept an open mind. A commonly expressed view was that the wee bugger had got guts and the best of British luck to him.

Even the usually imperturbable Sammy Green was feeling the strain of the tense atmosphere which was affecting the whole country. He arrived at Billy's apartment shortly after breakfast, accompanied by Betty and Mrs Brown to whom he had given strict instructions to try and keep Billy's mind occupied. Betty in particular was filled with foreboding but made a determined effort to carry out her orders by sitting with him on the chintz-covered settee and trying to recapture some of their carefree dreams before the winning of the Pools had become a reality while Sammy busied himself on the telephone tying up last minute details.

The only other two people whom Sammy allowed in the apartment were David MacWhirter to whom he had given exclusive coverage and Richard Willerby who had appointed himself as Sammy's general aide. Lunch when it was served was not a successful meal. The food seemed to stick in their throats while the few beers which Sammy had allowed Billy only had the effect of making him feel sick. The men drank weak whiskies and water, conscious of the need to keep cool heads for the next few hours. Only Mrs Brown, overcome by the occasion, again succumbed to the sherry bottle and was soon drowsing happily in an armchair.

Sammy and Richard Willerby had given a lot of worried thought as to how to get Billy to the factory gates. The reports

that dense crowds were lining Dock Road made it seem like a bad
idea to stick to the original plan to drive him up to the gates. The
danger of aggravating the unfriendly section of the crowd by
seeming to turn the occasion into a triumphant procession was
too great. On the other hand it was more than the bravest heart
should be called upon to do to make the pilgrimage on foot.

In the end it was decided to enlist the co-operation of the
police.

Sharp at one-thirty a plain police van drew up outside the
Beacon Hotel and Billy and Sammy scrambled into the back. The
rest were to follow in an inconspicuous aged Austin.

There was little traffic in the streets and by the time they
reached the end of Dock Road it had almost ceased altogether. The
size of the crowds however had not been exaggerated. As the van
proceeded slowly between the lanes of people as if on normal
patrol duty Billy and Sammy could hear clearly the sound, not
quite a roar, not quite a murmur, which is typical of a great con-
course of people waiting for the teams to trot out of the tunnel at
a big football match.

Then the van stopped suddenly. Sammy, peering out of the
barred back window, gripped Billy on the shoulder.

'This is it, kid,' he whispered. 'You're on your own now. Good
luck.'

A moment later the back door opened and Billy found himself
alone on the roadway, surrounded by a sea of faces and, in front
of him, the factory outer gates standing open.

The silence lasted only for a second and then a great roar
went up as flash bulbs popped and a television camera mounted
on the back of a truck focused him in its baleful eye.

Suddenly Billy felt he could not move. He was stuck rooted to
the spot, more frightened than he had ever been in his life before.

There is no saying how long he might have stood there whilst
the police cordon linked arms and strove to hold back the crowds
if a burly figure had not suddenly burst from the ranks and
grabbed him by the arm.

'You'll be all right, Billy lad,' he said. 'You just walk straight
ahead. I'll be alongside you.' With a rush of gratitude Billy recognized the solid figure of Sam McGee.

The distance from the outer gates to the factory door was only
about fifty yards but as Billy started to walk it stretched before

244

him like an eternity. Then he was vaguely aware that the animal roar of the crowd had died away and in its place there swelled the sounds of cheering. Somewhere someone struck up 'For he's a jolly good fellow' and the theme was taken up until the whole air was filled with a holocaust of noise. Somebody shouted 'Bloody scab' but it was greeted with angry shouts and there was a violent scuffle behind the sorely tried ranks of the police.

Next, as if in a dream Billy heard a voice shouting urgently. 'Billy! Billy! It's me. I'm coming in with you,' and Chick Brown was alongside him. Together the three of them started the long walk but with every step they took others broke from the crowd to join them. Willie Jameson was amongst them and a score of other familiar friendly faces.

He was not aware of the picket line until he was only ten yards away. The first face he could make out was Winstanley Jackson, one of Daniel Cooley's mates, then he saw Joe Kidd and beside him the bristling eyebrows and the halo of red hair of Barney Corcoran. They stood in the middle of a solid phalanx, grim-faced and bearing their placards aloft. Although Billy looked, there was no sign of Harry Birdsall.

At this stage Sam McGee and Willie Jameson stepped in front of Billy and marched purposefully forward. For a moment it looked as if they would have to bludgeon their way through when miraculously, as the crowd fell suddenly silent, the ranks of the picket broke and with another few strides Willie Jameson pushed open the small wicket gate and they were inside, surrounded by the silent machinery and a smell of emptiness.

They stood silent, some of them near to tears now that the tension had broken. Then somebody opened the double doors and at first a trickle and then in a flood men started to crowd in, some in their Sunday best, others in their working clothes.

Finally Jim Cantlie stepped inside.

'Right lads,' he said. 'Let's get the shop open. You're not paid to stand around here doing nothing.'

*   *   *

A sound that could almost be heard ran round the country like a wind gently soughing in the trees. It was a sigh of relief. Some stayed glued to their television sets. Others flooded out to the pubs. A few went into the churches to pray. However they reacted there was a general feeling that they had been delivered from a fate that they could only now allow themselves to recognize.

At six o'clock there came the news that the Camel strike had been declared over. In Paris student demonstrators outside the Elysée Palace were broken up by angry citizens who tore their placards from their hands and threatened to throw them in the Seine. One by one reports came in from all over Europe that Unions were recommending a return to work pending further negotiations.

The Prime Minister made a moving broadcast at nine o'clock in which he said, 'The will of the people has been made known. The voice of sanity has once more been heard in the land.'

At Ochil Castle Lord Ochil carefully removed all the pins from his operational map and stored them away in an old cigar box. Then he sent a message to all his commanders. 'Well done. To us is the victory.'

In his office in Borough High Street Shamus O'Donovan spent a long time gazing at the ceiling. Then he too sent a message to faceless men in shabby offices all over Europe and America.

'Fear not. Our day will come.'